I0652343

# VEIN
# &
# VOW

# VEIN & VOW

### THE BOUCHERS
### BOOK ONE

Nicole Jacquelyn

LN
♡P

**Vein & Vow**
Paperback Edition
Copyright © 2025 by Nicole Jacquelyn

Love N. Books Press
An Imprint of Wolfpack Publishing
1707 E. Diana Street
Tampa, FL 33610

www.lovenbookspress.com

Cover design by Jennilynn Wyer Designs
Edited by My Brother's Editor

Paperback ISBN 979-8-89567-079-8
Ebook ISBN 979-8-89567-999-9
LCCN 2025935747

*To the person who told me Vampire novels don't sell.*
*Crossing my fingers that you were wrong about that.*

# VEIN & VOW

# BEAU

I'd seen a lot of dead people. Conservatively, I'd seen thousands. They'd died in war, natural disasters, accidents, suicides, murders, and plain old age. I'd long ago stopped being shocked or feeling much of anything when I came across one.

But nothing had prepared me to see my baby brother laid out on a stainless-steel table.

I reached desperately for the usual detachment, but I couldn't find it. I couldn't actually hold on to any single emotion or thought beyond the fact that they'd obviously tried to spare us by placing his body parts close together to give the illusion that he was all in one piece.

He wasn't.

The sheet dipped ominously between his torso and head. His thighs and knees. The ball of his shoulders and most of his arms. His wrists and hands.

I swallowed down the bile in the back of my throat.

"You know who did this?" my father rasped, his eyes flickering between the normal blue and a deep red.

"Strike team three eliminated all of them," Arthur

assured him. The Commandant of the United States Vampire Command looked almost as sick as I felt. "It took them less than a day to get back into the compound."

"Why weren't we informed?" Ambrose, my eldest brother, stared at the commandant.

"It was a fluid situation."

"Bullshit."

"How much less than a day?" my brother, Chance, asked derisively. "A fucking hour? You can't tell me this didn't take a while."

I forced myself not to flinch. I refused to think about all that Zeke had gone through before the end. Not now. Maybe not ever.

"It took them twelve hours."

"We should've been there," Danny murmured. "We should've known."

"We did know." I swallowed hard. "All of us knew."

I'd known the moment Zeke was hurt. There was always a low vibration of connection between the five of us. When one of us was worried or injured, all of us felt it to some degree. Sometimes we didn't know which of us was in danger, and it became a process of elimination game, each of us reaching out to the others until we knew who was in trouble. Zeke had been the only one we hadn't been able to contact.

"You're sure this was some small group and not part of a larger—"

"They were locals who noticed that the team didn't get injured like they should've," Arthur replied, cutting our father off. "They knew what we were, and when given the opportunity..." He grimaced and shook his head.

"How the hell did they even have the opportunity?" Ambrose asked. "How the fuck did they keep him down?"

"That, we don't know," the commandant confessed.

"And no one thought to ask?" Chance snapped in disbelief.

"I give you my word—"

"Fuck your word," I said flatly, staring at the man who'd been like an uncle to us.

Our brother had been cut into pieces, and *Uncle Arthur* hadn't even called to let us know he'd been captured. We'd spent the last two days trying to find out what the fuck was going on. Our mother was frantic. We'd barely been able to convince her to stay home while we came into headquarters, and I wouldn't have been surprised if she came through the doorway at any moment.

He'd fucked us.

"Bjorn," my father snapped in warning.

"It's all right, Erik," Arthur said, shaking his head. His eyes met mine. "This is unprecedented aggression."

"What the hell did you all expect when you went public?" Danny spat.

"We went public sixty-four years ago, Daniel," Arthur reminded him. "And since that time, targeted assaults have been minimal. The benefits of no longer having to hide our species from the rest of the world far outweigh the consequences of living openly."

Danny scoffed. "Tell that to our brother."

"We're doing everything in our power to make sure that this is an isolated event," Arthur replied quietly. "And not part of a larger plot."

I didn't think a single one of us believed that some random local group in the middle of the jungle had the means and opportunity to hold my brother captive for any length of time, not without outside resources.

Our father stared at his friend. "You have all that you need from him?" he asked quietly, reaching out to brush Zeke's hair back from his forehead.

"We do," the commandant confirmed.

"I'll expect him back home by dusk tonight."

"I don't know if it'll be possible to—"

"Tonight, Arthur," my dad ordered, reaching into his pocket. "No later."

The commandant held our father's stare for a long moment before nodding. "I'll see it done."

With a nod, my father flipped open the pocketknife in his hand and reached out to cut a lock of Zeke's hair. My throat tightened painfully as he cupped it into his palm for a moment before closing his fist.

As everyone began to file out of the room, I looked down at Zeke again. His face was slack, and there was mottled bruising around his jaw and eyes, but he still looked like the little brother who had followed us around, trying to be a part of anything and everything we'd ever done. It was almost as if, at any moment, his eyes would open, and he'd tell me to get my shit together.

I wondered where he was now that he was no longer here.

"If she's there," I murmured quietly. "Send her my love."

"Let's go," Chance ordered from the doorway.

I nodded and followed him out of the room.

The flight home was silent. It wasn't until Danny had set us down on the property that our father finally spoke.

"Your mother never knows," he ordered quietly.

"Of course," Ambrose replied.

"Do we really believe that this wasn't a targeted blow?" Chance asked, looking around the cabin at each of us.

"Fuck no," I replied. "They knew what they were doing."

"They were trying to figure out what would kill him,"

Danny added, standing in the door to the cockpit. "Worked their way through—"

"Enough," our father snapped, slashing his hand through the air. "That's enough."

"Fuck," Ambrose muttered, looking out the window. "Mom's coming."

We were still lowering the stairs when our mom's ravaged face came into view. She stared up at the doorway, her eyes roving over each of our faces as we stepped off the plane. Chauncey, Ambrose, me, Daniel. When our dad stepped off last, her knees buckled.

We'd all known that Zeke was gone before we'd left the house that morning, but some part of her must've held on to hope while she waited for our return.

I froze, my eyes closing in pain as a horrific wail split the quiet of the forest.

"Dad's got her," Chance murmured, setting a hand on my shoulder. "Come on. Let's give them some privacy."

I followed my brothers down the trail toward the house, the sound of our mother's sobs ringing in our ears.

"How long do you think they'll keep us grounded?" Danny asked, glancing back at us.

"Probably a while," Ambrose replied. "Arthur will want to give Mama some time with us." He paused. "And he'll want us out of the game while they try to figure out this clusterfuck."

"Two teams down seems excessive," Chance muttered.

"They won't be down," I argued. "They'll merge our teams until we're back."

"Right."

"Why the fuck didn't he get out of there?" Danny muttered. "No way in hell they could've kept him there if he was trying to get out."

"Drugged?" Ambrose said.

I let out a huff of humorless laughter. There wasn't a single drug ever developed that worked on us for long. Our metabolisms flushed everything so quickly that I'd never even been able to get a buzz, and I'd tried everything.

"Cinderblock room," Chance said quietly. "Steel door."

"They had to enter the room at some point," Ambrose said, shaking his head.

"Maybe he was anemic," Danny murmured.

"No way in hell," I argued. Every one of us carried blood on us at all times. In all my years working for the command, I'd never been sent into any situation without being fully hydrated. It was nonnegotiable.

"I need a shower," Chance grumbled as we reached the porch. "I smell like the fucking morgue."

We went our separate ways as we entered the house, and I slowly followed Ambrose up the stairs toward our wing.

"He shouldn't have been on his own," he said without looking at me. "I should've taken that team spot."

"He wanted it."

"I'm the oldest," he shot back, his shoulders tight as he stopped at the top of the stairs. "He should've been on Team Two with Danny."

"They would've killed each other," I replied without thinking.

"Instead, someone else killed him."

"We'll find them," I called as he strode toward his room. He didn't bother answering.

All of us needed a few minutes to ourselves, and we took them, but it wasn't long before each of us wandered back down to the main part of the house. I felt numb. The world was still turning, but I felt outside of it like I was looking in a window, and I couldn't quite figure out what was going on inside. I'd felt that way only once before, and I dreaded the moment when I stepped inside, and everything hit me at once. I knew it would happen. I just wasn't sure when.

"I will not send another son to fight their battles," my mother shouted from the kitchen as she and my father stepped inside the house.

"We have a treaty—"

"Goddamn the treaty and goddamn the Vampire Command," she spat back.

"You know the rules."

"Those rules are ridiculous, and you know it," she argued. "You never fought for them."

"I fought."

"Not for some arbitrary command that doesn't even keep us safe."

"Matilda—"

"No," my mother shouted. "No! I will not give them another one of my sons."

"You know how tentative this balance is."

"I know that they allowed my son to be murdered and didn't even have the fucking respect to inform us that he'd been captured."

"And what would we have done?" my father bellowed. "Do you think that we would've fought any harder than the men he was with? I've been in their shoes, Mattie. I know those bonds. Those men were his brothers in every way but blood."

"They were *not* his brothers," our mother shouted. "His brothers would've never allowed him to be captured in the first place!"

She entered the living room almost at a run and stopped short when she realized that all of us were in the room. Chance and Ambrose were in a couple of chairs by the unlit fireplace. Danny and I were on the couch. All of us were silent.

"You're not going back," she ordered, her hand shaking as she pointed at us. "Not a single one of you."

"Matilda," my father said, walking in behind her. "You know they don't have a choice. What are you doing, my love?" His hand slid around her waist, and for the first time in my life, she didn't relax against his chest. "Ordering them not to fulfill their commitment will only make them feel disloyal to their mother when they do."

"Find your mates," my mother hissed, her voice breaking. "Find your mates so we can be done with this."

"We're trying," Ambrose replied quietly. "You know that we are."

"Well, try harder." With a shuddering breath, Mom finally rested back against our father, her shoulders curling forward as she hung her head.

I curled my hands into fists, the weight of her words like an anvil in my gut. The order hadn't been directed at me specifically, but everyone in the room knew that the chance of me finding my mate again was staggeringly low. It was more likely that I'd spend another hundred years or more in command. I just hoped that my brothers would be lucky enough to find their own mates so they could be done being whored out to the human forces.

Our baby brother's body arrived just as the sun began to set. Ignoring the pilot and co-pilot, we unloaded his plain wooden casket in silence and carried it to the clearing behind the house. There had been few Vampire funerals during my lifetime, and I'd never attended one, but we all understood the steps to take. We didn't celebrate the way humans did. There was no one but family in the half circle around Zeke's coffin. No music or words to commemorate my brother's life. Each of us was silent as we set the coffin on the pyre our father had built that afternoon.

We were silent as my mother lit the fire. We were silent as it licked up the sides of the coffin. We were silent as ash floated into the air and tears rolled down our cheeks.

We burned the youngest of us, my baby brother, Ezekiel Boucher, as twilight filled the trees.

## CHAPTER 1
# REESE

"I know you stole it, Kenny," I yelled, flipping him off as I rushed down the stairs. "Fucking *find it,* or we're going to have issues."

"I didn't steal your stupid hair dryer!"

"I let you borrow it, and you never gave it back."

"I did, too!" he called, leaning over the railing. "I gave it back that night that Salmon and I came over for cocktails."

"No, you didn't." I shoved the strap of my backpack higher on my shoulder. "Salmon probably took it home with her the next morning. Who the hell names their kid after a fish anyway? That should've given you a pretty good indication of what you were dealing with."

"Salmon was nice," he argued, yelling as I crossed the parking lot.

"Salmon was a raging bitch who gave you gonorrhea," I screamed back. "Find my fucking hair dryer!"

"I'll buy you a new one!"

"Sure, you will," I muttered as I raced down the sidewalk. We'd had the same argument at least five times, and

I still hadn't seen a new hair dryer on my doorstep. Leaving the house with damp hair was getting really freaking old, especially now that the weather was cooling down.

It took me fifteen minutes to walk to work, and I'd spent so much time trying to find a hat that I now only had five minutes to get there before I was late. I hadn't even found the one I was looking for, and I was currently jogging down the side of the road wearing a blue hedgehog beanie with spikes on it that I'd bought for a Halloween costume. I probably looked deranged.

Groaning as my backpack thumped against my lower back with every step, I slowed to a brisk walk just as my phone rang.

"What?" I barked, lifting it to my ear.

"Hello to you, too."

"Sorry, best friend."

"Why do you sound out of breath?" Rena asked suspiciously. "Are you in the middle of something?"

"Yeah, in the middle of running to work. What's up?"

"You have to stop leaving so late."

"It couldn't be helped. I had a hat issue."

"Please tell me you're not wearing the hedgehog hat."

"Fuck off."

"You are."

"Why are you calling me at eight in the morning?"

"Because I went on that date last night."

"With the dude bro?"

"He was really nice, actually."

"I bet that guy still has his mom wash his clothes."

"You can't know that from a picture."

"Oh, yes, you can."

"He has a good job—"

"Lemme guess," I said with mock excitement. "Tech start-up."

"Why do I even call you?" Rena bitched. "You always do this."

"That's exactly why you call me. I bring your happy ass back to earth."

"My feet are fully planted."

"They are not, as evidenced by the fact that you went out with that guy."

"Well, he asked me on a second date," she replied smugly.

"Of course he did." I hopped in place, waiting for the light to change so I could cross the street. "You're gorgeous, own your own business, and have an ass that won't quit."

"Stop trying to flatter me when you're being irritating."

"It's not flattery when it's true," I argued, finally crossing the street. I could see my office building in the distance, and I increased my pace. "And I'm always irritating."

"I just want to find a guy I can settle down with," Rena said with a sigh. "I'm not like you."

"Gee, thanks."

"You know what I mean. You're all, I'm an independent woman, I can butcher a deer and make mouthwatering steaks, why would I need a man?"

"That happened one time."

"But I want a partner," she whined. "Like, a solid, not going anywhere, sees me at my worst and still thinks I'm hot, brings me coffee in the morning, and puts a ring on it —partner."

"See, you think I can't sort through that shit and pull

out the important piece, but I can. Get a fucking maid and have her bring you coffee in bed."

"I need a Vampire."

I groaned, long and loud. "When are you going to stop with that shit? We're not thirteen anymore. For all you know, Vampires are shit in bed and out of it. They probably don't even drink coffee."

"I heard that they're devoted to their mates."

I snorted.

"Oh, stop it. I read all about it."

"You realize it's probably all bullshit, right?" I asked as I reached the front of my building. I waved at the security guard, Larry, as I pulled open the glass door. "They're notoriously private. Anyone giving out information is probably lying out of their ass."

"It was a news article, actually."

"Sure, it was."

"I don't know how you're so blasé about it all. You work with them, so it's not like you don't have—"

"I don't work with them," I corrected for the thousandth time.

"Yeah, yeah. You just prepare their meals. You're their chef."

I let out a startled laugh and choked on the spit in my mouth.

"I mean, basically," she said innocently.

"I'm a blood tech," I corrected as I made my way down the carpeted hallway. "I literally move blood from tiny containers to larger containers."

"So gross."

"I make good money, and I don't have to talk to people. It's the best job ever."

"You know I could match your salary if you come work for me."

"Did you miss the part where I said that I don't like to talk to people?" I asked distractedly, opening the door to our offices.

A man in jeans and a pea coat was talking to our receptionist as I scooted quietly through the waiting area. The lobby was mostly for show. It was so rare to have anyone stop in that it was kind of startling to see Abby speaking without a telephone propped between her shoulder and cheek.

"No, but you'll talk to Vampires," Rena said sarcastically.

"I don't talk to Vampires," I hissed, pushing through the door and into the lab. "There are two couriers. One is a brown-haired girl who looks like she's about twelve, and the other is an old man who looks like he's ninety."

"Sure, they are."

"I have to go," I said quickly, hanging up as my boss leaned out of his office doorway.

"Late," Noah called, raising his wristwatch into the air. "Don't you live like three blocks away?"

"They're long blocks."

He just stared at me.

"I was having a hat problem."

"Still no blow dryer?"

"Kenny says he's going to buy me a new one."

"He said that last week."

"Well..." I came to a stop in front of his door.

"I can order you a hair dryer," he said calmly, watching as I pulled the blue spiked abomination off my head. "If you can't afford—"

"You know I can afford it," I replied, waving him off. "It's the principle of the thing."

"You'd rather bitch about it and wear that thing on your head," he mused, wrinkling his nose at my hat.

"Basically."

Noah shrugged. "You're the one who looks like a six-year-old boy."

"Hey, I resent that comment," I shot back. "Just because I don't have boobs—"

"You cannot say *boobs* in here, Reese," he hissed, his eyes wide as saucers.

"You're the one who said I look like a boy!"

"I meant the frigging hat!"

"Sure, you did."

"Jesus," Noah mumbled, pinching the bridge of his nose.

"You can't fire me, or your husband would murder you in your sleep," I reminded him cheerfully.

"I'm aware of that, you menace."

"Mr. Miranda would help me bury a body," I continued, looking at my bitten-down nails. "*Your* body if needed."

"Sometimes I hate you a little."

"You love me."

"You're a pain in my ass."

"I swear I won't be late again."

"Yeah, yeah."

"I really am good at my job."

"Any animal with opposable thumbs could do your job."

"But would they be as discreet as I am?" I asked, leaning against the doorway as he walked behind his desk.

"I heard you talking about your job to Rena when you walked in here," he replied dryly.

"Yeah, but I didn't tell her anything."

"You don't know anything."

"Exactly."

"You're giving me a headache."

"We still on for dinner on Thursday?"

"Pete's making some Italian recipe," he confirmed.

"Pedro," I corrected cheekily.

"I know my husband's name."

"Then why don't you use it?"

"He's going to have to help *me* bury a body," Noah muttered as he dropped into his chair.

"Just because he went by Pete growing up in order to fit in with the whiter-than-white kids at his school doesn't mean we can't honor the name his parents gave him now that he's an adult," I murmured gently, my lips twitching.

Noah stared at me for a long moment. "He still goes by Pete," he ground out through his teeth.

"Whatever you say," I replied breezily.

"You call him *Mr. Miranda,* for fuck's sake!"

"Well, yeah, because he was my math teacher. It would be weird if I called him Pete. Some bonds cannot be broken."

"I love you," he said, his eyes a little wild.

"Aw, I love you too."

"No, I'm reminding myself. I do it when I want to toss you out the window."

"Does it help?"

"Sometimes."

"Oh, good. You know we're on the first floor. At best, tossing me out the window would end in a bruised ass."

"Might be worth it to see the look on your face." He took a deep breath. "But I can't today. We've got a potential client coming in at nine."

"Really?"

"He said he wanted to see the lab while it was in use."

"Strange."

"It's fine. At least you're not wearing that stupid hat anymore."

"My hair look okay?"

"Not even close."

"Ah, well," I shrugged, running my fingers through the tangled locks. "You win some, you lose some."

"Go do your job," he ordered, pointing.

"Plus, I think he's already seen me in the hat," I said, tapping the doorframe.

"What?"

"There was a guy out at reception when I came in."

Noah was out of his seat and shoving me toward my sterile work area before I'd even finished my sentence.

"Good luck," I called out as he hurried toward the front.

Walking over to the scrub area, I stashed my backpack under the counter and pulled off my jacket. I dropped my rings into a little bowl on the countertop, pulled my hair back into a tight bun, and pushed my sleeves above my elbows so I could start washing. I did it all without conscious thought, the ritual second nature.

The smell of the disinfectant soap was calming as I scrubbed underneath my fingernails and soaped up my hands and forearms. When Mr. Miranda had first offered me the job—much to Noah's dismay—I'd been a little skeeved out about dealing with other people's blood all day. I'd felt almost frantic as I cleaned up before and after mixing, but that anxiety had disappeared pretty early on. It was just blood. It wasn't as if I was actually having to deal with the people it came from.

I hummed a song from beginning to end and then rinsed my arms, using the massive roll of paper towels to dry. I'd learned the hard way that if I didn't dry off well, it would be nearly impossible to get my gloves on.

I'd just gingerly shaken the sleeves of my base layer and sweater down, both wool—it was cold as hell in the sterile area—when Noah and the man from the lobby stepped into the office area. I didn't turn to look as their voices grew closer. I had a job to do, and I wasn't kidding when I'd mentioned how important discretion was. Vampires didn't like anyone knowing where they sourced their blood. We didn't advertise. There was no sign outside the door. Somehow, our clients just knew who we were and what we sold. Rena was the only person who knew what I actually did for a living, and even though she was a bit of a blabbermouth, she'd never say a word to anyone else about it.

I pulled on my smock with the attached gloves, still keeping my back to the hallway, and then stepped into the mixing room.

"Hello, my beauties," I murmured, taking in the space. "Start playlist."

Music immediately started through the speakers, and I smiled as I strode across the room. Noah hadn't liked me wearing headphones as I worked, so he and Mr. Miranda had come in and wired in a sound system one weekend. He'd tried to act like it wasn't a big deal, but the system must have cost a mint because it was excellent.

The night guy—I'd never bothered to learn his name—had already unpacked everything, so all of my blood was ready and waiting. We had a contract with local hospitals. All of those little vials of blood that were taken but never used? They ended up in my workstation. I wasn't sure what the criteria was or if there were certain viruses and diseases that were automatic disqualifiers. As far as I knew, could drink any blood, no matter how sick the person was, and it wouldn't affect them at all.

As a human, blood-borne illnesses were definitely a

concern for me. I had to be very careful not to accidentally come into contact with any of it—hence the scrubbing, smock, and gloves. One of the hardest things I'd had to get used to was not scratching my face once I was gloved up. My nose had itched for two months straight while I worked. Agony.

The process of mixing blood was easy. Noah hadn't been completely wrong when he said anyone with opposable thumbs could do it. I thought I added a little flair to the whole process, though. Some of our competitors mixed on a large scale, using industrial vats and computers. I was sure that they sold more in a month than we sold in a year, but we were considered a boutique facility. It was kind of like the difference between buying something from a big box store and a family-run business. Volume versus quality.

Some clients preferred specific blood types. Some wanted a mix. On the wall, a large screen detailed each of the orders I'd fill that day. One crate of four-ounce jars of A-positive. Two crates of two-ounce jars of any mix. Five crates of AB positive or negative, mixed was fine, ten-ounce jars. Someone must be throwing a party. On and on it went.

All of the identifying labels were gone. It was completely anonymous, but most of the time, the hospital was kind enough to label the blood types. Occasionally, I had to test for them, which wasn't exactly hard, but it definitely slowed me down.

Lip-syncing to the song that played around me, I pulled out a flat of vials and turned toward my workstation beneath the row of windows that opened to the hallway. I nearly dropped them when I came face-to-face with the man from the lobby.

He was unnaturally attractive. I mean, I'd seen attractive guys. I knew plenty of them. I passed them on the street. I watched movies. But this guy was something different. He was *beautiful*. Just imperfect enough to be the most striking human I'd ever seen and somehow... familiar. Which was strange as hell because I'd definitely remember meeting someone who looked like he did.

And he was staring.

"Reese," Noah called, gesturing at me. "Come out here a moment."

I jolted and looked away from the chiseled jaw I'd been staring at in wonder. "I just scrubbed," I replied, lifting my hands out to show him my gloves.

"You can re-scrub."

"Do you know what a pain in the ass that would be?" I asked dubiously.

"Come out here, please."

"Seriously?"

"*Reese*," Noah ground out, widening his eyes as he glanced at the man standing next to him.

Right. Noah was my boss. The other guy was a client.

I pasted on a phony smile and nodded, pushing the flat of blood further back onto the counter so there was no chance of it falling off. The room was small, so it was only a few steps to the door, and by the time I was through it, I was peeling off my smock and gloves. I'd have to re-dress on my way back in with a new one.

"Mr. Boucher, this is Reese," Noah introduced as I stuffed the used smock into the trash. "She's our blood tech. She does all the mixing for this facility."

"And I'm damn good at it, too," I said cheekily, striding toward them. "It's an art, really, and I'm an artist." I lifted my hand and my head at the same time, prepared to shake the client's hand and scoot back to work, but I froze.

NICOLE JACQUELYN

"Reese, this is Beaumont Boucher. He and his family are—"

"What the flaming fuck?" I whispered as a wave of heat hit me, rolling from my scalp to my toes.

"Is everything okay?" Noah asked, taking a step toward me. "Reese? What's wrong?"

"No," Mr. Boucher barked, taking a quick step backward. He looked like he'd seen a ghost. "Fuck, no."

I fought the urge to take a step forward.

What the fuck was wrong with me? The guy was looking at me like I'd grown two heads. I shouldn't be trying to get closer to him. Not only was that pathetic in the extreme, but I should be running in the opposite direction before he decided he'd take his business somewhere else. Noah would have a conniption.

"Reese?" Noah called again. I really should give him more credit. When it came down to it, his only concern was me and not the client, who was wearing clothing that cost more than I paid in rent each month.

Another wave of heat rolled over me, and I grit my teeth, trying to ignore it. Had I caught the flu? I'd felt fine that morning.

"Nice to meet you," I ground out, looking at the client's chin. I wanted to turn away from him, but I couldn't seem to do it.

"This isn't happening," Mr. Boucher muttered.

"What the hell is going on here?" Noah barked, finally at the end of his patience. He took a couple of steps forward and pushed his way between me and the client, his back brushing against my arm.

I recoiled as fire flashed from the point of contact to the tips of my fingers.

"Reese, go back to work, honey," Noah ordered gently, still staring at the client.

Mr. Boucher took another step backward, and I took an involuntary step forward. Unfortunately, the step brought me into contact with Noah, and I nearly fell on my ass as I jerked away again, my entire body twanging with the wrongness of the feeling.

"Stop," Mr. Boucher ordered, his eyes on me.

"If you'd let me know what the problem is," Noah said, lifting his hands in supplication. "We would love to have your family's business, Mr. Boucher."

"I'll be in touch," the Vampire replied. He stared at me for a long moment before turning on his heel and striding away.

By the time he disappeared through the doorway, it felt like I was coming apart at the seams. My entire body burned like I had the most wretched fever in existence. My eyes watered as sorrow beat behind my eyes. My hands shook. Beneath it all was a sense of overwhelming panic. What the hell was wrong with me?

## CHAPTER 2
# BEAU

It wasn't possible. I staggered to my car, my hands trembling. It just wasn't possible.

I'd been waiting so long. Two lifetimes. I'd been patient. I'd sacrificed.

All of this was wrong. She was rude. Dismissive, even of her boss. Full of herself. She dressed like a child. It looked like a strong wind could blow her over. Her lips...

I'd barely started the engine when a call came through the speakers.

"Yeah," I rasped out.

"Was it you?" Chance asked dubiously.

"It's all wrong," I replied, the hoarseness of my voice giving me away. "It's not right."

"What do you mean, it's not right?"

"She's—no, it can't be. Something's wrong."

"I'd say something's right," he argued, relief making his tone shift. "What's she like? Where'd you meet her? Didn't you have that appointment at the bank this morning?"

I stared out the windshield, stunned. "She's *wrong*," I

repeated. The past few minutes played on a loop. The conversation she'd been having when she came through the lobby. The stupid hat she'd been wearing at a jaunty angle. The wrinkle in her nose as she sang along to the music in her workroom. The way she'd argued with her boss. The sarcastic swagger as she'd called herself an artist. The way her eyes had traced over my face through the window. How those same eyes had widened in confusion when the heat rolled over her.

"You knew it wouldn't be the same," Chance said quietly. "Mordecai warned you it wouldn't be."

"I have to go," I rasped. "I'm headed back to the house. We'll talk then."

"You're leaving her?" he asked in disbelief.

I hung up without answering. I needed to get the fuck out of there. Pulling into traffic, I ignored the pit in my stomach that intensified as I got onto the freeway headed north. Half an hour later, I was pulled onto a side street, vomiting violently.

It would pass. I knew it would. I just had to wait it out.

EIGHTY-ONE YEARS EARLIER

*"This is a fucking nightmare," Zeke muttered as we picked our way through the rubble. "I don't know why we're not in Germany ending this."*

*"You know exactly why," I replied quietly, listening.*

*The treaty between our kind and humans had lasted a millennia for one reason—neither side crossed the line, ever. It was a solid truce by the time my brothers and I were born, but the elders remembered a time when the peace was a fragile thing, and they never let us forget it.*

25

"We can alleviate suffering, but we cannot change the course of any war or conflict," Zeke spat. "Which is bullshit, and you know it. How many times have we stepped in when asked, changing the course."

"They have to ask."

"Why the hell aren't they asking?"

"No clue," I breathed, looking over the destruction of the London street. There were people everywhere, calling out for family members and neighbors, the sounds of their fear grating along my skin.

"They're so fragile," Zeke whispered, striding forward.

I paused to listen for whatever he'd heard. There. Someone was weeping, mumbling words I couldn't make out. It sounded like a woman, maybe a child. So quiet the humans around us would never hear her.

Zeke was already tossing pieces of stone and debris behind him when I joined him on the pile. The Luftwaffe had been hammering London for months, and the results were catastrophic. We'd spent the better part of our time in England searching for survivors in the mess they left behind.

America hadn't joined the war, but anyone could see that their involvement was inevitable. The president was fooling himself if he believed that the mad Austrian would ever stop in Europe. The United States was unwilling to send troops, and for once, that included the Vampire legion who'd been guarding their shores since 1785. It was a mistake of massive proportions. Roosevelt was fully aware that our kind had flatly refused to support the Austrian. The Vampire Federation was morally opposed to demonizing any group the way the Nazis had, which made any alliance with them impossible. Vampires who had joined the Fuhrer were quickly and quietly erased from existence.

So we'd been forbidden from the fight, our hands tied. We had, however, been sent as a humanitarian force. I wasn't *happy about it, the awareness that I could be making a differ-ence like a spider crawling over my skin, even as I slept. Only the knowledge that our brothers, Chance and Danny, were currently spying from different resistance cells in France and Poland kept me from breaking. I looked up at the sky. Nearly noon. My oldest brother Ambrose should be halfway to Switzerland with a group of children. We'd know in a few days if they'd made it.*

*"Why here?" Zeke asked under his breath. "We could be anywhere."*

*"This is where we were sent," I reminded him.*

*"To clear rubble?" He shook his head. "There are more dead bodies on this street than live ones."*

*"I know," I breathed, reaching for another piece of the crushed building. I could smell the bodies too, their stench mixed in with the scent of soot and garbage.*

*"Who are we saving? What difference are we making?"*

*"Patience," I murmured. "It's only a matter of time."*

*"How many will be dead by then?" he hissed, straighten-ing. "What is the point in all this?"*

*"Keep your voice down."*

*"It's insanity, Bjorn," he barked, making me jerk in surprise. He hadn't used my childhood name in years.*

*"Lower your voice," I ordered again. The last thing we needed was to bring attention to ourselves. Our cover was excellent, our reasons for being in England mundane, but if anyone looked too closely, everything could go to hell. Our exis-tence was a closely held secret within the top levels of many governments for good reason. Historically, the human popula-tion was anything but welcoming to anyone perceived as other. The human war we were in the middle of was living and dying proof of that.*

*"Please," a weak voice called out. "Please, I'm in here!"*

*My entire body jolted with recognition, and Zeke's gaze flashed to mine.*

*"No," he whispered, fear filling his eyes.*

*We started in on the pile again, my knuckles bleeding as I clawed my way into it. The debris created a large mound as we tossed it behind us, every second feeling like an hour until large brown eyes and curly dark hair came into view.*

*It felt as if I'd been submerged for a lifetime, and I'd finally come up for air. Her face was covered in dust, and there was a long scratch down her cheek. Her nose was thin and upturned at the end, her lips a perfect cupid's bow, and her eyelashes were long and clumped together with tears and grime.*

*She was mine. I'd been waiting my entire life for her, and here she was, on a random street in London, buried under hundreds of pounds of rubble.*

*"Are you hurt?" Zeke asked, pulling more debris away.*

*"I don't think so," she said, using her hands to shove at the opening. "Please get me out."*

*"Well, we've gotten this far," I said slowly as I grabbed a large piece of brick and yanked it away from her. "I don't think we'll stop now."*

*She let out a little huff of laughter, and my stomach tightened into a knot. "Good news," she murmured tearfully. I could smell her blood, but most of it had already dried. She wasn't badly hurt. The scent still nearly brought me to my knees.*

*"Is anyone else with you?" Zeke asked, grunting comically as he jerked the last piece of rubble away.*

*"No," she said, shaking as she made to stand up.*

*I'd just reached out to her when a deep voice from down the street made the woman turn.*

*"Millie," he yelled.*

*"Alan," she called back, her face crumpling. "Alan, I'm here!"*

"Millie," he yelled again, the anguish in his voice making it break.

Before Zeke or I could move, he was scrambling over the mess, reaching for the woman we'd uncovered.

"Sweetheart," he said, his voice hoarse as he pulled her out of the hole. "Oh, my love."

I staggered back.

"It happened so fast," she said, crying as her hands framed his face, moved to his hair, and wrapped around his neck. "I was asleep."

Zeke's hand wrapped around the back of my arm, holding me in place.

"Thank God, you're all right," he said, kissing her cheeks. That upturned nose. The cupid's bow I was already obsessed with.

"Steady," Zeke murmured, too quiet for human ears to detect.

"You're all right?" she—Millie—asked.

Her name was Millie. It fit her. Now that she was out of the hole, I could see her in her entirety. There wasn't an angle anywhere. Every part of her was soft and sloped.

She was mine. My body tensed as I fought the urge to step forward and break the man's neck.

"My darling," she sobbed. "You're not hurt?"

"No," he whispered into her neck.

"I was so frightened," she breathed, her dirty fingertips digging into his back.

We watched like a couple of voyeurs as they composed themselves and were still standing frozen as they turned toward us.

"Thank you," the man said, keeping his arm around my mate as he reached out to shake our hands. "Thank you."

Zeke shook his hand first. I forced myself to do the same.

"I'm Alan Davies," he said. "And this is my wife, Millie."

*That's when I noticed where the arm wrapped around her waist ended. His hand was placed protectively on her slightly curved stomach.*

*All the air left my lungs.*

*"Zeke and Beau Boucher," Zeke said for both of us. I was glad of my brother's presence. My entire body had locked as I forced myself to look away from my mate's abdomen.*

*"Please, let me buy you dinner."*

*"No need," Zeke replied. "We're just happy to do our part."*

*"You're Yanks?" Alan said in surprise.*

*Their voices faded in and out as I stood there, fighting every instinct I had. She was married. My mate was married to a human. It made my skin crawl. She was standing too close to him. Her hands were all over him, still moving as if to assure herself that he was really there. His hold was possessive. Loving. I fought the bile rising in my throat.*

*"We actually have an appointment," I heard Zeke as if from far away.*

*I nodded, meeting Millie's eyes for a moment before forcing my feet to move. Zeke no longer had a hand on my arm, but his presence beside me was bracing as I made myself walk away from her. My ears were ringing. Heat rolled over me, pulsing with every beat of my heart.*

*Zeke tried to talk to me, but I couldn't hear him. Every step away from her was agony. My skin was on fire. My chest ached, and my stomach roiled with nausea.*

*By the time we got back to our lodgings, I was sweating.*

*"He's already been called up," Zeke said, pushing me until I'd dropped onto the sofa. "Didn't you hear him? He's leaving in a few days, and Millie is going somewhere in the country."*

*"What?" I asked distractedly. She'd been so close, I could've touched her. Why hadn't I reached her before that miserable human showed up?*

*"He's shipping out in a couple of days, brother," Zeke said,*

*handing me a drink. "He'll be gone. With the way this war is going, he won't be back."*

*That jolted me out of my stupor.*

*"He could."*

*Zeke scoffed. "Doubtful."*

*"She loves him."*

*"She'll forget him."*

*I thought about the way she'd gazed at him, the adoration and relief in her expression.*

*"She won't," I said, throwing the drink back. It burned pleasantly. I'd need the entire bottle to keep me seated inside that small flat. "She's carrying his child."*

*"Many things could happen before—"*

*"Don't say it," I ordered sharply. The thought of my mate losing the man she loved and the child she carried was almost as bad as the fact that she had them.*

*Our mother had lost two children before she met our father. Even at her happiest, there was a shadow behind her eyes a hundred years later.*

*"You've found her," Zeke said in awe, dropping to the chair across from me. "You've actually found her."*

*"Too late," I breathed, bracing my elbows on my knees.*

*"It's not," Zeke argued. "You wouldn't have found her if it was impossible. That's not how it works."*

*"How the hell would you know?" I snapped.*

*"Have you ever heard of such a thing?" he asked, throwing his arm out. "You just have to be patient."*

*I ground my teeth together. I didn't have the capacity to argue with him, not then. I couldn't stop thinking about her eyes. Deep brown. Like the coffee my father drank in the morning, not even a splash of cream. The small huff of laughter she'd let out when I spoke. I'd done that. I'd made her laugh. Me. The curve of her hips and shoulders, the full-ness of her breasts, the small roundness of her belly. The bare*

31

feet, slender and delicate, that had curved carefully over the rocks.

Had Alan Davies picked her up after we'd left, or had he ignored her scratched feet and made her walk? They'd surely get infected. My hands clenched into fists.

"I think we should go over there for supper," Zeke said after a few moments. "At least get to know them a little. Maybe she's not as attached as she seemed. The man could be an awful husband."

"No."

"You know you want to."

"It's a bad idea," I rasped, even as every part of me yearned to find her again.

The other half of my soul.

"I'm going," Zeke said, watching me carefully. "You can stay here if you'd rather."

He knew I'd never let him go alone.

BY THE TIME I pulled into the garage at our family estate, the shakes had stopped, and my stomach had mostly settled. It would be hours before I stopped sweating.

"Beaumont," my mother called excitedly, her feet barely touching the cement as she raced for my car. "You found her."

"No," I said, putting up a hand to stop her. "No, something's wrong."

"What do you mean?" she asked in confusion. "I can feel it." She paused. "I can *smell* it."

"She's not right," I said desperately, my words curt. "It's not her."

"It is..."

My chest tightened, distant memories mixing with

new ones in a kaleidoscope of confusion. It could *never* be her.

"Bjorn," my dad barked in rebuke from the doorway.

"Sorry, Mama," I murmured.

"Come inside," she ordered, waving off my apology.

I followed her numbly into the house.

"It's her," my father said flatly as I passed him. "I can smell it."

"I already told him that, my love," my mother admonished. "He knows."

"It can't be," I argued. "She's..." I shook my head. She was everything I'd never wanted. Her eyes were wrong. Her face was wrong. Her body was wrong. Her personality was appalling. She bounced when she walked. She was too short. She was too small.

"Tell us," my father ordered, crossing his arms.

"She's *wrong*," I replied. I didn't know how else to explain it. My body told me that she was the one. It ached to get back in my car and race back to the bank. But my mind, my gut, said that a mistake had been made.

"What's wrong with her?" my mom asked worriedly, chewing the inside of her cheek as she leaned against my father. "Is she ugly?"

"Yes," I said quickly. "No."

"Which is it?" my father asked.

"Looks are just window dressing," my mother said before he'd even finished speaking. "They don't matter. Not really. It's what's inside that counts. The bond—"

"She's not ugly."

My parents stared at me.

"She's not *right*."

They continued to stare.

"Son," my father said after a few minutes, his voice gentler than I'd heard since I was a child. "You knew she wouldn't be exactly the same. You were warned back when—"

"I know that," I snapped.

"Mordecai told you—"

"I know what Mordecai said."

"It's a blessing," my mother reminded me quietly. "One you've been granted *twice* now."

"I've waited before," I said, a new wave of cold sweat dripping down my back as I thought of going through it all again. "I can do it once more."

"You will not," my father said sternly, glaring at me in admonishment. "How dare you defy the Gods again?"

"I'm not defying—"

"Quiet," he ordered. "Your brothers have waited as long as you. Ambrose even longer. To throw away this chance *after doing it once before* would be the height of entitlement. You made your mother a promise."

"She's not *right*."

"Who are you to decide that?" he thundered, losing the leash on his temper. "Do you question the Gods?"

"Erik," my mother murmured as my back snapped straight.

"You will complete this bond with the mate of your soul," my father ordered, pointing at me as his eyes flashed. "As you should have done before."

"Don't speak of my mate," I shot back, getting to my feet, his aggression fueling my own.

"Which one?" he asked nastily.

"Beaumont," my mother snapped, holding up her hand as I moved away from the counter. "Not another step."

"Your selfishness ends now," my father growled.

"My *selfishness*?" I argued in disbelief. "You believe it

was selfish to allow my mate to live the life she'd chosen for herself?"

"If you'd allowed fate to unfold as it should've, you would've been living within your bond for the last eighty years," he said flatly.

"This argument has grown tedious," my mother said, her hand wrapping tightly around my father's forearm. Her tone softened. "We urge you to give this considerable thought, Bjorn. You have been given a gift, one which our kind spend their entire lives waiting for. Don't waste it."

Without another word, she towed my father out of the room. Their low voices fell into an argument before they'd reached the other side of the house.

Pulling out my phone, I strode toward my wing of the house. I needed to change my clothes and find something to occupy my mind. I wished I could call Zeke. He remembered our time in London far better than I did. Fighting the bond had left spots in my memory that I was sure I'd never recover.

Someone had left a voicemail on my phone. I pushed play and set the phone on my bed as I began to strip out of my damp clothes.

"Hello, Mr. Boucher. This is Noah Miranda-Whittaker from Accord Blood Works. We met this morning." A long pause. His voice lowered. "I'd like to apologize. It took me a few moments to understand the situation, and as such, I behaved inappropriately this morning. *Reese Matthews* is a close friend, more of an adopted child really, to me and my husband. Naturally, I'm very protective of her." Another pause. "Please return my call at your earliest availability. Reese was feeling unwell and has gone home, but I will be in the office until five o'clock."

The recording stopped abruptly, and I realized I was standing frozen, my shirt hanging limply around my neck.

Reese Matthews. Even her name was wrong.

I finished stripping as I strode toward the bathroom and hopped in the shower. By the time I was done, the achingly familiar sensation—like someone was yanking at a cord lodged in my chest—had started again in earnest. It was miserable, perhaps even worse than the first time.

Every molecule in my body was screaming. I loathed the idea of her, but she was mine. No matter how many times I told myself that she was wrong, that I just needed to stay the fuck away from her, I also knew that I couldn't go through it again. The thought of it made panic pound through me.

I dressed quickly, the relief of my decision-making my movements swift and jerky.

Minutes later, I was in the car, waiting impatiently for the garage to open.

"Thank God," I heard my mom mutter from the front porch as I drove away.

"One down," my father replied.

It wasn't hard to find where Reese Matthews lived. Once found, a Vampire's soul match was like a beacon, always lighting the way home.

## CHAPTER 3
# REESE

"It's probably the flu," I told Rena, pulling aside the blinds for the thousandth time in the last hour. "Don't come over."

"Are you puking?"

"Not yet," I mumbled. "But I have a fever."

"Poor thing."

"Yes," I said, dropping the blinds back into place. "Feel sorry for me."

"I'll drop soup on your porch later."

"I think I'm just going to try and sleep," I said, moving through the apartment.

Food hadn't helped. Water hadn't helped. A shower hadn't helped. I was currently striding around the apartment in a tiny tank top and panties, and I still felt like it was too much. My skin felt raw and hot.

"Well, call me later, and let me know you're okay."

"Will do," I replied. I set the phone carefully on the counter.

Noah had to be wrong. He'd been reading the same bullshit that Rena loved. There was no way some random

Vampire had imprinted on me, or however he'd explained it. That shit didn't happen to regular people. It happened to pretty people. Rich people. Famous people. It didn't happen to normal, average people. That would cause pandemonium. The masses would flock toward anyone they even suspected might be a Vampire.

I must've caught something. I'd gone grocery shopping in the afternoon two days ago, and the place had been crawling with kids. I'd probably picked up some bug. Resisting the urge to walk outside into the cool air in my underwear, I poked at the thermostat, turning it down another couple of degrees. Maybe I needed another cold shower. At least the last one had taken the edge off.

If this was some kind of Vampire mating ritual, they could keep it. I was fucking miserable. I'd never been more uncomfortable in my life. It wasn't painful exactly, more of a throbbing heat throughout my body, like an itch I couldn't reach. It was driving me insane.

Laying down in the kitchen, I pressed my cheek against the cold linoleum and finally found a little relief. If I turned over every few minutes, moving to a different area of the floor that I hadn't warmed with my body, I could make the sensation dissipate enough that I didn't want to crawl out of my skin.

I was lying there, wondering how the hell this had become my life and trying to reach the random macaroni noodle I'd missed when I swept, when someone knocked on my front door. I wanted to ignore it, but I was moving before I'd even made the decision to get up. I told myself that it was probably Kenny with a new excuse as to why he didn't have my hair dryer.

I knew better.

Forgetting that I was practically naked, I swung open the door.

It wasn't Kenny.

"You," I muttered, staring. Noah had been correct when he warned me that if he was right, the Vampire wouldn't last a day before contacting me.

Mr. Boucher was standing outside my door, his hands gripping each side of it like he was holding on for dear life.

"Reese," he greeted calmly.

"What the hell are you doing here?" I blustered.

Oh, shit. I wanted to throw myself at him. It wasn't even attraction, though there was plenty of that. In any other circumstance, I would've been scheming already with ways to get him naked. Whatever I was feeling was beyond that. It was need—pure need. It didn't matter if he was clothed or naked. It wouldn't have mattered if he looked like an ogre and his body was covered in boils. Every instinct inside me was urging me forward. I needed to wrap myself around him. Hold him to me. Feel his skin against mine, his breath on my face. I wanted to drink him in.

"I think you already know why I'm here."

"Yeah, my boss may have mentioned you'd be stopping by. Not interested," I bluffed flatly. That was as far as I could get with it. I couldn't even make myself shut the door in his face.

He let out a bark of laughter that stunned me.

"I'm guessing you've got a fever," he said quietly, leaning down a little. "Your skin's ultra-sensitive, and it was worse before I got here. You've probably tried a cold shower, right? Turned your heater down. Nothing's helping."

My back snapped straight. He was right. The sensation had abated. Not completely, it was still there, but it was manageable.

He licked his lips, and my breath caught in my throat.

"I can help you."

"I don't think I want your kind of help," I replied instantly.

He tilted his head a little and stared at me. "Invite me in."

"Not happening."

"You sure?"

My heart started to hammer, and the heat engulfed me again.

"What the fuck are you doing?" I asked suspiciously, taking a step backward.

He stayed just outside the door.

"I'm not doing anything."

"Bullshit."

"Invite me in."

His light brown eyes flared as he inhaled deeply.

"Why is this happening?" I asked, freaked the fuck out.

"The universe has a perverse sense of humor."

"The universe?"

"The universe. The old Gods. The new one. Take your pick."

"I can't be your mate or whatever," I blurted, shaking my head. "I don't even know you. I'm not even interested in Vampires, okay? That's my friend, Rena. She thinks you guys are rad. You should go meet her. Maybe this is a fluke, and you're like, supposed to find her through me or something."

"That's not how it works."

"How would you know?"

"Because I know," he ground out. "Let me in."

"No."

"Let me the fuck in." His fingers tightened on the doorframe, making it creak.

"Fuck you, asshole," I spat back, fear making my heart skip its steady pounding and shift into a jackrabbit rhythm. I still couldn't make myself shut the door between us, and that was almost more frightening.

His entire expression changed in an instant as his hands dropped.

"I'd never hurt you," he said softly. "Never. Don't be frightened."

The words were soothing, like a cool breeze against my flushed skin.

"I don't want this," I replied stubbornly, the inevitability settling over my shoulders like a cloak.

I'd ignored the rumors for years. Paid no attention to the stories. Vampires were only a part of my daily life in one way: I mixed their food. I didn't interact with them. I didn't read articles about them. I basically forgot they existed most of the time. But everyone on the planet was aware, even when they chose not to think about it, that Vampire mates were sacred in their culture. Not a single human who'd mated with a Vampire had ever given any indication that they weren't happy with their circumstances. Not even a whisper of a story. While humans were marrying and divorcing in a matter of years, Vampire mates were happily living together for very long lives.

"I don't either," Mr. Boucher said, snapping me out of my panic spiral.

"What?" I felt irrationally hurt by the words. He didn't even know me.

"I don't want this either," he said calmly.

"I heard you." I swallowed hard. Well, wasn't that a nice kick to my self-esteem? "Why not? I thought it was a big deal to find your mate."

"Invite me in."

I crossed my arms over my chest.

"I'm standing at your door where everyone can see me," he said quietly. "You want your neighbors over here asking questions, calling the news, paparazzi—"

"Come in," I said, cutting him off.

"Fuckin' finally," he muttered under his breath as he strode inside.

I let out an inappropriate giggle.

"What?" he asked, closing the door behind him.

"So, that part is true," I said, my voice quivering. "A Vampire has to be invited inside."

"No," he replied, looking around the apartment. "That's been distorted."

"How so?"

"We can discuss it later," he replied, his eyes moving back to me. He pulled his jacket off slowly and tossed it onto the couch. I wasn't the only one who'd changed clothes. He was wearing a different shirt than he'd been when we met at the office. "Come here."

"Why?"

"Do you argue about everything?"

"Basically."

The pull was so strong that I dug my toes into the carpet, forcing myself to stay where I was.

"Because I want to hold you," he ground out.

"Hold me?"

I watched in fascination as his tongue briefly slid out to wet his bottom lip. The fire under my skin flared. "It'll help."

His body was unnaturally still as we stared at each other. I knew without a shadow of a doubt that if I didn't move, he would continue to stand there. Comprehension finally hit as I glanced down his body. Whatever I was feeling, he was feeling it too. But he was still leaving it in my hands. I held the power.

As soon as the decision was made, I was moving. Five steps separated us, but they felt like a mile as I launched myself toward him. He didn't falter as our bodies collided, and I practically climbed him like a tree.

The relief was instantaneous as I wrapped my arms around his neck and my legs around his waist. I groaned as his hands gripped my ass, holding me in place.

"Fuck me," he breathed, the tendons in his neck bulging as he tipped his face toward the ceiling.

I was beyond caring about what he was doing or feeling. The relief was so good, the feel of him like the best massage I'd ever had wrapped in the best orgasm. I couldn't get enough. I wanted to burrow under his skin and live there. I didn't understand how all of it worked or what the hell was wrong with me, but I didn't care. He was the antidote to everything, and I needed more.

Tightening my thighs around his waist, I let go of his neck and pressed his jaw between my hands, tilting his face toward mine. I closed my eyes and inhaled deeply as his breath feathered over my face.

He smelled like winter. Peppermint and pine.

I didn't even know I was crying until he reached up to gently wipe away the tears with his thumbs.

"I need more," I rasped out as he walked further into the room and sat down on my couch, his arm around my waist.

He swallowed hard and nodded. "I know."

"This is really embarrassing," I muttered. I didn't let go of him, though.

"Most natural thing in the world," he corrected, his voice tight.

"But I don't—" I gasped and forgot what I was about to say as his face dipped and his lips ran from my chin to my jaw. "More."

His fingers burrowed into my hair, and everything in me clenched as he jerked my head back, his mouth running down my throat.

Half of me begged him to keep going, knowing that we weren't even close to slaking this thing between us, but the other half of me was screaming that a predator's teeth were at my fucking *neck*.

"Mine," he muttered against my throat, a shudder running through his body.

I let out a groan of disappointment as he pulled away, holding our faces just inches apart.

"Better?" he asked quietly.

"It's not gone," I replied, my voice as low as his.

He nodded shallowly, his gaze softening. "It'll never be gone."

"What?" I whispered. Panic struck like a needle in my chest.

"It'll get better, Reese. It won't always be this bad." He swallowed. "But it won't ever go away entirely."

"That's insane."

"It's how we're made."

"It's not how I'm made," I argued angrily. I couldn't even imagine spending the rest of my life with my skin crawling and fire in my veins. I could manage it for a while, but eventually, I wouldn't be able to take it anymore.

"It *is* how you're made," he replied, his hands in my hair tightening. "Or you wouldn't be grinding your pussy into my cock five minutes after you invited me in. I'm good, but I'm not that good."

"You're a fucking dick," I said in surprise, jerking against his hands.

I wasn't sure why I did it. It wasn't as if I'd let go myself. If it was up to me, he'd stay right where he was forever. Under me. Over me. Around me. Preferably with his mouth shut.

"I'm yours," he replied easily, his hand gently sliding out of my hair. It drifted down my neck, over my collarbone, to my breast, the tips of his fingers toying with my nipple.

"Whoa," I gasped, my hips jerking. "It's worse now."

Heat poured through me like lava, each point of contact between us the only relief.

"I think it'll get worse until we fuck," he replied, pinching my nipple between his fingers.

"You *think?*"

"It's never been this bad before," he muttered, his breath hitching.

"Before?" What did he mean before? Didn't Vampires only have one mate?

My train of thought broke into a thousand pieces as his hand slid down my belly, jerking my panties to the side. His other hand tightened in my hair, forcing me to lean up.

And then his fingers were there, sliding over my clit.

I couldn't stop the loud moan that fell from my lips as his fingers pressed inside.

He muttered something in a language I couldn't understand.

"More," I demanded, chasing his fingers as they pumped inside me. "It's not enough."

"May I have you?" he asked, his fingers still moving as he pulled my face close to his. The phrasing was oddly formal, but the words were gravelly and rough. A shudder ran through my body. I felt delirious with sensation, my palms burning as I ran them under the collar of his shirt, touching anything that I could.

"Reese," he growled, his eyes intent on mine. "May I have you?"

"I thought I was already yours," I bit out, grinding my pussy against his hand.

"That's not an answer." His hand stopped, and my body snapped, taut as a wire.

"Will this ever go away?" I asked, trying desperately to focus. The question felt important, but I was having a hard time remembering why. "If we stop now—will it go away?"

My stomach lurched at the thought.

"For me, never," he ground out. "For you—partially."

"What does that mean?"

"It means, you can live with it. With distance, it'll be manageable."

"How manageable?"

"I don't know."

I squeezed my eyes shut, trying to reason. He could leave. My hands tightened on his shoulders.

I tried to convince myself that this didn't have to be forever. I could stop things now and still go back to my normal life. I could manage it. In time, it could just be a wild memory that I brought out to impress people at parties. I was once a Vampire's mate, but I'd walked away.

The thought made my chest feel like it was going to cave in.

I could continue on with my normal life.

I opened my eyes again and met his weary ones. "Do you want to stop?"

"Yes."

His hands didn't loosen, so I asked again.

"Do you want to stop and walk away?"

He was silent for a long moment before he let out a strangled, "No."

"What's your name?" I asked, my voice shaking as I stared into his eyes. I remembered the last name, Boucher —but for the life of me, I couldn't remember what his first name was.

"Beaumont," he breathed as I slid my hands up his neck. "Beau."

"Beau," I whispered, testing it out. Something inside me settled. The name felt familiar. Welcome, somehow. "You can have me."

Within seconds, Beau had shoved his jeans down his thighs, and my tank top was gone. The underwear I was wearing tore away like paper, my hips barely jerking at the force of it.

I ran my lips along his jaw, my entire body vibrating with anticipation. He smelled so good and tasted better.

A hand around the back of my neck forced my head backward, and I mewled in protest as he jerked me down, filling me with one smooth thrust.

"Oh my god," I whispered, my eyes widening in shock as he pulled me closer.

"Quiet," he ordered as I grappled for something to hold on to. My fingers tangled in the hair at the back of his head, my other hand gripping his shirt when he struck.

The teeth at my neck *burned*, but it wasn't painful. Confusion filled me. My mind told me to jerk away, to fight him, but instinct had my body loosening, curving around him as he rolled his hips beneath me. Holy hell.

The orgasm hit me so fast that I couldn't even breathe as it pounded through me. I wept as his tongue laved where he'd bitten.

It wasn't enough. I stared in disbelief as he raised his head, meeting my eyes.

"It's all right," he whispered, his hand on my hip still urging me to move.

"I feel like I should apologize," I babbled, the words garbled. I didn't understand what was happening, and I tried not to sob in frustration. I'd just come, but it felt as if I hadn't. I wasn't even close to satisfied. The burn under my skin was excruciating. "It's not—it wasn't good. This isn't good. Maybe we were wrong." My hands loosened, and I dropped them to his shoulders.

A small smile played around his lips, and I had the sudden urge to hurt him. None of this was funny. My nails dug into his shoulders as he lifted the meaty part of his thumb to his lips. When he pulled it away, two puncture marks stood out in stark relief, little beads of blood barely showing.

"No," I muttered, pulling away a little as he pressed his hand to my mouth.

"Trust me," he ordered, pressing harder.

I glared at him, prepared to tear him a new one until the blood hit my tongue, coppery and warm. A wave of coolness flowed through me as he began to thrust harder beneath me. It was ambrosia. The best thing I'd ever had in my mouth. My heart thundered as my eyelids fell.

"Enough," he ground out, yanking his hand from my mouth.

"Please," I groaned, chasing it as I opened my eyes.

With both hands free, he controlled our movements completely, slamming me down and yanking me back up over and over again. My breath shuddered as I leaned toward him. Before I could reach his mouth, his hand urged my face toward his neck.

The second time I came, my teeth were wrapped around the tendon in his neck, instinctually gripping him as I sucked hard.

The room was silent when I came back to myself.

The heat was a soothing beat, no longer agonizing.

I lifted my head slowly, wincing at the hickey I'd left on his neck like a high schooler.

"Okay?" he asked, brushing my hair away from my face.

There was something in his tone that made alarm bells ring in my head, but I ignored them as his fingers soothed over the bite on my neck.

"I'm okay," I rasped. "Are you okay?"

He let out a huff of laughter.

"Sorry, I, you know, bit you," I mumbled.

"Did you draw blood?" he asked calmly.

"No." I looked at the hickey. "Was I supposed to?"

"Sometimes," he replied. "Not always."

"Is that—" I swallowed uncomfortably. He was still inside me. *Hard* inside me. "Is that why you bit your thumb yourself?"

"Most mates don't draw blood the first time. The ability is rare."

"What, my teeth aren't sharp enough?" I joked.

"Your canines haven't dropped down yet."

"Say what, now?" I asked dubiously.

"It's the exchange of blood that finishes the bond," he said. "That's why you needed mine, too."

I felt better. For the first time ever, I felt like I was *home*, and it was freaking me the fuck out, but I liked it. I didn't know this guy. He could be the biggest sleaze on the planet, but he was mine now. Irrevocably. It both frightened and thrilled me. Actually, about a million emotions coursed through me. It felt like I'd discovered the meaning of life or something. It was almost euphoric. If this was what drugs felt like, I knew why people ruined their lives over them.

But he seemed...detached somehow.

When he didn't say anything else, I awkwardly lifted away from him and scooted off his lap.

"Um...I'm going to, um, get dressed."

Beau nodded.

I flew to my room like my ass was on fire and threw on the first thing I could find. My skin still felt too sensitive for clothes, but I forced myself to pull on a sweater and jeans. I needed some kind of barrier between me and... everything. Plus, it was frigid in my apartment. When I got back out to the living room, he was still seated on the couch, his pants buttoned, and his shirt straightened. Cool as a cucumber.

"I'm starving," I blurted, searching for anything to say to this stranger that I'd just committed my life to. Oh, god, what had I done? "Are you hungry?"

I'd always been impulsive. I'd gotten into so much trouble because I never thought shit through, but this was by far the worst. It was even worse than the year I'd spent in juvie after beating the shit out of Rena's boyfriend after he'd roofied her when we were sixteen.

"Oh, shit," I muttered, my eyes shooting to Beau's. "Do you eat? Like, food? You know, human food?"

"Of course we eat food," he said flatly, getting to his feet.

"Well, excuse the hell out of me," I shot back. "But I spend my days mixing blood for you guys, so I wasn't sure."

The glare he aimed at me made my shoulders inch toward my ears.

"We eat just like *humans,* and no, I'm not hungry."

"Right, okay then," I said, clapping my hands together. "Well, it seems like you're ready to go, so—" I waved toward the door ignoring the way my stomach twisted.

He stared at me like I was an idiot. "All right. I'll call you," he said finally, stepping toward the door.

I barely held back a gasp as it felt like a cord was being yanked from the center of my chest. He seemed fine, his expression unchanged as he swung open the door.

It must've been only me who felt the pull. That wasn't exactly fair. It was his stupid species that caused all of this. A human man wouldn't make me crave him like air.

Well, I refused to let him see how badly I wanted him to stay. I wasn't a needy girl. I did my own thing. If he wanted to fuck like animals on my couch and then take off, that was his business. I'd gotten what I wanted from him, too. He could kick rocks, the jerk.

"See you soon," I wheezed, my hand on the wall.

With a nod, he stepped outside and closed the door. Within seconds, the pain in my chest felt like a living thing, clawing to get out.

I dropped to my knees in agony.

# CHAPTER 4
## BEAU

I wasn't sure if she was the most impulsive woman I'd ever met or just had the least self-preservation of anyone on the planet. Vampires liked to tell stories, especially the elders, and more often than not, human mates initially rejected the bond even though it hurt them. They didn't trust it, were wary of tying their life to someone they'd just met, and held misconceptions and biases against our kind. The reasons were endless, and most of them were valid, especially from a species that rarely stayed with the same partner for an entire lifetime.

It was almost a rite of passage to court and woo your mate until they were ready to commit. Males boasted about how quickly they got their mates to fall in love with them.

Unless every mated male I'd ever met had been lying, I was pretty sure what had just happened in her apartment wasn't normal. The sex was typical. Phenomenal, actually. And the exchanging of blood was pretty standard. The speed at which we'd cemented the bond, though, left me reeling.

My brothers and I had been taught what to do when we reached maturity. It had been a conversation with our father that each of us had come away from both mortified and fascinated. There were almost as many stories of Vampires and mates neglecting to finish the bond as there were success stories. Some went years before their mate's canines dropped and the instinct to bite came into play, leaving them in a perpetual state of frustration. Thankfully, information had become more available as the years passed, and it didn't happen so often anymore.

I stepped reluctantly away from Reese's door. The woman had clearly wanted a little space, shooing me out the way she had, and that wasn't normal either. Separation was possible once the bond was cemented—we wouldn't be able to live our lives if we were forced to never leave our mates—but never so soon. My chest burned.

It took months for the bond's effects to lessen enough that mates could go hours and, in rare cases, days without each other.

Slowly, I walked toward the stairs, the burn increasing with every step. At any moment, I expected her to throw open the door and follow me out. If the burn in my chest was getting worse, then her symptoms must've been incredibly painful. For humans, the need to be in close proximity to their mate was even more imperative—an evolutionary design that protected them until their immortality was locked.

I made it to the car before I realized that she wasn't actually going to follow me. By then, my thoughts were so muddy that I was having a hard time concentrating. I had a mate. There was no turning back. No one gave up their fated mate, not when our lives depended on finding that other half of ourselves.

It had nearly killed me the first time I'd done it, and the only reason I'd been able to was because I'd never touched her. Time and distance had eventually lessened the effects. A lot of time and an entire ocean of distance.

My hand was on the door handle when I came to my senses.

There was absolutely no way that Reese was happily watching me walk away. My mate was just so stubborn that she refused to tell me she'd made a mistake, no matter how much it hurt.

Turning on my heel, I jogged back toward the building. Taking the steps two at a time, I jerked around a long-haired man who was meandering down them.

"Where's the fire?" he asked, watching me go.

Ignoring him, I hurried down the breezeway. Reese hadn't locked the door, and I swung it open, ready to chastise her for it.

"Did you forget something?" she wheezed snarkily.

"Gods," I muttered, slamming the door behind me. "Was it so hard to ask me to stay?"

She was kneeling on the kitchen floor, the top half of her body bent downward so far that her forehead was nearly touching the linoleum beneath her.

"It was pretty clear that you wanted to hit it and quit it," she said with a groan, her shoulders losing a little of their tension. "Who was I to stop you?"

"Come here," I muttered, helping her off the floor. "You're my *mate*."

"Not your *keeper*," she stated as she got her feet under her and tilted her head back to look at me.

"How long did you plan on writhing on the floor in pain?"

"It would've passed eventually," she replied, brushing her hair back from her face.

I didn't have the balls to tell her she was wrong. If anything, it only would've gotten worse.

"I don't think I like this," she said, looking away from me. "Uh, I think we should've thought this through a little."

"What's to think through?"

"Oh, I don't know, tying ourselves to each other?" she said with a humorless laugh. "I mean, the sex was great, but is that really enough to sustain a long-term relationship? Probably not."

"My father would tell you that the Gods don't make mistakes."

"You have a father?"

"Why wouldn't I have a father?"

"What about a mom?"

I stared at her. "Really?"

"Mom, too, huh?" She nodded. "Okay."

We stood there for a long moment, neither of us sure what to say. Our bodies didn't have any problem connecting, though. Her hands had slid under my t-shirt to press against the skin of my stomach, and mine were wrapped around the sides of her neck. I didn't even remember putting them there.

"You're hungry," I said, finally.

"I'm fine."

"You said you were."

"I mean, I could eat, yeah." She hedged.

"Come on. Let's go get some food."

Now that we were connected again, I had a hard time stepping away. My hand never lost contact as I lowered it from her neck and slid it down her arm.

"You're a hand holder," she said as I tugged her toward the door. "Interesting."

We only paused long enough for her to pull a small

wallet and set of keys out of the backpack she'd worn that morning. I was relieved to see that she did, in fact, have enough common sense to lock her door.

"What kind of food do you like?" she asked as the cold air slapped me in the face.

"Do you need a jacket?" I asked. It was cold outside for anyone, but she didn't have a whole lot of insulation on her petite frame.

"Nah, this sweater is plenty."

I nodded as we headed toward the car. I wasn't even surprised when her fingers slid between mine again, just relieved that I hadn't had to reach for her first.

It was a complete mindfuck.

"Reese," the long-haired man from before called, standing at the bottom of the steps. "Who's your friend? He's pretty."

I jolted with surprise. Somehow, I hadn't even noticed him.

"None of your beeswax, Kenny," Reese answered as we reached him. "But he's gonna kick your ass if my hairdryer isn't in front of my door by the time we get back."

Kenny lifted his hands in surrender and took a couple of steps backward. "On it."

"I mean it, Kenny," Reese said, looking over her shoulder as she pulled me along. "Give it back."

"What was that?" I asked as we crossed the parking lot.

"Nothing," she replied, waving me off. "He borrows shit and never gives it back. I swear, you'd think I'd learn."

"You really want me to rough him up?"

Reese shot me a look. "Of course not."

"All right."

"Wait," she said, putting her hand over mine as I

reached to open her door. "That's it? You'd just beat him up because I asked you to?"

"Where do you want to eat?" I asked, ignoring the question. Would I beat up Kenny if she asked? Probably. Mating bonds didn't exactly make Vampires rational when it came to their other half.

"I'm good with whatever," Reese replied slowly as I opened her door. "I'm like a raccoon. I'll eat anything."

"Great." I closed the door and rounded the hood, ignoring both the feel of her eyes on me and the anxiety that pulsed while I wasn't touching her.

I didn't even like her.

It felt as if I was going insane.

Reese was quiet as I pulled out of the parking lot, and I had no idea what to say to her. My hand had already found the hole in the thigh of her jeans, and my fingers rested there, the feel of her skin like a balm to my nervous system.

"You know, I usually make the guy buy me dinner *first*," she said a few minutes later. "Especially if I know he's good for it—which you clearly are." She waved her hand toward the dash.

I fought the snarl that took me by surprise and barely glanced at her.

"I don't need to know about the men you've been with before."

"It's not like there's been a lot," she mused. "I mean, I don't think my number is super high or anything, but I obviously have experience. I mean, I'm twenty-seven years old, and I've only had one relationship that lasted longer than three months, so obviously, I've been with more people than, say, someone who got married at twenty-two."

"Reese—"

"You're probably much older than I am, so I'm going to assume that your number is way higher, too." I refused to meet her eyes even though I could feel her staring. "I hope you were a gentleman and bought them dinner first since we've already established that Vampires *do* eat food. How many long relationships have you had? And how does that work exactly with your super long life? Doesn't the woman get older while you stay, you know, like this?"

"Stop speaking," I snapped.

My heart was pounding. Her words hit a little too close to home.

"I'm just trying to get to know you," she shot back. "You don't have to be a dick."

She shoved my hand off her thigh with a huff and crossed her arms over her chest.

"I don't give a shit how many people you've been with," I ground out. "You'll only fuck me from now on."

"Pretty fucking presumptuous of you," she scoffed.

"Go ahead and try," I replied with a chuckle. "See what happens."

Out of the corner of my eye I could see Reese pause. Her entire body stilled.

"Are you threatening me?"

"No, I'm not fucking threatening you." I looked at her in disbelief. "Feel free to do whatever you want. Try and pick some guy up. I'm sure Kenny would be willing to give you a ride."

"Ew. Kenny and I are barely friends. I would never sleep with him."

"You won't want to sleep with anyone," I explained. "You're bonded now. You're not going to find anyone else attractive."

"Yeah, right," she scoffed.

"Even if you convinced yourself that you had," I

warned. "Their touch won't be welcome. It'll be uncomfortable at best."

"You're kidding. I can't even touch other men?" she ground out angrily.

"You can touch them," I clarified. "But not sexually or with the intention of fucking them."

"This just gets better and better."

"You work at a bank," I replied, glancing at her as I pulled onto the freeway. "You must've known at least a little about how the mating bond worked."

"You're the first Vampire I've ever seen there," she shot back. "It's not like there are any Vampires in my social circle. How the hell would I know how the frigging mating bond worked?"

"You acted like you knew it was a forever thing," I said slowly, horror making my heart pound. "You said—"

"Yeah, I know that mates are forever," she said quickly, her voice sharp. "But beyond what they say in fucking magazines—that I don't even read, by the way. My best friend reads them and passes on what she thinks is pertinent info while I try to tune her out. I don't know shit."

"Nothing in those magazines is real."

"I fucking knew it!" she shouted.

The longer we were in the car, the more agitated she got. She was mumbling under her breath, the words too garbled for me to understand. Her knee bounced. Eventually, not touching became too uncomfortable for both of us, and with a curse, she jerked my hand back to her bare thigh.

Instead of taking the exit that would've brought her to a quiet Italian restaurant like I'd planned, I stayed on the freeway. I needed reinforcements.

"It's gonna be okay," I reassured her, my fingers gently smoothing back and forth.

"Easy for you to say," she said tiredly. "Your entire life wasn't just upended because you invited a Vampire in to fuck you on your couch."

I held back a laugh. She wasn't what I wanted. It still felt like the Gods had fucked me for a second time, and a simmering rage at the universe still pulsed under my skin, but I couldn't deny that she was kind of funny. She had so much fucking energy. I bet she'd never sat still for more than a few minutes in her life. She had an answer or a comeback for everything.

I wasn't sure how I'd deal with any of that long-term, but it was a bit amusing for the moment.

"Actually, you're wrong."

"I'm never wrong."

"My life won't be the same now either."

"How's that?" she asked snidely.

"Well, for one, I have to quit my job."

"I'm going to pretend that makes sense." She reached over and patted my thigh condescendingly.

I shook my head. Jesus, she was exhausting. "I have a contract with your government," I explained. "Once a Vampire finds their mate, they're no longer allowed to fulfill that contract."

"That's bullshit," she snapped, suddenly pissed on my behalf. "So, don't tell them."

"Doesn't work that way," I replied. "It's against our laws for me to continue once I'm mated. To do so would be a pretty flagrant breach of ethics."

"How so?"

"Difficult to explain." I hedged. "It's just not done."

"So, you have to find another job?"

I shrugged and slid my hand deeper into the hole in her jeans. Reese let out a little whoosh of air and relaxed into the seat. Shit. I'd forgotten that the tension that was building in me was magnified for her. No wonder she wouldn't shut the hell up. She was trying to distract herself.

"I'm good for a while," I said, tightening my hand on her thigh. "Our family has made plenty of investments that have paid off over the years."

"You're loaded, aren't you?"

"We're comfortable."

"That's what rich people say." She shuddered. "I'm not quitting my job."

"I didn't ask you to."

"I like working there. I get to see Noah every day, and sometimes Mr. Miranda stops by, and I get to see him, too."

"Mr. Miranda?"

"Noah's husband. He was my teacher in high school, and we've stayed close."

That sounded...off.

"Don't make that face. Number one, Mr. Miranda is very gay, and number two, he isn't a sleaze. They're like my dads."

"I didn't say anything."

"No, your face was speaking for you."

"Where are your parents?"

"Who knows," she replied with a shrug. "They lost custody when I was five and dropped off the face of the earth."

"You want me to find them for you?"

"Jesus, *no*." She paused. "Wait, you can do that?"

"Money helps."

"I fucking *knew* you were loaded."

I couldn't stop the chuckle that came out of my mouth.

"Dear God," Reese murmured. "Laughing makes you more attractive. *How is that possible?* Do it again."

"Ha."

"No, laugh. Do it."

"I can't laugh on command."

"Fine, I'll tell you a joke." She hummed and tapped her finger on her chin. "Okay, got one. *What does one traffic light say to the other traffic light?*" She paused. "Stop looking at me. I'm changing."

"Was that supposed to be funny?" I asked, my lips twitching.

"It's hilarious!"

"To a five-year-old."

"I don't even know any five-year-olds," she grumbled.

"No nieces or nephews?"

"No siblings, period," she said with a snort. "I do have Rena. She's my best friend. We're practically sisters. She doesn't have any kids yet."

"The magazine reader?"

"Oh, yeah. She loves that shit. Says she wants a Vampire of her very own." She let out a huff of laughter. "Man, she's gonna be pissed. Do you have any siblings?"

"Four—three brothers."

"You don't know how many brothers you have?" she asked dubiously.

"Had four," I replied quietly. "Three now."

"Oh," she breathed. "I'm sorry."

I nodded. The reminder of Zeke was like a splash of cold water.

"Are you close with them?" Reese asked cautiously. "I always wondered what having siblings would be like."

"Yeah, we're close."

"That's cool."

The car was quiet for a while. I wasn't sure what Reese

was thinking about, but I couldn't get over the fact that Zeke would've loved her. Their personalities were startlingly similar now that I thought about it. The same sharp tongue, the same compulsion to get the last word, the same ability to irritate me.

"Wait, where are we going?" Reese asked, leaning forward as I pulled onto my driveway. "This isn't a restaurant."

"Our place."

"What do you mean, *our*? It's not my place."

"My family's."

"You're taking me to your parents' house?"

"Calm down."

"You still live with your parents?" Her voice rose with each word.

"Jesus, calm down."

"I didn't agree to this."

"We're already here."

"No," she snarled. "Take me back."

"They know we're here," I said, tightening my hand on her thigh. "At least say hello."

"Mother of God," Reese breathed as we pulled up in front of the house. "This place is fucking massive."

"Yes."

"No wonder you still live here," she mused, leaning down to see better. "I'd never move out either."

"I have a fucking apartment to myself," I muttered defensively. "It's not like I'm still in my childhood bedroom."

I didn't know why I felt defensive. Most adult Vampires lived with their parents. Some moved out when they were mated, but even then, there were a lot who stayed put. It was a community, more than anything. When you lived in a world where those who understood your life were few and far between, you tended to stick close to the ones who did.

"I can't go in there," Reese whispered, trapping my hand between her thighs as she clenched them. "I can't—" She looked at me worriedly. "It's getting bad again."

"Hurts?" I asked quietly.

"Like I'm going to come out of my skin."

"You hid it pretty well."

"I was trying to ignore it."

I nodded. Instead of hitting the button to open the garage, I circled back around and pulled back down the long driveway.

"Wait, what are you doing?" Reese asked as I found a spot in the grass halfway to the main road.

"You've got two options," I said, throwing the car in park. "You can stick it out until we've made it through introductions and dinner."

Reese groaned.

"Or I can satisfy it here."

"Someone could see us."

"No one's going to see us."

"What if someone drives up?"

"They won't."

"How can you be sure?"

"What's your choice?" I asked, refusing to keep going back and forth.

Reese bit her bottom lip and glanced out the windows. "Here."

"Good."

I got out and rounded the hood before she could change her mind.

"What, you mean out in the open?" she asked as I opened her door. "This is dumb. This—"

She wasn't resisting. Her mouth might be going a

million miles an hour, but she was pliant as I helped her out of the car and ushered her toward the trunk.

"No one will see us," I assured her, spinning her toward the car. My hands were at the waistband of her jeans in a moment, and they were so loose that they fell to her ankles as soon as I'd unbuttoned them.

Our fingers tangled as we shoved at her underwear. I held back a laugh at the sight of them. Boxer briefs. Almost an exact match to the ones I was wearing. This woman was so fucking wrong for me.

I swallowed hard as Reese bent over the trunk, her back arching as she pressed backward against my hips.

"Why are you still dressed?"

It took seconds to shove my trousers and boxers out of the way. The moment I was bare, I pressed forward, and her hand was there to meet me, her fingers between her legs positioning me at her entrance.

We both groaned as I slid inside.

"Yes," Reese whispered, bracing her hands against the side of the car.

It was better than the first time, and I hadn't realized that it *could* be better than the first time. Reese was so wet that the sound of me sliding in and out of her was obscene. Her muscles clenched as she panted, her back arching even more.

She felt so good it was fucking terrifying. Nothing else would ever feel as good as being inside Reese. Nothing else would even come close.

"Please," she gasped, her hand sliding back between her legs. The tips of her fingers brushed against my balls as she manipulated her clit.

I clenched my teeth. We were scratching an itch. It was nothing more than that, but I refused to come so soon. I doubted she'd ever let me live it down.

"Beau," she gasped. "Jesus, bite me already."

"You're not in charge of that," I argued, wrapping my hand gently around the front of her throat. The moment I bit her, it was over. There was no way I could hold out.

"Please, I'm already on edge," she breathed. "I don't want to come the other way. It's not as good. It's—" Her words broke off on a moan as I urged her up until her back touched my chest. It wasn't an attractive position. To anyone else, we probably would've looked ridiculous. She was so much shorter that I had to widen my feet and bend my legs to compensate. We were half bent over the trunk, fully dressed, and I could feel the heat in my face from trying to hold back—but it felt so fucking incredible.

Letting go of her throat, I pulled my hand to my mouth and nicked the skin. The moment I had it in front of her mouth, she latched on, pulling so hard that I felt it in my balls. *Gods*. Jerking my head forward, I bit into the tender skin of her neck and groaned as her pussy pulsed around me and the taste of her flowed over my tongue. The orgasm went on for so goddamn long that my legs were rubbery by the time she let go of my hand, licking it softly before dropping her head back on my shoulder.

"Holy fuck," she murmured, sagging against me. "Is it always going to be like that?"

"I think so."

"Why does anyone ever get out of bed?"

I let out a huff of laughter as I pulled out of her and helped her steady herself against the car.

"Dammit," she griped, glancing at me over her shoulder. "I missed it."

After quickly yanking my trousers back up, I reached for the boxers around her ankles.

"Why do you wear men's underwear?"

"Really?" she asked, helping me pull them up. "That's what you want to talk about?"

"I've never been with any other woman that does."

She sent me a sharp look over her shoulder and jerked her jeans up her thighs. "I don't need to hear about your other conquests."

"Oh, now you *don't* want to talk about it?" I asked in amusement.

"Nope."

It was strange to watch the bond strengthening in real-time. It had been less than an hour since she had talked about other lovers, but suddenly, the idea made her angry.

"Is my hair a mess?" she asked grouchily, stomping toward her door.

"It looks the same," I replied, following her so I could open it.

"I can get my own door."

"I'll get it."

"Maybe I want to do it," she argued.

"Sorry."

"Next time, I'll do it myself."

"No."

"You're so fucking irritating."

"I'm hurt," I replied dryly.

It was actually amusing to see her so discomposed. I threw the door shut as soon as she'd climbed inside and heard her screech of frustration as I walked around to my own door. By the time I sat down, she'd pulled the mirror down in the sunshade and was desperately pulling her fingers through her hair.

"You said it looks the same," she snapped, turning toward me with wide eyes, her reddish blond hair wild around her face. "Are you serious?"

"Yes, I'm serious." I started the car and pulled back onto the driveway, turning back toward the house.

"It's a mess!"

"It's exactly the same as you had it at work this morning."

"It is not!"

"That's not how you normally wear it?" I asked curiously. I thought the wild mane of hair was a deliberate choice.

"I can't meet your parents like this."

"Sure, you can."

"No, really. There's a hole in the ass of my jeans, I look like I put my finger in a light socket, and I'm not even wearing a bra."

"You're not?"

"No," she retorted. "And just to be completely transparent, a little nipple play goes a long way when you're having sex, especially when they're just out there for the taking!"

Her mouth snapped shut, and she stared at me in horror.

Before she knew what I was doing, I'd reached across the car and slid my hand up her sweater. When my fingers brushed over her nipple, she swore, but she made no move to stop me as I pinched one and then the other.

"Better?"

"A little," she grumbled, leaning into my hand.

"I'll give you more later," I replied, pulling my hand away so I could hit the garage door opener on the ceiling.

"I don't think I like you very much," she mused, yanking her sweater into place.

"Sucks for you."

"Jesus, how many cars do you guys have?"

I ignored the question as I pulled into my spot and

turned the car off. My mother was probably pacing the floors, wondering what the hell we were doing. She would've known the moment we drove up the driveway the first time. My father, on the other hand, probably knew exactly what we'd been doing.

"I'm not good with parents," Reese said, opening her door before I was even out of the car. "They're going to hate me."

"No, they won't," I assured her. By the time I got out of the car, she was already standing next to my door.

"No, really," she said, taking my hand as she winced. "I'm an acquired taste. Most people don't like me at first. I have to kind of grow on you."

"That's a relief," I muttered, tugging her toward the door to the kitchen. "I was getting nervous."

It took her almost a minute to understand what I'd said, and I was already opening the door when she replied.

"You're such an asshole!"

Reese froze behind me when she got a good look at the faces staring at us from around the counter.

"So, it's going well, then," Chance said dryly, toasting me with his drink.

"Fuck my life," Reese muttered under her breath.

I probably should've warned her that every person in the room had heard everything she'd said since the moment we'd pulled into the garage.

# CHAPTER 5
# REESE

I f there was ever a good moment for spontaneous human combustion, it was the moment that Beau pulled me into the kitchen full of people that just heard me call him an asshole. I tried to tell myself that they already knew he was an asshole—it wasn't as if he tried to hide it—but I still couldn't meet their eyes. What a fan-fucking-tastic first impression.

"This is Reese," Beau announced, his hand tightening on mine as he led me further into the room. "Reese, these are my parents, Erik and Matilda, and my brothers, Chance and Daniel."

"Call me Mattie, please," his mom said kindly with the smallest hint of a southern accent. "Matilda is so stuffy."

She moved forward to shake my hand, and I gave her a pained smile as I took it. "Nice to meet you."

"Wonderful to meet you, too, darlin'," she replied, her smile bright. She was gorgeous. Not in a way that said she worked for it, but like it just radiated from somewhere inside of her. It was slightly disconcerting that she didn't look older than her forties, though. I mean, I knew that

Vampires didn't age the way we did, but she definitely didn't look old enough to be Beau's mom. His older sister, maybe.

Beau's dad was different. He only looked too young to be Beau's dad until you met his eyes and realized that the guy had seen some shit. His beard was long, with just a few light red streaks through it, and there were tattoos down both sides of his neck, disappearing into the collar of his shirt.

"Erik," he said gruffly, nodding at me. "Good to meet you."

"You, too," I murmured.

Okay, one friendly parent wasn't so bad. I could maybe win his dad over later.

"That one is Danny," Beau said, pointing at the brother with short hair. Then he pointed to the brother with longer hair and a full beard that looked like a carbon copy of his dad. "And that one is Chance."

"Ulf called earlier," Erik said. "He wants you to call him back when you get a moment."

"He could've called me himself," Beau replied.

"Didn't want to interrupt."

"Those first few days are a bit of a whirlwind," Beau's mom said conspiratorially to me, wrinkling her nose happily. "Make sure you take the time to soak it all in."

"I think they're letting it soak in just fine, Ma," Chance said, laughter in his voice.

"More than once, even," Danny muttered.

My face was so hot it felt like it was going to melt off my skull. How the fuck did they know? I glared at Beau. Someone must have seen us.

"Enough," Erik barked, glaring at his sons. "What the fuck is the matter with you?"

Beau let go of my hand to drape his arm over my shoulders. "Ignore them."

"Dinner's almost ready," Mattie said, reaching out to give Beau's bicep a squeeze. "Why don't you show Reese around, and I'll call you when it's on the table."

"Sounds good," Beau replied.

Chance and Danny had barely moved to leave when their mom spun on them. "Where do you think you're going?" she snapped. She pointed at Danny. "Set the table." Then at Chance. "Ice water and wine glasses for everyone."

Beau's chest jerked with silent laughter as he led me out of the room.

"You said no one would—" My words cut off as Beau's hand covered my mouth. He shook his head.

"This is the common living area," he said, his hand still over my mouth. "We each have our own spaces, but if we're spending time as a family—we come down here. There's a big television that drops down above the fireplace, but it barely gets used. Come on. My rooms are this way."

He tugged me up a flight of stairs and down a hallway.

"If you turn the other way at the top of the stairs, that's my brother Ulf's rooms." He finally dropped his hand.

"You have a brother named Ulf?"

"His name is actually Ambrose, but we've always called him Ulf."

"Interesting."

"My dad's never called any of us by the names my mom gave us."

"Why not?"

"Probably to be a pain in her ass," he replied dryly.

"What does he call you?"

"Bjorn," he replied, swinging open the door at the end of the hallway. "He calls Danny, Arne. Chance is *Happ*."

Inside was a living area that was pretty much the same size as my apartment. A couch and recliner sat in the center around an old wood coffee table. Actually, all the furniture looked old and expensive.

"This is the living room," Beau said, closing the door behind us. He pointed to the left. "That's the kitchen—but I don't have anything up here except eggs and beer."

"So, all the food groups, then," I replied sarcastically.

"I mostly eat downstairs," he said, following as I moved toward the kitchen. "Sometimes I make a couple of eggs up here if I'm in a hurry."

"You like eggs, huh?"

"It's the only thing I make well."

"Typical," I muttered. There was a small kitchen table that looked straight out of a historical museum.

"My mom likes to decorate," Beau said as I stopped to look at it.

"Your mom decorated your bedroom?" I asked, pressing my lips together in amusement.

"This is my dining area," he shot back. "My bedroom is that way." He pointed toward the other side of the living room.

"Tell me the truth," I ordered jokingly as I walked toward the bedroom. "She decorated in here, too."

The door was open, and I swanned through like I owned the place, only to pause when I got a good look at it. The bed was massive. There were two chairs in the corner, one of them draped with the shirt he'd been wearing when we met that morning. The dressers were matching and older than I was. Everything was dark and luxurious and incredible.

"I know you didn't decorate in here," I mused. There was no way.

"I chose the bed. The rest of the shit came with it."

"Nice bed," I murmured as he stepped in behind me.

The fire that was becoming almost familiar under my skin began to thrum. Knowing that I could slake it made it only slightly less disconcerting. We'd already had sex twice. It made absolutely no sense that I was already itching for more.

"Your mom said dinner is almost ready," I rasped as his cool palms slid under my sweater.

"We've got a little time."

"Not enough."

"We'll see," he said quietly, pressing against my back until I started toward the bed. I'd barely reached it when my sweater was tugged up and over my head, leaving me completely topless.

Beau hummed deep in his throat as he turned me and pressed his hand in the center of my chest.

"Lay back."

"We don't have time," I argued half-heartedly as I dropped to the bed, letting my shoes slide off my feet as I lay back.

Beau stared.

"What?" I asked, frowning. Looking down, I couldn't see anything out of place. I mean, breasts were present and accounted for. Nipples were hard as rocks and pointing toward the ceiling. I didn't have a dryer sheet stuck to me or anything.

"So pale," he murmured, kneeling on the bed by my hips. His hands tucked under my arms and scooted me up the bed. "And pink."

"It's not like they see a lot of sun," I replied, rolling my eyes.

Bracing on one arm, his other hand slid up my stomach, and I arched against it. His hands were so cool on my heated skin.

"How long is this supposed to last?" I asked, letting out a relieved breath as his fingers brushed over my nipple. "We literally just had sex, and I'm already on fire."

"I'm not sure," he mumbled, leaning down to lick my nipple.

I damn near shot off the bed when he wrapped his lips around it and tugged.

"That's not comforting," I replied, holding his head to me. My toes curled against the comforter as I arched toward him.

"It's normal for things to be heated in the beginning."

"Is that a joke?" I asked dubiously. "Did you really just make a joke?"

"What?" He glanced at me in confusion.

"*Heated*?" I replied dryly. "Really?"

"It wasn't intentional." He shook his head as he nuzzled between my breasts. "The desire is normal. Most mates don't leave their rooms for days—sometimes weeks."

"What's different about us?" I asked, trying to hold on to my train of thought. It was nearly impossible to focus as he dragged his teeth gently over one of my nipples. "Why did you bring me here?"

"It usually takes longer for a human mate to accept the bond," he said distractedly. His tongue slid around the underside of my breast, and I nearly screamed.

"What?" I was having a hard time following. Threading my fingers through his hair, I yanked his head up so he'd meet my eyes. "What do you mean it usually takes longer? People just—just live with it? I thought this was normal?" My voice rose in volume and pitch with each word.

"It's uncomfortable," he clarified, his eyes on mine. "But most humans are more distrustful of the bond. They don't want to give up their lives, or they're too nervous to make that kind of commitment. It usually takes months to finally cement it."

"I could've waited," I murmured, understanding hit like a bucket of cold water. "I didn't—You made it seem like—No, you said—"

"I asked you," he flatly cut me off. "I asked you every step of the way."

"You made it seem like it was inevitable. That nothing would help except if I fucked you."

"It is inevitable," he gritted out. "Even if you'd wanted to wait, we still would've been uncomfortable until you came to a decision."

"That wasn't discomfort," I argued, shoving him off of me. "That was impossible. It was *painful*. It burned."

Beau shrugged as I scuttled off the bed and reached for my sweater. "Other mates choose to deal with it until they're sure."

"I didn't know that was an option!"

"You could've said no at any time."

"No, I couldn't."

Beau stiffened and crossed his arms over his chest. "I didn't force you."

"What, so I'm just weaker than all the other mates?" I spat, glaring at him. "Is that what you're saying?"

"I'm not saying anything beyond the fact that no one forced you to accept the mating bond."

"It's not like you were trying to wait either," I shot back. "You wanted it just as much as me."

"It's a biological need for me," he replied calmly. "I've

always known that I would have a mate at some point. Why would I want to wait?"

"You don't even know me!"

"It doesn't matter."

"Of course it matters!"

I wanted to hit him. The realization that I was the only mate who hadn't held out long enough to actually get to know their partner? That stung. I wasn't some weak woman who'd been waiting for Prince Charming to come rescue her or who threw herself onto the dick of any handsome man who smiled my way. I was discerning. I had self-respect. I didn't need some full-of-himself Vampire to come sweep me off my feet. I'd never even *wanted* that. The pull to Beau hadn't been rational. It was visceral. Agonizing.

Even as I wished I could clock him, my body still ached for his. It was already protesting the lack of contact.

"Son, dinner is on the table," a voice called from the speaker in the wall, making me jump.

"You have a fucking intercom system?" I spat. For some reason, that made me even angrier.

"The house is big," he replied evenly. "Come on."

"I'm not just going to go down to dinner with your family when we're in the middle of a conversation," I argued, my eyes widening as he walked toward the door.

"She went to the trouble of setting out a nice meal for us," he replied. "I'm not going to keep her waiting just because you're having some kind of identity crisis."

I sputtered as I hurried after him. "I'm not having an identity crisis."

"It's not my responsibility to make your choices for you," he said flatly as he led me toward the door to the hallway. "You can deal with your own regrets."

"Take me home," I whispered, my voice shaking with rage.

I hated him. He was cold and distant, and it didn't matter how much my body craved his. He was an awful person. There was no shred of understanding or empathy in his gaze. No words of comfort for my understandable panic and confusion. There was just...impatience.

"I'll take you home after dinner."

"I'll call a ride share."

I moved to walk past him, but I didn't make it far before his hand clamped down like a vice on my arm.

"You may be angry or scared about your change in circumstances—" I scoffed, and his hand tightened. "But my mother is fucking ecstatic that I've found my mate. She's down there right now making sure everything is perfect for your first dinner with our family. You will not fuck this up for her."

"Or what?" I ground out between my teeth.

"The bond is cemented," he said quietly, leaning further into my space. "There's no going back. You can make this easy or hard on yourself."

"I hate you," I whispered back.

"That's fine," he replied, straightening. "You wouldn't have been my choice either."

I followed him silently out of his apartment, telling myself that it didn't feel as if I'd just been slapped. Foster care had taught me a lot of lessons, some good and some bad, but I was grateful for it as I followed him down the stairs, digging my fingernails into my palms to keep my eyes from watering. The tactic worked. By the time we reached the kitchen, I'd gotten my emotions under control again.

"I wasn't sure if you had any food sensitivities," Beau's mom—Mattie—told me as she gestured toward the food on the table. "And it always takes a while for the mating bond to—"

"Mama," Beau said, cutting her off with a shake of his head.

"What?" I asked, glancing around the table.

"We can talk about it later," Beau said easily. "This looks great."

"Not sure why she made my favorite," Beau's brother, Chance, said happily. "But I'll take it."

"I thought this was Beau's favorite," Mattie said, slapping her hands onto her hips.

"Sit down, love," his dad ordered gruffly, patting Mattie's hip. "If we need anything else, one of us will get it."

"I think everything is already here," she replied with a smile, sliding into her seat. "Open the wine?"

"She always gets our favorites confused," Beau's brother, Danny, said quietly, leaning toward me a little. "It never fails."

"I can also hear you," Mattie said easily. "And I know this is Beau's favorite."

"Is it?" Chance needled.

"So, Reese," Beau's dad, Erik, boomed. "What do you do?"

"Uh..." I glanced at Beau, but he wasn't even looking at me. "I'm a blood tech."

"No shit?" Danny asked in surprise.

"No shit," I confirmed, my lips twitching. "If you guys tell me your favorites, I can hook you up."

The silence at the table was deafening.

I nearly slid to the floor in embarrassment when Erik finally let out a bark of laughter. "I've had a lot of offers, but I can easily say that's a first."

"I'm sorry," I breathed, glancing around the table. "Did I just put my foot in my mouth?"

"Hell, no," Chance said with a huge smile. "I'll make you a list."

"I'm not picky," Danny added. "Just get me the good stuff."

"I have no idea what the good stuff is," I confessed.

"O pos," Danny and Chance both replied at the same time.

"Good to know." My lips twitched. I looked over at Beau, who was still sitting there silently. "What about you?"

He shook his head.

"What, you don't have a favorite?" I joked. The fact that he was silent really bothered me. He'd asked me to make an effort with his family. He'd forced me to the table. The least he could do was act like he wanted me there.

"Mates don't use banks, honey," Beau's mom said kindly, passing the bottle of wine down the table to Chance.

"You don't?"

"Banks are only for those who haven't found their mates yet," Erik confirmed.

"But, why—?" My words cut off as the realization hit, and I turned wide-eyed back to Beau. "You'll only have my blood from now on?"

A stiff nod was all the reply I got.

"But, how is that possible?" I asked in confusion. I knew the amount of blood that we sent out on a daily basis. I knew how much the average Vampire ingested. There was no way, even if we were having sex regularly, that Beau would take that much from me.

"Fuck, Bjorn," Chance said, his eyebrows high on his forehead. "Have you told her *anything*?"

"There hasn't been time," he replied darkly.

I jerked back in my seat.

"It has been a bit of a whirlwind," Mattie said sweetly, smiling at me. "We only found out about you this morning."

I swallowed uncomfortably. Now that I knew that most humans didn't immediately fall into bed with their mates the way I had, I felt like a fucking idiot.

"A mate's blood is composed perfectly to meet a Vampire's needs," Beau told me, finally turning his head to meet my eyes. "It doesn't take nearly as much to satisfy."

"Think of it as quality over quantity," Daniel added helpfully.

"Oh," I murmured. I looked over at his brothers. "So, neither of you have mates?"

"Free as a bird," Chance said as Daniel shook his head.

"None of my brothers are mated," Beau clarified.

"I've got a friend," I joked with a huff of laughter.

"It doesn't work that way," Beau snapped.

"Bjorn," Erik growled chidingly.

Mattie studied the two of us for a moment before speaking.

"Mates are very hard to find," she told me softly. "It's not a matter of meeting someone and falling in love the way humans do. It's instinctual and instant. There is no choice."

Her gaze slid to Beau for a moment before looking back at me.

"The love comes after."

I held back the inappropriate bark of laughter that filled my throat.

"So, you just have to wait until your mate falls in your lap?" I asked, looking at each of them.

"Pretty much," Daniel answered. "I mean, we're actively looking, but when you don't know where to look or who you're looking for—"

"Talk about a needle in a haystack."

"More like a needle in a needle stack," Chance quipped.

"I had to cross continents to find mine," Erik said, his eyes on Mattie.

She smiled softly back at him.

The conversation grew quiet as the food was passed around. Mattie had made some kind of pasta with shrimp and sausage in it, and I didn't care whose favorite it was because it was divine. The wine flowed freely, and there was no shortage as Erik opened bottle after bottle. By the time we'd finished eating, and Mattie got up to make a round of espressos, my head was spinning.

"Do you have any family?" Erik asked thoughtfully. I'd watched him drink at least four times more than I had, but he looked completely fine.

"Nope, no family," I said, my eyes widening in horror as I let out a small hiccup. "I'm sorry!"

Erik laughed and waved me off.

"I grew up in foster care. No siblings, no parents. I have some found family, though. My best friend, Rena, and my boss, Noah, and his husband, Mr. Miranda. I actually knew Mr. Miranda first. They're like my dads, sort of. The kind that threaten to throw you out a window but also braid your hair for a volleyball game." I shrugged. It was impossible to explain my relationship with the two men. We were a weird little trio.

"All of my family is gone, too," Erik said with a nod.

"Found family. I like that term. I have two best friends that we consider family, too."

"Uncle Sven," Chance bellowed deeply.

"Mordecai," Daniel added, drawing the name out.

"We fought together long ago," Erik said, his eyes crinkling at the corners. "Those bonds never fade."

It was on the tip of my tongue to ask him which war he'd fought in—I was pretty fucking sure it wasn't anything even remotely recent—when Mattie walked back in carrying the espresso.

"Why didn't you call me?" Erik scolded as he shot up from his seat to take the tray from her.

"You were visiting," she replied easily. "The pie is still on the counter."

"Sit. I'll grab it," he ordered, setting the tray of espresso cups on the table.

"We'll have to have your found family over for a visit," Mattie said as she handed out the coffee.

I snorted before I could stop myself.

Beau glared.

"No, no, I'd love that," I said, grinning. "And you can just call them my family. It's just that my best friend is obsessed with Vampires, and she's going to lose her mind."

"Obsessed with Vampires, you say?" Daniel asked, leaning forward with his chin in his hand.

"Don't do it," I warned jokingly, pointing at him. "She wants a mate, and it sounds like unless you win the lottery, she's not it."

"Never know," he said with a shrug.

"Mind your manners," Mattie warned.

"But, yes, they'd all be happy to come for dinner," I continued, raising my eyebrows at Daniel. He glared playfully. I liked him. I looked back at Mattie. "I mean, once they know about the whole mate thing."

"Your family doesn't know?" Mattie asked, pausing.

"Well, no." I looked to Beau for help, but unsurprisingly, he was watching the conversation with little interest. "I mean, it all happened kind of fast."

"Lucky bastard," Chance mumbled.

"Noah and Mr. Miranda know," I added. "I mean, they suspect. Noah warned me after I met Beau this morning that he thought that's what was happening, but they don't know for sure or anything. I told Rena I thought I was getting the flu."

Mattie let out a little laugh. "The flu?"

"Well, that's what it felt like," I shot back, throwing my hands up in the air, making her laugh again. "That heat stuff is no joke. I wanted to crawl out of my skin."

"Enough," Beau said quietly. He was glaring at me like he wanted to throttle me.

"What?" I asked, widening my eyes at him. "It's not like they don't know what I'm talking about. You knew what it was, right? So, I'm guessing your brothers do too. Plus, I mean, your mom's been through it—"

The words weren't even out of my mouth before Beau had shot from his seat and was dragging me out of mine. He wasn't rough by any means, but I was pretty sure if I hadn't gotten to my feet of my own free will, he would've tossed me over his shoulder.

"What is wrong with you?" I griped as he pulled me through the house.

"Beau," his mom called.

He completely ignored her.

We didn't stop until we'd reached the front porch, and he'd slammed the door closed behind us.

"On what planet is discussing our sex life an appropriate conversation to have with my mother and brothers?" he spat, rounding on me.

"Our sex life?" I asked dumbly. That's what he was pissed about? "I didn't say that you bent me over the fucking car, Beau. All I mentioned was how uncomfortable the heat was. That shit was painful."

"So, it's okay if you mention your arousal to my entire family, but fucking on my car is inappropriate? *That's* where you draw the line?"

"I don't know what kind of sex you've been having, but that wasn't arousal, you idiot. That was some kind of *torture.*"

"*Heat,*" he ground out. "It's called mating *heat* for a reason."

My jaw dropped in surprise. "You've gotta be fucking kidding me," I shot back, my voice rising. "Like a fucking *dog*?"

"No, not like a dog. Lower your goddamn voice."

"I'm not lowering anything!"

"Makes sense, since you can't seem to distinguish what should and shouldn't be private!"

"Well, how the fuck was I supposed to know?"

"You're drunk," he replied derisively.

"Your dad kept pouring me wine!"

"You didn't have to keep finishing it."

"I was trying to be polite."

"Well, you fucking failed."

"Holy fuck," I muttered, spinning away from him. I'd talked about sex with his mother. *His mother.* I didn't think I'd ever been more mortified in my life—and that was saying something, considering I'd shit my pants running the mile in eighth grade because my sadist of a PE teacher wouldn't excuse me when I told him I wasn't feeling well.

"This is a nightmare," Beau mumbled tiredly behind me. "Come on. Let's say our goodbyes, and I'll drive you home."

"Just—" I waved him off without looking at him. "Just give me a minute, okay?"

My heart thudded like a drum as I tried to calm my breathing. It wasn't the end of the world. No one had ever died of embarrassment. No one had ever died from humiliation. No one had ever died because they'd tied themselves to a Vampire that was a complete asshole but handed out orgasms like candy—I didn't think. I needed to start reading those tabloids with all the salacious details.

I'd impulsively tied myself to a guy who sneered at me and treated me like crap. That was overwhelming enough. I didn't need to overthink the fact that I'd said the wrong thing to his mother. That was inconsequential. In the larger scheme of things, that was nothing. They'd forget about it in less time than my classmates had the pooping incident.

I was strong. I was independent. Sure, I sometimes said shit that was embarrassing. Who didn't? I was funny as hell. I knew from experience that made up for a lot of faults. I'd just go back in there, make fun of myself, and the whole thing would be laughed off. Easy.

"Okay, let's go," I said, pushing past him. I threw open the door and marched right back into the dining room, pretending that my face wasn't on fire.

Mattie looked at me with concern, but the brothers watched in amusement, like they were waiting for the next unhinged thing that would come out of my mouth.

"I'm sorry for bringing up our sex life at the dinner table," I announced, throwing my hands out at my waist and wriggling my fingers as I shook my hips. "Didn't even realize that was what I was describing. Who knew?"

Chance and Daniel burst out laughing, their eyes on Beau.

"It's all right, honey," Mattie said, rounding the table. "I'm sure it's all very confusing."

I took a step back as she reached me. If she put her hand on me or tried to comfort me, I was sure I'd burst into tears. Beau's mom was so fucking nice. I didn't understand how he could've come from her.

"Beaumont," Erik said firmly, his eyes on his son. "A word."

"Have some pie," Mattie said to me as the two of them left the room.

I dropped into my seat, glancing behind me, but they'd already disappeared from view.

Maybe his dad was going to berate him for finding the absolute worst mate in the history of mates. I hadn't been lying when I'd told Beau I had to grow on people. I was usually either loved or hated on the spot, but eventually, the ones who hated me warmed up enough to at least find me amusing. I didn't think that there was any way out of the mating bond beyond death. I really hoped they weren't making a plan to off me.

"Don't worry about it," Chance said softly to me, pointing his fork in my direction. "Seriously. You didn't say anything embarrassing."

"Tell that to Beau," I joked. "I thought that vein in his neck was going to burst."

"So, the heat thing is real," Daniel mused.

"It's not—" I looked over my shoulder to make sure that Beau hadn't come back yet. "I didn't realize what it was, I guess. It's not, like, *sexual*. Not really. It's just the need to be near the other person, like an ache." I huffed in frustration. "I'm not explaining it right."

"That's pretty accurate," Mattie confirmed, nodding. "It's the urge to be close to your mate, in whatever form that takes. Even just holding Erik's hand eases it."

"You're still dealing with it?" I asked in shock.

"It's not how it was in the beginning," she assured me. "But we can't be apart for long, even after all these years."

I was just about to ask just how long they'd been together when the sound of Erik's voice barreled through the wall.

"This is not how I raised you," he shouted. "How dare you treat your mate the way you've treated her tonight? You've been given a *gift*, Bjorn."

"More like a fucking curse," Beau's voice filtered through, making me burn with shame.

I curled my hands into fists on my lap.

"That sweet girl is doing everything she can to make a good impression, and you've sat there glowering at her from the moment you walked into the room."

"She wouldn't know how to make a good impression if it slapped her in the face."

I focused on breathing. In through my nose and out through my mouth. I stared at the pie in front of me—some kind of berry—so I didn't accidentally meet anyone's eyes.

"If you ever put your hands on her again the way you did tonight—"

"I didn't hurt her! I wouldn't fucking hurt her!"

"If you ever put your hands on her in anything but a loving manner, I will take you out of this world," Erik roared.

"Nice," Beau spat back derisively.

"Better for her to live a human's lifespan loved than a

Vampire's lifespan without it," Erik replied, his voice lowering. "You, my most selfless son, have lost your way. You've given up too much, and it's twisted you—"

"This conversation is over."

"It's over when I say it is."

"I'll make it work," Beau yelled, cutting him off. "I'll make it fucking work. I have no other choice, do I? I'll deal with her inability to behave appropriately, and I'll ignore the sarcasm that she can't seem to contain and the self-confidence that seems to spring from *nowhere*."

I really hoped that no one noticed the shaky hiccup that burst from my throat. They would be done soon. He'd stop speaking soon. Then he could take me home, and I could be by myself for a minute. It wasn't as if I liked him either. He was a pompous asshole with absolutely no sense of humor. I'd had better. I'd had loads better. Other men fucking loved me. I'd never been short on partners. This was a Beau problem—it wasn't a Reese problem. Reese was just fine exactly how she was.

"I'll keep my touches *loving*, and I'll fuck her—"

Beau's words were cut off with a loud thud, and Mattie was instantly out of her chair and rounding the table.

"Stay here," she ordered the boys, pointing at them without even looking at them.

I couldn't hear what she said to Beau and Erik. She kept her voice too low, but less than thirty seconds later, she came back into the room. Erik was right behind her.

"I apologize," he said kindly, his eyes on me. "I was unaware you could hear us."

"You were being kind of loud," I joked.

He dipped his chin in acknowledgment. "Vampire hearing is much better than that of humans. I always assume my family can hear, but I underestimated yours."

"No worries," I replied, shooting him an uncomfortable smile.

"Beau will be right in," Mattie said, patting my shoulder as she passed my seat. "If you want to finish your pie before he gets here."

"I'm pretty full," I replied.

When Beau walked in a few moments later, it took every piece of willpower not to jump up from my seat and run toward the garage door. I wanted to get out of there more than anything.

"What?" Beau barked.

My head snapped up to find him staring at Daniel.

"You're a fucking asshole," Daniel replied, pushing up from his seat.

"Enough," Erik ordered, making Daniel drop back down again.

"Sorry, Danny, this one's taken," Beau said snidely, setting his hand on the back of my chair.

"Could've fooled me," his brother muttered. "Amazing how one person can fuck up the same thing twice."

I jerked in confusion, my gaze moving back and forth between them. What the hell was Daniel talking about?

"Let's go, Reese," Beau ordered. He didn't reach for me or even look at me as he said it.

"Thank you for dinner," I said, my voice barely wobbling as I looked at Mattie and Erik.

"Absolutely," Mattie replied.

"It was nice meeting all of you."

As I stood, Erik stood with me.

"Would you like me to drive you home?" he asked seriously, his voice low.

"Oh." I floundered for a moment. "No. No, thank you. Beau can drive me."

"All right."

The brothers called out their goodbyes as Beau ushered me into the garage. The moment we were alone, I let out a breath of relief.

I didn't need to pretend anymore. I didn't need to put on a happy face or act like I was okay or tell jokes or hide the wobble in my voice.

"I've got it," I bit out as Beau reached for my door.

"Of course you do," he mumbled under his breath, walking back to his side of the car.

I counted to ten before opening my door and getting into my seat.

I must've done something right in a former life because the ride back to my apartment was blissfully silent, and I was able to process everything that had happened.

It took me that long to realize that what I was feeling wasn't sadness. I didn't feel bad because Beau didn't like me. I didn't wonder what I could do differently or how I could change into a person that he would appreciate. I was already pretty fucking great.

My hands shook, and my breath seesawed in my lungs, not because I was embarrassed or upset. It was because I was fucking terrified that one impulsive decision had forever tied me to an asshole who couldn't stand me.

The moment Beau pulled into a parking space, I whipped off my seat belt. The car wasn't even parked before I shoved out of my door and hurried toward the stairs. I didn't want to be anywhere near him. I ignored the heat that burned in my chest and down my arms as I got farther away. The fire was preferable to staying in his presence for one more minute.

Unfortunately, he caught up with me before I was even able to unlock my front door.

"You can't come in," I said, spinning to face him as soon as I had it open.

"Give it a rest," he said tiredly, reaching up to rub his eyes with his fingertips. "You know that's not going to go well. It's already fucking building again. If I can feel it, I know you can."

"I don't care."

"Right," he replied sarcastically. He waved his hand at me like he was shooing me into the apartment. "Come on."

"You're not coming in," I repeated, standing my ground.

"Stop fucking around," he said shortly.

"Go home, Beau," I ordered, lifting my chin. *I'll call you.*

It was supremely satisfying to slam the door in his face, even if the aftermath felt like I was burning alive.

# CHAPTER 6
## BEAU

Tightening my fingers around the steering wheel, I stared at Reese's front door. I'd been sitting outside for two hours, and she still hadn't come outside again. The fire in my veins had begun before she'd slammed the door in my face, but the nausea hadn't started until about fifteen minutes earlier. It was fucking miserable. Every molecule in my body was urging me toward her.

I hadn't even been able to drive away. The thought of moving any further from her was abhorrent.

Taking her back to the house had been a mistake. It was inevitable that she would know them eventually, but I shouldn't have put us in that position until we'd had a bit longer to get used to each other. She made me want to put my head through a wall, and that was before she'd made a fool of herself at dinner.

I just couldn't get over the fact that the entire thing, meeting my parents, getting to know each other, cementing the bond—all of it should've been different.

She should've been different. Quiet and kind and lovely. I'd known that she wouldn't be the same person as Millie. I'd known that since I let Millie go, and my father's best friend, Mordecai, had come to me in London, berating and comforting me in equal measure.

He'd warned me to be sure of my decision because there was no going back. He'd been separated from his mate after only meeting her twice, and he'd never found her again. It was two hundred years before he found his mate once more, and she'd been nothing like the original women he'd met. He'd been so shocked he'd nearly lost her a second time. He'd warned me that even knowing that it was the same soul that he had connected to the first time, he'd nearly walked away from the new woman.

He'd spoken so earnestly that I'd listened intently at the time, but I'd rarely thought about our conversation again. I hadn't been able to even imagine finding my mate again, and for a long time, I knew it wasn't even possible. Millie had lived for fifty more years after we'd met on that London street. She'd had children and grandchildren and a full beautiful life, though I'd never seen it.

Zeke had been the one to check in on her from time to time. He'd never gotten close enough to say hello, even after we Vampires had gone public. I appreciated him for that. Knowing that he'd been able to speak with her while I couldn't would've killed me. Once I'd decided to let Millie live the human life that she was so enamored with, I'd left the country entirely and hadn't gone back until she was already gone. The mating bond would've forced me into doing something I'd already promised I wouldn't do, or it would've driven me insane, and neither was a preferable outcome.

I thought about the old conversation I'd had with

Mordecai while I sat in my car, waiting for Reese to pull her head out of her ass and let me inside. He'd been full of warnings not to let my memory of the mate I'd known interfere with the mate I'd eventually meet, but he'd never even hinted that I might actually dislike my new mate.

I hadn't even known it was possible to dislike the person the Gods had chosen. Sure, there were always bumps in the beginning, but I'd never heard of a Vampire actively detesting their mate. Every story I'd heard since the time I was able to listen described Vampires who were obsessed with the other half of their souls from the moment they met her or him.

The whole situation would've been so much easier if she wasn't so goddamn obnoxious.

My stomach twisted, and I grit my teeth as my neck and back began to sweat.

I needed a distraction. Less than a minute later, my brother Ambrose's voice was filtering through the speakers.

"You fucked up, little brother," he answered, amusement in his voice. "What the hell is going on over there?"

"When you figure it out, let me know," I replied dryly. "This whole thing is a clusterfuck."

"Sounds like it. Mom called to tell me you'd found her, practically bubbling with excitement—"

"Of course she called you," I grumbled under my breath, making him laugh.

"She was pissed when she called me after dinner."

"Yeah, I know."

"What the fuck is your problem, Bjorn?"

"She's a fucking nightmare," I blurted, digging my fingers into my eye sockets. "She never stops talking. She's loud. She's obnoxious."

"She's your mate."

"Fucking hell."

"I'd like to point out," Ambrose said quietly. "That you've found her twice, and the rest of us are still waiting."

"Don't you think I know that?"

"I think you're pretty blasé about a situation that the rest of us would kill and die for."

"I'm not blasé," I shot back. "I'm fucking angry."

"So be fucking angry," Ambrose replied. "But don't be a fucking idiot. The universe doesn't make mistakes, Bjorn. This woman was *meant* for you. Maybe take a minute to figure out why the hell that is before you burn it all to the ground."

"Is this the only reason you were trying to get a hold of me?" I asked tiredly. My hands were starting to shake, and I was pretty sure the symptoms were getting worse because I knew that Reese's symptoms must be a whole hell of a lot worse than mine were.

I refused to acknowledge why that was.

"Actually, no," Ambrose said, his tone changing completely. "I found something."

"What?" I sat up straighter in my seat. Ambrose and his team had taken the last two months following every thread that led to the group who'd killed our baby brother.

"We came to the camp." He paused for a long moment, and when he began to speak again, his voice was hoarse. "We found where they did—where he was tortured. Where they held him. Zeke left some shit behind."

"What kind of shit?"

"You gonna be home tomorrow?"

"What kind of shit, Ulf?"

"I'll be home tomorrow," he said, ignoring the question. "I'll talk to everyone together."

"That's bullshit."

"Don't wanna go over this twice, brother," Ambrose said softly. "Tomorrow, yeah?"

"I'll be there."

"Good." He let out a sigh. "Now go love on your mate."

I scoffed.

"Find some gratitude, Bjorn," he said tiredly. "And go convince your mate that you're not the biggest asshole on the planet."

"That's Chance," I replied, almost as a reflex.

"Exactly." Ambrose chuckled. "Love you. Talk soon."

"Love you, too," I replied as he hung up.

Ambrose was right. I needed to just suck it up. I knew Reese wasn't all bad. There were moments when I found her funny. Some of her facial expressions were cute—usually when she'd just embarrassed herself. I couldn't deny that she was beautiful, even if she wasn't my normal type. She was lean, yes, but the curves she had were exquisite.

We needed to figure out a way to make things work. *I* needed to figure out a way to make things work.

On that thought, I reached for the door handle but paused when a beautiful brown-haired woman sauntered toward Reese's apartment. She was tall and voluptuous, and by the way she pounded on Reese's door, I figured she must be the friend that Reese had mentioned. Rena.

"Reese, open up! It's cold as hell out here!" She stood impatiently, resettling her purse on her shoulder. "I know you're in there! You said you were sick." She waited longer. "Fine, I'm calling your phone. If I hear it ringing, fair warning, I'm kicking this bitch down."

She dug through her purse and pulled out a phone, putting it to her ear.

"Where the hell are you?" Pause. "You *said* you were sick." Pause. "I drove all the way out here, you pain in the ass." Pause. "Yeah, yeah. Text me later."

She waved both hands in frustration at the door and turned on her heel, stomping back down the breezeway before disappearing down the stairs.

So, that was the best friend who was *obsessed* with Vampires. Maybe I should've gone and enlisted her help in getting me back into Reese's good graces. I had a feeling after that dinner, I'd need all the help I could get.

If my mate hadn't called me back in—I checked the clock—three hours, all the while the heat from the mating bond grew more and more excruciating, I had a feeling that I was dealing with one of the most stubborn or masochistic women on the planet.

Or she just really hated me, which was valid.

As soon as Rena pulled away in her car, I headed up to the apartment. It was quiet on the other side of the door, even after I'd knocked.

"Reese," I called out, trying to peek between the living room curtains. "Open up."

I waited for a minute. Knocked again. Watched between the curtains for any movement.

"Come on," I called, glancing down the breezeway. If she didn't let me inside soon, someone was going to notice me standing out there like an asshole. "Reese, let me in."

Five minutes passed while I searched for Reese's number in the command database. You really could find anything now if you knew where to look. It rang and rang, but Reese didn't answer.

My heart sounded in my ears, growing louder the

longer she didn't open the door. From what little I'd learned about her, Reese would've never let me stand out there for so long. She wouldn't want the neighbors wondering why I was there, and I was pretty sure she wouldn't give up the opportunity to tell me to go fuck myself.

Wiggling the knob, I looked closer at the door. She hadn't locked the dead bolt.

Idiot.

With another wiggle, I lifted the door slightly as I butted my shoulder against it.

When it swung open, there was barely a sound, but I'd cracked the frame. I swung it closed behind me and locked the dead bolt to keep it that way.

There was no sign of Reese, and the apartment was as silent as a tomb and completely dark as I moved through it.

"Reese?" I called out, hurrying down the short hall-way. The door to the bedroom was wide open and as dark as the rest of the house. When I flipped the light switch, it illuminated a messy space, filled with a million textures and colors, but no Reese. The bathroom was a different story.

As I blindly reached for the light, my stomach lurched in panic at the sight of her pale face barely visible over the edge of the tub.

"Get out," she moaned, weakly throwing her arm over the edge of the tub.

"What the hell are you doing?" I barked, hurrying toward her.

"Cool bath," she said, not even trying to hide her naked body.

She was curled up on her side in the fetal position, her knees beneath her chin, shivering.

"Fuck," I muttered, soaking the sleeves of my shirt and jacket as I lifted her from the tub.

"Get out of my apartment," she hissed as I carried her out of the tiny room. "I told you I'd call you."

"Hard to do when you don't have my number," I argued, carrying her into her bedroom. "I was right outside. Why didn't you come get me?"

"Figured you left," she said, pressing her forehead against my neck. "Oh, god. That's good."

I dropped to the edge of the bed with her in my arms. Now that I'd gotten her out of the bath, I couldn't seem to put her down. The burning in my veins had calmed to a slightly uncomfortable sensation, and the nausea had disappeared.

"I don't want you here," she said, her hands sliding inside my coat. "You're a fucking prick."

"I know," I murmured, pulling a throw blanket from the end of the bed to cover her.

"I'm great. You're the one that needs a personality adjustment."

I ground my teeth together, rubbing my hand up and down her cold thigh as her hands burrowed beneath my shirt.

"You're probably right," I replied as her breath warmed the spot between my shoulder and neck.

Fuck.

"Your parents loved me," she said smugly. "And I think Daniel is my new best friend."

"Stay away from Daniel," I barked idiotically.

My brother would never behave inappropriately with my mate, and it wasn't as if she had the ability to cheat anymore. Physically, at least.

"Jealousy," she said with a huff. "Interesting."

"I'm not jealous."

"Sure, you're not."

We sat quietly for a few minutes as the effects of the mating bond calmed. The urge to let my hands roam was there, but manageable now that she was pressed against me.

"How did you get in?" she asked abruptly, lifting her head to meet my eyes.

"Broke the latch on your door."

"What the fuck, Beau?"

"You didn't lock the dead bolt."

"I wasn't expecting anyone to barge in," she griped, pushing away from me.

"It's a good thing I did," I said calmly as she got to her feet.

Reese really was beautiful, especially when she was angry. She stood glaring at me, completely unconcerned with the flesh she was baring, her hands in fists at her sides. With her hair piled on top of her head in some kind of clip and her cheeks once again flushed, it took all of my willpower not to reach for her while she berated me.

As she called me every filthy name she could think of, something seemed to click in my head.

This was my mate. This woman had been chosen for me specifically.

She could've lived a different life. If she'd lived some-where else, worked somewhere else, been out sick that morning, or if one of my brothers would've gone to the blood bank, we never would have met. She could've been married, and I would've had to make the choice again, whether or not to completely obliterate the life she'd built.

Instead, she was right there in front of me, the mating bond already cemented, angry and beautiful and mine.

The embarrassment from her unhinged behavior at dinner melted away like it had never existed.

"Are you done?" I asked, cutting off her tirade.

"No, I'm not done."

"You keep licking your lips."

"They're chapped," she snapped, her gaze moving from my neck to my face. The lie wasn't believable.

"Come here and let me help," I said softly.

"I don't want your help," she shot back, crossing her arms.

"I was a dick—"

"That's the understatement of the fucking century." She threw out her arms. "I can't stand you. If I had the choice, I'd never see you again. Ever."

"I understand."

"I doubt that very much."

She glared as I rose to my feet and lifted my hand to my mouth.

"Here," I said, reaching out. She allowed me to tangle my other hand in her hair, making the clip fall to the floor. "It'll help."

"I'm not going to fuck you," she blurted before greedily sucking the meat of my thumb between her lips.

I would've been embarrassed at the jerk of my erection if I thought she'd noticed, but she was wholly focused on my hand as I moved closer.

The blood in her veins was practically singing to me. My mouth filled with saliva as I stared at her pulse point. It was so close.

"No," she ordered, jerking her mouth from my hand.

"What?" It took me a moment to follow.

"You're not biting me again," she said, pulling away. "I'm never letting you that close to my neck again."

I stared at her blankly, my blood on fire as she crossed the room.

"What do you mean, you're never letting me bite you again?" I asked.

"You heard me."

"Never is a long time."

"Let me know your favorite type, and I'll hook you up, just like your brothers."

The sound of my growl surprised us both.

"Thanks for the blood," she said with a shooing motion. "You can go now."

"You really want to go through all that again?" I asked, gesturing to the bathroom.

"Well, not especially," she barked. "But I don't really have a choice, do I? I don't want you in my space."

"Then come home with me," I replied automatically. I hadn't meant to say the words, but once I had, it made sense. Every argument I'd made to myself just an hour before seemed stupid and childish. My parents already knew her at this point, and she'd be surrounded by other Vampires that would keep her safe. I had to be home to meet Ambrose the next day anyway. I also didn't feel like sleeping in my car, and I was almost positive that I wouldn't be able to drive away from her.

"Oh, fuck *off*," she spat dismissively.

"Come back with me," I pressed. "These symptoms aren't going to get any better, at least not for a while. You can't deny that they're at least manageable when we're close."

"Yes, but when we're close, I also have to deal with you, which is actually worse," she replied, her tone less biting.

"Less cold baths, though," I joked badly.

"I have to work tomorrow."

"I don't think Noah will expect you."

"It doesn't matter. I have responsibilities."

"Look," I said, dragging my hands through my hair. Now that I'd asked her to come back to the house, I desperately wanted her to. It was such a change from earlier in the night that I felt like I had whiplash. From the look on her face, she was feeling the same way.

I'd never felt so out of control.

"I'll sleep on the couch if you want."

"Well, isn't that sweet," she drawled.

"I'm trying here."

"You should have been trying before," she ground out. "You know, earlier when you took me to meet your family and showed every single one of them how much you dislike me—which is pretty interesting since you'd spent the hours before that fucking my brains out!"

"It was a mistake," I conceded, hiding my wince. The argument with my father had been one of the lowest moments in our relationship, and I'd done some pretty terrible shit in the past.

Reese turned back to me and stared at the small closet. It was full to bursting, with random pieces of fabric spilling out onto the bedroom carpet.

"Fine," she said finally.

I let out a quiet breath of relief.

"Just so you know," she said after a moment. "The only reason I'm agreeing to this is that I don't want to spend the next week feeling like I'm boiling from the inside, and I don't trust that you won't leave me here—completely fucked—whenever you decide you don't like me again."

"I didn't want to leave the first time," I pointed out.

"Wait in the car," she ordered. "I'll be out once I pack a bag."

Instead of arguing with her, I strode out into the living room. I couldn't make myself actually leave the apartment, but at least I'd be out of her way while she did whatever she needed to get ready. My focus had been distracted when I'd been in her home earlier, and I finally took the time to look around the room. The couches seemed to be the only thing in the entire apartment that were newer. The rest of it was worn and colorful. The coffee table was definitely mid-century unless it was an excellent replica. There was a hurricane lamp that was made long before Reese had even been born. I wondered where she'd found it. Books were tightly packed on a bookcase along one wall. There were too many of them to fit neatly on the shelves. She'd decorated her space to reflect her perfectly. Loud and chaotic.

I couldn't say I hated it.

"I thought I told you to wait in the car," she said flatly as she carried a duffel bag into the room.

It was as good of a time as any to tell the truth.

"I couldn't make myself leave the apartment," I replied evenly.

Her gaze shot to mine.

"Couldn't leave the parking lot earlier," I continued with a shrug.

"It's—I—" She stuttered to a stop and took a deep breath. "Right. It's just as bad for you."

"In some ways," I agreed. The physical symptoms were worse for her, but she didn't have the Vampire instincts I was fighting.

"Well, let's go," she said, moving toward the door.

By the time we'd pulled out of her parking lot, the tension in my shoulders had dissipated to almost nothing. The burn in my gut was still there, churning, but the knowledge that she was coming home with me was making it easier to ignore.

I wasn't sure how long I'd be able to go without her blood. The thought of it made my skin crawl. I didn't even know if I could stomach the banked blood anymore. I'd never heard of a mate rejecting the exchange, but surely it had happened before. I was beginning to realize that the stories I'd been told may have been exaggerated. There was no way that all mates not only ignored their instincts and waited for weeks or months for the human partner to decide whether or not they'd accept the mating, but that once they had, everything was great.

The mating bond had made me want to protect Reese from harm and crave her to a tortuous degree, but it hadn't made me dislike her any less.

Or maybe it had. Maybe that was why I felt more accepting of her filthy mouth and chaotic presence all of a sudden.

"I don't know anything about you," Reese murmured sleepily as we pulled onto the freeway.

"It'll come," I assured her, reaching out. We had unlimited time to learn everything. Being in such close proximity without touching her was uncomfortable at best. It must've been bothering her, too, because she allowed me to lace her fingers with mine.

"When were you born?" she asked curiously.

"December 13, 1870," I replied, glancing at her.

Her hand tightened, but she valiantly tried to hide her shock.

"No shit?"

A laugh rasped out of my mouth at her strangled words. I nodded.

"Jesus, you're old."

"I haven't aged since around 1901," I corrected.

"So your body is, like, thirty-one years old?" she said, turning toward me just a fraction.

"Why? Does it seem older?"

"No," she replied instantly, making me laugh again.

"How old is your dad?" she asked in fascination.

"Old," I replied, my lips twitching.

"Your mom can't be more than twenty years older than you," she mused. "Women married young back then." She whistled. "This is so weird."

"My mother was twenty-two when I was born," I corrected, looking over at her.

"Old lady," she joked.

"She was married before my father," I explained, something inside me settling at the surprisingly normal conversation we were having. No sniping. No misunderstandings. "And she had two daughters."

"Oh," Reese murmured, her face falling. "What happened?"

"The war," I replied quietly. We'd only ever heard bits and pieces of what our mother's life had been like before she'd met Erik Boucher. "Her husband was a soldier. My sisters died of typhoid."

"Damn," Reese whispered. "Your poor mother. When did she meet your dad?"

"After," I replied. "He fought for the Union—"

"Hell yeah, he did," Reese enthused, making me smile. "I knew I liked that guy."

"He'll be so glad," I joked. "He was in her town buying a horse or something. The story changes each time he tells it, but the result was that he saw my mother gardening out in front of her little house and knew instantly that she was his."

"Must've been a shock for her, though," Reese mused.

"You should ask her about it," I offered. "I think she's downplayed that part for us."

"Aw," Reese replied. "She wanted you to be under the illusion that your mates would jump for joy when you found them."

"Something like that, I'm sure," I agreed.

"Sorry, *not* sorry to disappoint," she quipped.

It took me a moment before I could think of something to say that wouldn't make her angry. If I told her she hadn't disappointed me, we'd both know I was lying. If I confirmed that she had, it would be like rubbing salt in the wound.

"I'm sure I'm not your first choice," I said finally.

"Oh, I don't know," she said almost breezily. "If you kept your mouth shut, I'd like you just fine."

I let out an *oof* in mock pain, and she chuckled.

"You haven't been so bad for the last fifteen minutes," she said slyly. "Keep up the good work."

"No promises," I replied as we turned onto the driveway.

My parents were in patio chairs on the front deck as we pulled into the garage.

"Shit, I thought they'd be asleep," Reese grumbled, sitting up straighter.

"They stay up late," I replied, shutting the car off. "It made it impossible to sneak out."

"What was there to do in the eighteen-seventies anyway?" she asked snarkily.

"There were cows to be tipped back then, too," I replied.

"Are you serious?" She stared in disbelief.

"No, I'm not serious. We lived in the city. There were prostitutes and gambling halls."

Her mouth dropped open. "You better not have given

me syphilis. I know all about those turn of the century sexually transmitted diseases."

"I'm going to ignore that you know an obscure fact about prostitutes a hundred and fifty years ago." She glared. "And tell you that Vampires can't catch human infections."

"Thank God for small mercies," she grumbled as she threw open the door and climbed out.

I stopped her at the hood of the car and pulled the duffel bag from her hands.

"My father will punch me again if he sees you carrying your own bag," I told her as she opened her mouth to protest. "And since sneaking inside is impossible, let's get this over with."

"He punched you?" she asked, a smile playing on her lips as I tugged her toward the garage door.

"Oh, so you didn't hear that part, huh? Figures."

"Actually, I did," she replied smugly. "But it's nice to get confirmation that it wasn't just wishful thinking. Do we really have to go say hi to your parents?"

I stopped short in the driveway. "I should've told you earlier," I murmured, leaning down to speak in her ear. "But Vampire hearing is very sensitive. They can hear pretty much anything you say in or around the house."

Reese choked and started to sputter.

"Even in your room?" she hissed.

My eyes widened in horror. "No, absolutely not. The apartments are about as soundproof as they can get. Someone would have to be outside the door for anyone to hear what was happening inside."

"Oh, thank God," Reese blurted.

My father's laughter drifted toward us.

"They just heard us, didn't they?" Reese asked, her head dropping in defeat.

"Unfortunately."

Reese stood with her eyes closed for another moment, then jerked her head as they snapped open and started marching forward, towing me along behind her.

"This is a surprise," my mom called happily as they came into view.

"Your son is a pain in my ass, but I've agreed to stay close to him so as to not burn alive," Reese announced.

"Logical," my dad replied.

"I thought so."

He looked at me. "You've come to your senses."

"He didn't really have a choice," Reese answered for me. "He can't seem to stay away from me either."

"As it should be," my mom sniffed.

"That remains to be seen," Reese replied. "If I murder him in his bed, I hope you won't hold it against me."

My dad grinned. "Not at all, dóttir."

"Consider this your home," Mom said sweetly. "With or without Beaumont."

"Well," Reese said, a little loudly. "I'm exhausted and surprisingly cold. So, we're going to bed."

It might've been the first time in my life that I'd seen Erik Boucher work so hard to contain his laughter.

"Good night," my mom said, smiling at me.

"Night," I replied, following Reese to the door.

"Ulf will be home by nine," my dad called out as we moved inside.

"The famous Ulf," Reese said, stomping toward the stairs.

"I'll introduce you tomorrow."

"Great."

"Are you pissed again?"

Reese paused halfway up the stairs and turned to me with a deliberate grimace, and I suddenly understood the problem. I was surprised by the new knot of concern that pulled in my gut.

When I threw her over my shoulder, she let out a huff of air, but the contact must've felt good because she melted into me, resting her forehead against the small of my back, her arms sliding around my chest.

Maybe she'd changed her mind.

I took the stairs two at a time, anticipation making my hands shake.

# CHAPTER 7
## REESE

I'd never wanted anyone as much as I wanted Beau Boucher. He was gorgeous when he was scowling, but smiling? It was hard to even look at him. The way he moved was mouthwatering. His body was impossibly defined with muscle that I couldn't wait to get a good look at but had already mapped with my fingers.

It was too bad that he was such an asshole.

"Okay, put me down," I said as he swung the door shut behind us.

Knowing that his parents and brothers could hear anything we were saying outside his little suite of rooms made me want to vomit. I wasn't even sure what they'd heard. Probably the argument on the porch. Definitely anything I'd said in the garage.

Oh, god. Had they heard us fucking when we'd fucked in the trees halfway down the driveway?

The minute Beau set me on my feet, I took a step backward, and his hands tangled in my hair.

"No," I said instantly, reaching for his wrists.

"I know this is painful for you, too," he replied in confusion, his hands tightening. "Why don't you want to make it better?"

"I don't sleep with people who can't stand me," I replied evenly. "Even if I know it'll feel good."

"We're getting to know each other," he said carefully. "I haven't been at my best. I know that."

"You called me a curse," I reminded him quietly. "You said that my self-confidence *stemmed from nowhere*—"

"I didn't mean—"

"Let's not lie to each other, at least," I said with a sigh, dropping my hands from his wrists. I wasn't about to get into a wrestling match with him. When he realized I was serious, he'd let go. "And that self-confidence? That was hard won. I spent hours in the mirror telling myself that I was fucking great until I finally believed it."

"Fuck, Reese," he muttered, wincing.

"Until we can figure this out, I agree, we need to stay close. That doesn't mean that I'm going to let you into my body in *any* way."

"Understood," he replied after a moment, gently untangling his hands from my hair.

"I think we can contain ourselves and share the bed," I said, moving farther into the room. His couch wasn't big enough for me to sleep on. There was no way Beau would be able to. "If that works for you?"

When Beau nodded, I hid my relief. Just being in the same room with him calmed my heart rate and made the heat mellow into the feeling of being toasted by the sun. I wasn't anxious for it to ratchet up to eleven again.

"Go ahead," Beau said with a chin jerk toward his room. "I'll be in soon."

I hesitated.

"Just going to turn off the lights." He nodded toward his room again.

"You have my bag," I reminded him.

"Oh, shit."

Once he'd handed me the duffel I'd had since the first trip Rena and I had taken as adults, I turned and hustled into his room. Without Beau looking over my shoulder, I was able to appreciate the space even more than I had when I'd seen it earlier. The décor was like some fancy hotel filled with antiques or a castle or something. The headboard looked like it weighed three hundred pounds. I walked over and pulled on a drawer in one of the dressers. The empty drawer smelled like cedar.

There were no knickknacks or tchotchkes in the room, but there was a very old, framed photograph showing five boys dressed to impress and staring unsmiling at the photographer. Even with the lack of color, it was easy to pick Beau out of the lineup. There was something about the tilt of his head and the way he held his shoulders that was recognizable even as a boy.

Noise from the living area startled me into movement, and I headed for the bathroom to get ready for bed. I hadn't been lying to Beau's parents. The events of the day had worn me out, and my body felt like it was moving on autopilot as I pulled my toothbrush out of my bag. I began to brush and turned in a circle, taking in the room. Everything was pristine. There were plush towels hanging on the wall and a bottle of heavenly-smelling soap next to the sink, but it was the shadow of something big behind the glass shower door that had toothpaste almost dripping onto my shirt.

A claw-foot tub was tucked behind the large shower, its feet resting on the tile floor but far enough back that it missed any spray from the dual showerheads. The thing was absolutely magnificent, and the placement was genius. I stared at it in awe.

"Do you want me to leave any lights on?" Beau called from the bedroom, snapping me out of my adoration.

"You have a bathtub in the shower," I replied, walking over to the doorway.

"Really?" he asked in mock surprise.

"It's beautiful."

"It's a bathtub."

"To you it's a bathtub," I mumbled around the toothpaste foaming furiously in my mouth. "To me, it's heaven."

"Climb in," he offered.

I was seriously tempted as I turned back to the sink and finished brushing my teeth, but every muscle in my body urged me back toward the bedroom and massive bed that was calling my name. I stripped to my t-shirt and underwear and barely made it under the covers before I was yawning, but my body decided in that moment to send a spiral of heat from the center of my chest to every single finger and toe.

When Beau's hand crossed the center of the bed and slid beneath my t-shirt, I didn't resist. The cool pressure of his hand on my belly lulled me to sleep.

I couldn't tell how long I'd slept, but when I opened my eyes, I was instantly aware that Beau wasn't in bed with me. His side of the bed was cool, and he'd messily pulled the blankets up and tidied the pillows while I'd slept right through it. Groggy and irritated at the heat pulsing in my abdomen, I shuffled out of the room to find him bent forward on the couch, his elbows on his knees.

"What are you doing out here?" I rasped, trying to ignore the expanse of skin not shielded by his boxers.

"Hey," he whispered, lifting his head. "Go back to sleep. It's early still."

The pallor of his skin was terrifying. He looked *gray*.

"What's wrong?"

"Not feeling great," he replied with an unconvincing smile. "Probably just a bit of anemia. It's all right. Go back to bed."

I let out a bubble of laughter that cut off when I realized he wasn't making a joke.

"What do you mean, anemia?" I asked, heading for the kitchen. It only took me a minute to find the cupboard of glasses and fill one with tap water.

There were two empty bags of AB negative in the bottom of the sink. Bags. Pfft. They obviously hadn't come from us. We used glass jars.

"We can't get sick," Beau said with a sigh. "But anemia can knock us out for a minute."

By the time I turned back toward him, he'd listed toward the back of the couch and was lying there with his eyes closed.

"How the hell do Vampires get anemia?" I asked, bringing him the glass of water.

"Lack of blood," he muttered, barely opening his eyes to look at me.

"If you don't drink blood, you become anemic?" I asked dubiously.

"Basically," he replied with a small smile. "It's a little more complicated than that, but yeah. It hasn't happened to me for years."

I knew that Vampires needed blood to survive, but I'd never even considered the biology of it all. Racking my brain, I tried to remember anything I'd learned in high school health class about anemia. All I could recall is that it sometimes made the person dizzy or caused headaches.

"Didn't you just have blood before bed?" I asked, glancing at the sink.

When there was no response, I looked back to find him passed out.

"Beau," I called, reaching forward to shake his shoulder. His entire body started to slide sideways, and I was unprepared for the panic that tightened around my throat like a vise. "Beau!"

I looked back and forth between the door and the unconscious Vampire, remembering that no one could hear me if I called for help. Less than a second later, I was vaulting over the couch in a move that would've made my old track coach proud and throwing open the door to the hallway.

"Help!" I screamed, wondering if anyone would even hear me from their own rooms. "I need help!"

I rushed back to the kitchen and tore open the drawers until I found the steak knives. If Beau was sick because he needed blood, then logically, the blood of his mate, *composed specifically* for him, would help. Since there was no way I could carry him anywhere, and I couldn't stomach the idea of leaving him alone while I searched the monstrosity of a house, I figured it was worth a try. Climbing onto the couch until I was straddling Beau's thighs, I tried again to wake him up.

"Come on, you handsome bastard," I called, tapping at his cheeks. "Wake up and be a dickhead again."

After a few moments with no response, I held my breath and sliced over my wrist.

I hadn't anticipated gagging at the feeling of dragging a serrated knife over my own flesh or the way little stars surrounded my vision as I swayed. Dropping the knife before I accidentally cut myself again, I lifted my wrist to Beau's mouth and used it to pry his lips open.

Just as his teeth clamped down, his mother came flying into the room, and it was lights out.

When I came to, I was lying on the couch with a furious Beau leaning over me, his skin the color of parchment. It was an improvement, barely.

"What the hell were you thinking?" he asked.

"How did this happen?" his mom asked worriedly. "Why are there bags in the sink?"

"Sit down before you fall down," his dad ordered Beau. "I'll get the medical kit."

My gaze shot back and forth between them, trying to get my bearings.

"I told you I'd be fine," Beau said to me, ignoring both of them. "Why would you hurt yourself like this?"

"You said that a mate's blood is made for their particular Vampire," I replied, confused. Where was the appreciation for saving his ass? "You passed out."

"Oh, Beau," his mom murmured as Danny and Chance bumbled into the room.

"You said no blood," Beau grit out, his eyes on mine.

"You were obviously hurt or something. You—"

"It doesn't matter," he cut me off. "You said no."

"What are you talking about?" Beau's mom asked sharply, her tone switching from worry to anger.

"You didn't tell me that it was going to make you sick," I argued.

"It doesn't matter."

"Of course it fucking matters!"

"No," Mattie said flatly, her attention on me. "Vampires do not, under any circumstances, take blood from the unwilling or coerced."

"Informing me that going without would make you sick isn't coercion," I countered, looking back at Beau.

"You said no," he repeated quietly.

"What, none of you have ever bitten someone who didn't want it?" I asked, looking around. "That's bullshit. The banks haven't existed for more than fifty years at most."

Beau stiffened, his eyes darkening with disgust. "We don't bite anyone but our mate. Ever."

"It's been that way for hundreds of years," Danny added quietly. "For a Vampire to bite someone without the mating bond—" He shook his head.

"There are other ways for humans to donate," Chance added. "Both dead and alive. To bite one is as abhorrent to us as...cannibalism is to humans."

"You're kidding me," I replied, dumbfounded.

"You shouldn't have done this, baby," Beau said, peeking under the towel he'd wrapped around my wrist. "Dad's going to have to stitch it."

The endearment almost made me miss the second sentence.

"What?" I shot up from the couch and tried to pull my arm back. "Just lick it."

Danny started laughing.

"What?" I spat, glaring at him over the back of the couch before turning to Beau. "It works on my neck. Do it to my wrist."

"The punctures in your neck are tiny," he replied gently, his hand pressing on my thigh to keep me seated. "And I made them myself. This is something entirely different."

"Did you try?" I asked accusingly.

"He's right," his mom chimed it. "You'll need stitches and maybe an antibiotic. I'll call Alice."

She walked away while I stared at Beau. "Who the fuck is Alice?"

"Uncle Sven's wife," he replied calmly. "She's a doctor

of a sort."

"What the hell does that mean?"

"It means she went to medical school—"

"A couple of times," Chance said nonchalantly. "Medical advances, you know. Have to keep up with the times."

"But she specializes in Vampires."

"I'm not a Vampire," I reminded him, trying to ignore the pain in my wrist.

At least the mating heat seemed to have disappeared for the moment. I was thankful for small mercies.

"Yes, but you'll have biological changes happening now that we've cemented the bond," he replied distractedly, peeking at my wrist again. "Better to get advice from someone familiar with mate physiology."

"What the fuck are you talking about?" I asked, jutting my chin forward and tilting my head so he'd meet my eyes.

"Gods, you still haven't told her anything, have you?" Danny muttered.

"What exactly am I supposed to know?" I looked between each of them. The brothers seemed to be waiting for Beau to answer me, but he was conveniently not meeting my eyes. When he finally tilted his head up, he seemed nervous for the first time since we'd met.

"The mating bond has benefits," he said slowly, stretching his neck from side to side. "And not just for Vampires. *Both* mates become essentially immortal."

I let out a nervous giggle, waiting for him to start laughing with me. "What does *essentially* mean?" I asked sarcastically, playing along.

"You won't get sick. You won't age," Beau replied seriously. "You cannot be killed outright unless..." He paused and swallowed hard like he was trying to force himself to finish.

"Unless your head's cut off," Chance finished for him. "That whole stake in the heart thing? Bullshit. Garlic? I love the stuff. Danny's not a fan, though."

"Garlic's okay," Danny disagreed.

"Holy water tastes okay in a pinch, and it doesn't burn. Bullets always sting no matter if they're silver, copper, lead, or steel."

"So...everything is bullshit, and I'm going to live forever," I said, hysteria making my voice go all high and pitchy.

"I was going to tell you," Beau said, his thumb tracing patterns on my knee. "We hadn't gotten that far yet."

"Whose fault is that?"

"It's a closely guarded secret," Beau's dad announced as he came back into the room. "As far as humans know, we're blessed with a longer life than theirs, and we're harder to injure and kill—but we're still fallible—because we are before the mating bond."

"It's why we have to quit our jobs when we find our mates," Beau explained as he helped me to my feet and led me over to the kitchen table. "It would be too easy to ferret out the truth if we continued working with the military."

"That's the job you talked about having to quit," I mused as I sat down in one of the chairs.

"It's one of the reasons," Beau's dad agreed. He reached out and gently but firmly took my wrist from Beau and pulled until my arm was stretched out across the table. "But we also believe that a Vampire's priority is their mate *first* and anything else second. Leaving for long periods of time wouldn't be possible for years, if ever. The two responsibilities have never been able to coexist." He looked meaningfully at Beau, and a moment later, my mate's arms were wrapped tightly around my waist and chest, holding my uninjured arm against my body.

I yelped in pain when Erik unwrapped my wrist and his palm came in contact with my skin.

His eyes shot to mine in surprise. "That hurts you?"

"Like stinging nettles," I confirmed.

"Damn, Reese," Chance teased. "Got the hots for the old man, huh?"

"No, I don't," I shot back, my voice squeaking like a twelve-year-old's. I looked at Erik. "I mean, of course, you're attractive—" Beau growled almost silently in my ear. "Aesthetically pleasing," I rushed to say. "In a purely academic way. But I don't see you like that. At all. That would be—"

"Quiet," Erik ordered.

When had he become Erik in my head?

"I've never seen aversion this strong before," he said curiously, watching me as he carefully wrapped gauze around the back of my arm so our skin didn't touch when he gripped it. "I'd have Mattie do this, but the poor woman is squeamish. I'll do my best not to make contact."

"Or we could just slap some butterfly bandages on and call it a day," I offered hopefully.

"Nice try," Beau murmured, his lips against my neck.

The feeling of him there had my body unconsciously sinking back against him.

"You going to watch?" Erik asked easily.

I jerked my head quickly to the side and stared at the window behind the sink. The sun was beginning to rise.

My arm from my elbow to my wrist burned like fire for a few moments, and I inhaled on a hiss, trying to stay still, but only a few seconds later, the entire area was numb.

I continued to look out the window.

"Are you qualified to do this?" I asked Erik, leaning

back against Beau. "I mean, you guys are loaded, so it's not like we can't afford an actual doctor."

Beau's brothers laughed, and he let out a huff of amusement against my hair.

"I've been stitching knife wounds for a long time," Erik replied dryly.

"I didn't mean to make the cut so big," I confessed, still staring out the window. I was pretty sure that if I accidentally got a look at what he was doing, I'd vomit all over the table in front of me.

"That's good to hear," Erik said. "I'm still confused why you did it in the first place."

"Beau looked like shit, and then he passed out, and I couldn't wake him up." I began to turn my head, then realized what I was doing and glared at the window again. "He said at dinner that my blood is like his perfect meal or whatever."

Erik chuckled. "Are you not exchanging blood?" he asked curiously.

"I put a kibosh on that for the moment," I replied quietly.

Beau's lips pressed against the top of my head.

"It's not my place to interfere in a mating bond—"

"Then don't," Beau said, cutting him off.

"But as your elder," Erik continued as if he hadn't spoken. "I feel the need to inform you both that any blood not yours is no longer compatible with Bjorn's physiology."

"Shit," I mumbled, thinking about the empty bags in the sink.

"Blood donated by a mate will suffice but will still leave him feeling under the weather."

"But you said—"

"It is the act of exchanging blood that will keep you

both healthy," Erik said. "Not clinically giving each other a shot of blood on a schedule, but the skin-on-skin contact and bite. I've been told that it's something about the pH of the skin and the oxytocin present at the time of exchange, but you'd have to ask for specifics from someone more well-informed than I am."

"We'll figure it out," Beau stated.

"Bjorn, you'll be ill—"

"We'll figure it out," he repeated.

"Could you please just get to stitching?" I asked, recognizing the irritation in Beau's voice. If they got into it again and made this whole process even longer, I was going to scream.

"You're done," Erik announced, his voice laced with amusement.

I whipped my head around to find a neat row of black stitches across my wrist. My stomach gave a small flip, and I looked away from it to find Erik smiling.

"Do they meet your standards?"

"A real doctor would've bandaged it, too," I said somewhat weakly, making him roar with laughter.

"I'll get to it," he said, turning toward the bag at his feet.

"Don't ever hurt yourself like that again," Beau ordered quietly.

"You were sick," I countered, my voice equally low.

At some point, his arms had loosened a bit around my torso, and I hadn't even noticed. They were no longer holding me in place...just holding me. He cupped his palm under my chin and tipped it up until our eyes met.

"It doesn't matter if I'm dying," he replied firmly. "If you press your skin to my lips and tell me to drink, I will."

"He's not wrong," Erik said as he began to wrap my wrist. "I've seen it done. Instincts are a powerful thing."

"Well, that would've been nice to know," I griped, raising my eyebrows.

"You know now."

"Tough lessons are the ones that stick," Erik mused.

"If I never heard that sentence again, it would be too soon," Daniel complained from the living room, startling me. I'd forgotten he and Chance were still there. "It was his favorite phrase while we were children."

"He left me fifty feet up in a tree," Chance agreed.

"What were you doing fifty feet up a tree?" I asked, catching a small grin as Beau turned his head toward his brothers.

"I'd climbed there," Chance replied nonchalantly.

"That's nothing," Danny scoffed. "I fell in the river, and he watched the current take me downstream."

My jaw dropped in surprise.

"I told you not to get so close," Erik said, leaning back in his seat with his arms crossed.

"It took me miles downstream!" Danny shot back indignantly.

I let out a bark of laughter.

"That wasn't even the most irritating part," Danny said, looking at me. "He was *waiting on the bank* when I dragged myself out."

"I knew where it grew shallow enough that you'd find your footing," Erik informed him.

All at once, the four of them paused, and the room went silent.

"Ulf's here," Erik announced, standing. "I'll meet you all downstairs."

He strode out of the room with his sons on his heels.

"Ambrose has news," Beau said, letting go of me. He rounded the table and scooped up the bloody gauze and other medical paraphernalia, throwing it in the trash under the sink. "I need to go down and—" He paused and then turned to look at me. "Come with me?"

For some reason, the fact that he was including me made my skin flush with warmth that had nothing to do with the mating heat.

"I'm not wearing pants," I reminded him with a grimace. I'd been completely unworried about it while his family was there, but it suddenly hit me that I'd been not only walking around in my underwear but had passed out straddling Beau, and they'd all probably gotten a good look.

"Don't worry about it," he said, watching the emotions play over my face. "Those boxers cover far more than a swimsuit."

"They're underwear."

"Could've fooled me. They look like shorts."

"I don't bitch about your underwear."

"What is there to bitch about?" he asked, looking down at the black boxers he was wearing.

I had to concede that there was absolutely nothing to bitch about when it came to the skin hugging cotton.

"Do I at least have time to put on pants before we meet another brother?" I asked.

"Please do," he replied, following me slowly as I rose from the table and walked toward the bedroom. "I need to get dressed, too. It's freezing in here."

I stopped by the door of the bathroom and turned to look at him as he started pulling clothes out of one of the dressers. It wasn't cold in his rooms.

"You're still anemic," I said, making him turn. "That's why you're cold. That's a symptom."

"I'm fine," he assured me. "I feel much better."

"Well, you still look like hot garbage."

"Sorry to disappoint," he replied with a smirk, running his fingers through his hair.

I hesitated for only a moment before I crossed the room. All of my previous decisions had been valid. He'd said shitty things about me. He didn't like me. He'd basically been a giant asshole since the moment we'd met.

But.

I'd made an impulsive decision to tie my life to his. There was no going back now, and if I was honest with myself, I wasn't sure if I'd choose to if given the option. I'd lived my life pretty apathetically to that point. Nothing had ever been permanent, and I'd rarely allowed myself to care about anything based on the assumption that nothing ever would be.

The knowledge that I'd somehow been given something that could never be taken away, something purely mine forever? It was heady.

One of us had to flip the script on this shitshow we'd gotten ourselves into. It may as well be me.

"We have a few minutes, right?" I asked, sliding my hands over his bare chest.

I ignored the ache in my wrist.

"Reese," he murmured cautiously. "What are you doing?"

"It's been hours," I reminded him. The thrumming burn under my skin gradually increasing moment by moment.

"You're under no obligation—"

"Where's the asshole?" I asked, cutting him off. I looked him over mockingly like I was searching. "Because the man I climbed like a tree would already be fucking me."

I let out a whoop of surprise when Beau bent at the waist and wrapped his hands around the backs of my thighs. When he straightened, I scrambled for purchase, wrapping my arms around his neck.

"I don't have time to fuck you," he said, spinning toward the dresser.

My ass hit the top, knocking his clothes to the floor.

"What a shame," I replied breathlessly, tipping my head back.

The sight of him lifting his hand to his mouth had become the most erotic thing I'd ever encountered.

Forget that.

The way he lifted his hand to my mouth, little beads of blood standing out starkly against his skin? *That* was the most erotic thing I'd ever encountered.

I licked and sucked at the skin, the blood acting like an aphrodisiac as my nipples tightened and my pussy throbbed. My fingers tangled in his hair as I pulled his head toward my neck.

His resistance surprised me enough that I let go of his hand and turned my face toward his. The muscle in his jaw was pulsing as he gritted his teeth, and his eyes were hooded. He was doing his damnedest not to bite me.

"Take it," I ordered softly.

His eyes closed.

"It's yours," I reminded him.

The speed at which he struck was startling, but it wasn't why I cried out. Every inch of my body throbbed with pleasure. His hand pressed against my lips again, the blood there rolling over my tongue as he shoved his hand up the legs of my boxers. The moment he thrust two fingers inside me, I shattered.

It lasted a long time.

By the time I came down, he'd closed the bite on my throat and was gently brushing the hair back from my face while he waited for me to release his hand.

"We should probably just go back to bed," I said groggily as he smiled at me. "I don't think I have any bones left. They disintegrated."

"I could carry you downstairs," he replied evenly. "But you probably still want to put some pants on first."

I sighed and slumped forward, resting my head against his chest. "Fine," I muttered against his skin.

His hands were gentle as they helped me down from the dresser.

Unfortunately, as I walked back over to my bag, I missed the moment when he shucked off his boxers and traded them for a new pair. By the time I'd set my clothes on the bed, he was pulling up an incredibly faded pair of jeans.

"How old are those jeans?" I asked in disbelief. They were incredible, and they fit him in a way that made me debate stripping and climbing onto the bed. I figured that once I was fully bare and spread out, he'd forget he even had brothers that we were supposed to be downstairs seeing.

"Uh," he said, glancing down at them as he pulled on his t-shirt. "Fifty years?"

I choked. "You're kidding."

"They don't make shit that lasts anymore," he mused. "Chance still has bellbottoms that he pulls out every once in a while."

"I'd pay to see that," I replied, tearing my eyes away as I stripped out of my underwear and t-shirt.

Beau let out a low groan.

"I bet your mom's wardrobe is incredible." I pulled on a pair of my own jeans, only two years old.

"You're not wearing underwear?" he asked hoarsely.

"I'm wearing a bra," I countered, pulling it over my head. Bralettes may have been one of the best inventions in women's wear. It wasn't as if I had a lot to support, but at least they kept my nipples from staring everyone in the eye.

"But no underwear," he repeated.

"I rarely wear them," I reported, pulling a t-shirt on.

"You were wearing some the first time."

"That's because I'd been at work," I explained as I pulled on a pair of socks. "I wear boxers or nothing, otherwise."

"That makes no sense."

"I can't exactly go commando to work," I said, pausing to look at him. "But boxers bunch under my work pants, so briefs it is."

Beau just stared at me.

"Enjoying this little peek into my brain?" I asked jokingly, raising my eyebrows.

"I'm not sure yet," he confessed.

I turned and walked into the bathroom, leaving the door open. "Well, let me know when you decide."

As I ran my fingers through my hair he came to stand in the doorway, leaning his shoulder against the jam as he watched me.

"I forgot a hairbrush."

"Second drawer." He pointed.

I reached for it.

"You're letting me use your hairbrush? I guess this is getting pretty serious," I teased.

"I guess so," he murmured, his eyes on mine as I pulled the brush through my hair.

"Let me brush my teeth really quick, and I'll be ready."

He moved into the bathroom behind me and opened another drawer, pulling his own toothbrush out.

To say that the two of us mundanely brushing our teeth together was surreal would be an understatement.

I'd never brushed my teeth with someone before, and it felt oddly...competitive. Was I brushing less vigorously? Would it gross him out if I started brushing my tongue? Half the time, I gagged myself.

Hell would freeze over before I stopped brushing before he was finished.

His eyes danced as he watched the emotions flicker over my face. With a light hand on my hip, he scooted me out of the way and leaned down to spit and rinse his brush.

"You can stop now," he said with laughter in his voice. "Damn, you're stubborn."

I waited until he'd left the bathroom before spitting and brushing my tongue.

When we arrived downstairs, his family had already congregated in the family room and were speaking quietly. The new addition was as handsome as the other Vampire males I'd met. They were all similar enough that no one could mistake them as anything but brothers, but it was as if Ulf and Beau had inherited opposite traits from each of their parents. While Beau had his mother's brown eyes, Ulf had Erik's blue ones.

"So, this is her," a deep voice announced as we walked into the room.

"Apparently," I joked self-consciously.

"Reese, this is my older brother," Beau said, his hand on the small of my back ushering me across the room.

"Ambrose," his brother said, reaching for my hand.

I shook it, hiding my wince at the stinging nettle sensation.

"No touching," Beau said, pulling on my arm.

Ambrose frowned.

"The bond," Erik explained from his spot on the couch. "It's uncomfortable for Reese."

"So much that she slit her wrists?" Ambrose asked darkly, looking behind me at Beau.

"I didn't slit my wrists," I argued quickly, showing him the unmarred one.

"It was a misunderstanding," Beau said, wrapping his arm around my chest.

"He was anemic," I babbled, the tension between them making me a little nervous.

"You did it?" Ambrose asked Beau.

My mate jerked like he'd been hit.

"Of course he didn't," Beau's mom scolded. "What's the matter with you?"

"I'm fine," I announced loudly. "Nothing to see here."

"I passed out, and Reese panicked," Beau replied quietly.

"I did not panic," I countered.

"Looked pretty panicked to me," Chance drawled.

"I'd go so far as to say hysterical," Danny added.

Whipping around, I glared at Beau's brothers. "Forget that blood hook-up. You two can get leftovers."

"You cut your arm trying to give my brother blood?" Ambrose asked curiously.

I turned back to him reluctantly and nodded.

"Interesting," he murmured, looking from me to Beau.

"Everyone sit," Beau's mom ordered. "Ambrose has news."

I wondered what news he could have that would have everyone gathered around at the edge of their seats, but I kept my mouth shut as Beau led us over to a plush armchair. I knew better than to ask and remind them that I probably shouldn't even be in the room. Beau dropped into the chair and pulled me onto his lap.

"Not appropriate," I murmured, glancing at his parents.

"At least you're wearing pants this time," Beau replied.

I pinched the tender skin on the inside of his thigh.

"It looks like the group that took Zeke had a lot more connections than command previously believed," Ambrose said as soon as Beau and I shut up. "And they were incredibly well funded."

"Is anyone surprised by that?" Chance scoffed.

"The compound where he was held wasn't just some huts in the jungle," Ambrose continued. "It may have looked like that from the outside, but inside was a different matter. It's been deserted since the team took out—" He paused and glanced at me. "Should she be here?"

"She's family," Erik replied firmly as Beau's body tensed beneath me.

"She's human," Ambrose argued.

"So is your mother," Erik said in a deceptively soft voice.

"You know I'm not talking about Mom—"

"She stays," Beau announced, his hand tightening on my hip.

"That's a quick turnaround," Ambrose shot back.

I tensed to stand, and Beau's hand shot out lightning fast, wrapping around my waist to hold me in place.

"I can go back up to the room," I assured him, turning my head to look at him.

"You're not going anywhere."

Ambrose let out a long breath. "The place has been deserted since team three took out the group and recovered his body," he continued roughly. "We found where they tortured him."

I let out an involuntary hiss and turned to Beau again. "You didn't tell me—"

"Later," Beau replied.

I leaned further into him as Ambrose kept speaking.

"The walls and door were reinforced steel, and the entire thing was set up for exactly that. I don't think Zeke was the first."

"Corbin," Danny said with a curse.

"Keith and Gordy, too," Chance muttered.

"Possibly," Ambrose replied. "We took samples, and they're testing everything we brought back."

"You're saying he never had a chance." Erik's eyes looked like they were flashing or something, and it was so disconcerting that I had to look away.

Ambrose cleared his throat, and I laid my hand on Beau's arm, running my thumb back and forth. He was frozen.

"We also found where he'd been held. No windows, stone walls, same steel-enforced door," Ambrose informed them. "I didn't want to go in there. The place..." He shook his head. "But it's a good thing I did. There was lots of writing on the walls, but down near the floor on the northern wall was that symbol—" His voice broke, and Beau shuddered. I tightened my hand on his arm. "That symbol that Zeke used to draw all the time when we were kids."

"His *brand*," Beau said, his voice a whisper. "When he wanted to raise cattle."

"Fucking idiot." Chance let out a watery chuckle.

"That's the one," Ambrose confirmed, pulling something out of his pocket. "When I got down and got a better look at the stone, I found some shit behind it. A St. Christopher medal without a chain, a tooth, some ribbon, a lock of hair, a couple of rings—looked like wedding bands—and a photo."

He stood up and crossed to his parents, handing them something in a tiny plastic bag.

Beau's mother let out a sob, and I looked away. It felt intrusive to witness the private moment. Ambrose had been correct. I didn't belong in that room.

"Turn it over," Ambrose murmured.

When Mattie let out a keening wail, Beau pressed his forehead against my back, his breath coming in short painful sounding pants. Turning, I wrapped my arm around his neck and pulled him against me. Whatever was happening was bad. Somehow worse than the fact that his brother had been *tortured*. The air in the room felt heavy and thick when a few minutes later, Ambrose carried over the little bag.

Beau leaned up and took it, and I got a look at what was inside.

The tiny photo looked like it had been cut from one of those little columns you'd get from a photo booth. Black and white and just slightly blurry, like the people in it hadn't been able to sit still long enough for it to be taken. Of the two men pictured, it was easy to spot which of them was Zeke. He had the same strong jawline and nose as the rest of his brothers. His eyes were shaped like Chance's, and his lips could've been Beau's. The man with him had been caught mid-laugh, his head tilted back a little. Their arms were wrapped around each other, Zeke's hand cupping the man's neck just below his ear. They looked happy—no, more than that—they were practically glowing.

I swallowed back tears at the knowledge that at some point after the picture was taken, the happy man in the photo had been tortured and killed.

After a moment of staring at it, Beau flipped the photo over and inhaled a sharp breath.

"My mate" was written on the back in messy cursive.

Without a word, Beau handed back the photo so Ambrose could show Chance and Danny.

The room was silent. Beau was stiff as a post as he stared blankly at the fireplace.

"Was he there?" Mattie finally asked, breaking the silence. "Ezekiel's mate—was he there when they found him?"

"No," Ambrose said, leaving the photo with Danny as he sat back down. "Zeke was the only prisoner."

"Then where is he?"

"How the hell didn't we know?" Danny asked. "We *felt* it when Beau found his mate. *Both* times."

Beau jerked beneath me.

I stared at Danny as the words played over and over in my head.

"We need to find him," Mattie said fiercely. "We need to find Ezekiel's mate."

"We're already working on it, Mama," Ambrose replied gently.

"He could be in danger," she muttered frantically, looking at her husband. "He could be hurt somewhere."

"We'll find him, Mattie," Erik soothed.

"You need to take that back and have it analyzed," Chance told Ambrose as Danny handed him back the picture. "We might be able to figure out where it was taken."

"Where was Zeke in the last year?" Beau asked.

"South America, mostly."

"He went to Europe to meet that old friend," Danny said as he sat back down. "He was there for like two months."

"It had to have been pretty recent," Ambrose declared. "He knew as soon as he'd found his mate he was required to resign."

"He should've immediately," Mattie spat angrily. "What in the world was he thinking?"

"Their mission was active," Beau said calmly. "He probably didn't want to leave his team short."

"We could speak in circles all day and never get closer to an answer," Erik announced gruffly. "Unless Ezekiel had begun writing a journal, I doubt we'll ever know what led to his decisions."

*We felt it when Beau found his mate. Both times. Both times. Both times.*

Danny's words played on a loop. What had he meant by that? Had Beau found me before that day at the bank? I knew for a fact that I'd never seen him before. It wasn't every day that you came into contact with the most beautiful man you'd ever seen. Or Vampire, as it were. If Beau had found me earlier, why hadn't he approached me? The bond had snapped tight the moment I was within three feet of him. I didn't understand how he could've forced himself to wait. Had he just been dealing with the effects on his own, or did I have to feel it too before they started for him?

"I have to bring this back in a couple of hours," Ambrose said. "We'll run facial recognition and test it for particulates."

"Then we should know something soon," Erik soothed Mattie.

Heat started building, and I surreptitiously slid my hand inside the collar of Beau's shirt so I could press my palm to his skin. Talk about terrible timing.

"We'll head back with you," Chance announced, glancing at Danny.

Ambrose nodded.

Beau tensed. "You'll keep me updated?"

"Of course," Ambrose said sympathetically.

"You should go, too," I murmured.

Beau looked at me like I was crazy.

"You should."

"Not happening," he replied flatly, holding me in place as the others left the room.

"It's important," I said softly, running my fingers through his hair.

The pain in his eyes was staggering. I'd known that he'd lost a brother, but I'd had no idea how recently, and I hadn't really had any frame of reference for what that truly meant. His family was so extremely close. When they were all in the same room, it was almost as if you could feel the missing piece. The fact that Zeke had died horribly just added to the anguish that layered the space.

"It would be so incredibly painful for you," Beau murmured, lifting my hand to place a soft kiss in my palm.

"I could hack it."

"There's no way on earth I'd ever be the cause of that."

"He's your brother."

"You're my mate."

"You don't even like me."

"I'm a fucking idiot."

"I won't argue with that."

"There are plenty of things that I like about you."

"Name three," I sputtered sarcastically.

"You're tenderhearted."

"I am not."

"You cut open your arm with a kitchen knife because you thought I was dying."

"I didn't think you were dying."

"You didn't even wait for help to get there."

"They don't have the right blood!"

"They could have told you what to do."

"I don't like being told what to do," I hedged.

"You're so full of shit."

"I am not."

"You're funny," he said begrudgingly, making me snicker.

"I thought I was obnoxious."

"You are."

"Okay, what's the third thing?"

"You don't wear underwear."

"That's a bullshit third thing!"

"No, it's not."

"That one doesn't count."

"I think it does."

"Your entire family can hear this conversation," I reminded him.

"They're not paying any attention."

"I am," Ambrose called loudly from the kitchen.

"Oh, great," I mumbled. "Now they all know I'm not wearing underwear."

"Who cares."

"Um, me?"

"Ambrose picked his nose until he was in his twenties," Beau informed me.

"I did not, you asshole," Ambrose yelled.

"My parents used to go out every Friday night—"

"Don't you dare," Erik thundered from somewhere in the house.

"One time, they decided it was a good idea to get busy in the family car—"

"Beaumont!" Mattie screeched in warning.

"But my father forgot to put on the parking brake, and one of them accidentally knocked the gearshift into neutral."

I could hear Ambrose laughing.

"That was bad enough," Beau whispered, leaning

close. "But what was worse is they didn't notice it until they'd rolled down a hill and plowed into the side of some poor family's house."

"We couldn't get any privacy at home!" Erik yelled.

"Now you know their embarrassing secrets," Beau said, leaning back. "Feel better?"

"I'm wondering how you even knew the car thing happened."

"They had to call me to come pick them up," Ambrose called from the kitchen.

I let out a laugh, and Beau smiled, the shadows in his eyes lightening a bit.

We sat in the chair quietly, and by the time Chance and Danny came back downstairs with bags slung over their shoulders, I'd managed to turn sideways and was resting my head beneath Beau's chin. The guys said goodbye to their parents before striding back into the living room.

"We'll call you as soon as we know anything," Chance promised.

"Ignore everything he says, and you two should be fine," Danny advised me with a small smile.

"It was nice to meet you, Reese," Ambrose said, coming in behind them. "I hope we can have more time to get to know each other next time I'm home."

"I'd like that," I replied.

"Love you," Beau called out as his brothers headed toward the door.

"Love you, too," they called back one by one as they stepped outside.

I was a bit stunned as Beau let out a long breath and rested his head against the back of the chair. Rena and I said I love you all the time, but I honestly couldn't remember if I'd ever heard men do it. Even

Mr. Miranda and Noah hadn't ever said it in my presence.

Shit.

"I need to get my phone!" I shot up from the chair and lost my balance.

"What's wrong?" Beau asked as I raced for the stairs.

"I'm supposed to be at work!"

I was winded by the time I reached Beau's rooms, and when the receptionist picked up the phone at the bank, she could barely understand me because I was breathing so loudly. I had to repeat myself twice.

"Reese?" Noah answered just seconds later. "Are you okay?"

"I'm fine," I gasped.

"You don't sound fine."

"I just ran up an assload of stairs."

"Why?"

"I just remembered I was supposed to be at work like an hour ago."

"I just figured you were late again," he replied drolly.

"I am *never* this late, and you know it."

"There's a first time for everything."

"What if I was just dead in my apartment or something, and no one even came to look because you just assumed I didn't show up?" I asked indignantly.

"Well, if you were already dead, would it really matter how long it took for someone to find you? You don't have any cats, right? Because that could create a problem."

"You're the anti-Christ," I muttered, dropping onto Beau's bed.

"Does that make you an acolyte?"

"You're not as funny as you think you are."

"I assumed you were with Mr. Boucher," Noah said seriously. "Was I wrong in that assumption?"

"You weren't wrong," I grumbled. "But for all you know, he's an axe murderer."

"I've met his father—"

"You know Erik?"

"Meeting the family already, huh?" Noah mused. "Yes, we've met a few times. Pete and I both liked him."

"Pedro." I corrected.

"Is everything all right?" Noah asked. "You're okay?"

"This whole mate thing is a complete mindfuck," I confessed, falling back onto the comforter.

## CHAPTER 8
# BEAU

T he last two days had been so overwhelming that I was beginning to get a headache behind my left eye. Between that and the heat urging me to go into the bedroom and interrupt Reese's conversation, my mood was somewhere between punching a wall and pulling the blankets over my head just to drown everything out.

It was hard to imagine my baby brother with a mate. The thin thread of guilt over finding my mate twice while the others still waited felt a little thinner because Zeke had also found his. However, it was now wrapped in the guilt over being alive to enjoy it while Zeke wasn't. I couldn't believe he'd been so stupid as to continue on a mission when he knew the other half of his soul was back wherever he'd left him, waiting for him to return. I honestly didn't even understand how it had been possible for the two to part. Unless they hadn't completed the bond, which meant that my mother's heart would break all over again when she realized that the last piece she had of my brother would grow old and die long before any of us were ready for it.

I wondered what Zeke's mate was like. I'd always known that his mate would be male—all of us had. My little brother had never seen the appeal of women. He'd appreciated their differences, and he'd adored my mother, but he'd never been attracted to the fairer sex. Was his mate outgoing like Zeke or more reserved? Did he enjoy video games the way my younger brother had? How old was he? How had they met? How had he reacted when Zeke told him that he was a Vampire? I hoped that my brother's bond had started out less chaotic and messy than mine had.

Reese had gotten under my skin. I'd been so sure that something was wrong and the universe had epically fucked me, but I was beginning to wonder if I'd been the one who was wrong. She'd actually cut her arm in some misguided attempt to wake me up. And yes, it had helped, but it hadn't been necessary. If someone had asked me the night before I would've guessed that Reese wouldn't give a single fuck whether I lived or died. I hadn't given her much reason to. For some reason, she seemed to care.

I couldn't figure her out.

I'd been a dick, and to be completely honest, that was kind of my baseline. I didn't like most people, and I had patience for even less of them. Beyond some fantastic orgasms, it's not as if my presence improved her life any.

It was still early. We'd known each other for twenty-four hours and spent a lot of those hours apart, but in the last few, I'd developed an almost rabid need to be near her, and I didn't think it was the bond. The fire was still present. I could feel my back growing damp beneath my t-shirt, but that didn't explain the bit of relief I'd felt when she'd slid her hand into the neck of my shirt earlier or when she'd turned to comfort me when I hadn't asked for it.

I'd even been grateful for her smart mouth when she'd started arguing with me, making Ambrose laugh. She cut the tension. It wasn't appropriate. She was still obnoxious. But somehow, she'd also broken the ice when I'd felt like we were all trapped under it.

I walked around the living room and kitchen aimlessly, picking up the few things that were out of place. From what I remembered of Millie, she'd been soft. Soft-spoken and soft-hearted. I couldn't imagine her even knowing that someone had been tortured, much less sitting through the family meeting that we'd just had. She'd have been sweet and comforting and unobtrusive— but she wouldn't have cut through the tension. She wouldn't have urged me to go with my brothers, knowing full well the kind of agony it would bring her.

Making the comparison made me feel lower than a snake, but it was impossible to ignore.

"I talked to Noah," Reese announced as she strutted out of the bedroom. "He assumed that I was with you, so I'm not fired."

"Were you worried you'd be fired?"

"No way," she scoffed. "Mr. Miranda would divorce his ass. But I still figured they might be worried if I didn't check in."

"Was he worried?"

"Not at all," she replied wryly. "Apparently, they've met your dad and liked him, so they assumed you weren't a serial killer."

"I'm not sure that logic is sound."

"That's what I'm saying!" She smiled gently. "How are you doing?"

"What do you mean?"

"Shit downstairs got heavy."

I shrugged, not really sure what to say. Was I okay? Not really. Would I survive? Obviously.

"Do you think they'll be able to find your brother's mate?" Reese asked softly.

"I hope so."

"I'm sure they've got all kinds of gadgets to find out where that picture was taken."

"Probably."

"Do you wish you went with your brothers?"

I took her in, the messy hair and t-shirt, the white bandage wrapped around her arm, the way she'd braced the toes of one sock-covered foot on top of her other foot as she leaned against the doorframe.

"No."

"You seem like an action type of guy," she mused, straightening. "I can't see you content to stay behind."

"I'm needed here," I replied as she walked toward me.

"Another reason for you to dislike me." The words were light, but her eyes never left mine as if she was trying to read my answer before I spoke.

"I'm relieved, actually," I said, surprised that the words were true. Did I wish I was helping my brothers find Zeke's mate? Of course. But there was a sense of freedom in having a different responsibility.

The mate bond was my most sacred commitment, and no matter how I'd raged against it at first, the rightness of it was settling deep in my chest. Everything felt just slightly less important.

"I'm glad," Reese said, pausing when our toes were nearly touching. "Because I'm starving, and I was worried that if I asked you to get me food, you'd be even more pissed."

"Get your own food."

146

Reese's mouth dropped open in surprise.

"I'm joking," I said quickly, reaching for her as she took a step backward. "Too soon? Fuck."

"You were making a joke?" she said slowly, studying me like a bug under a microscope.

"Not a good one, obviously."

Her lips twitched, and I let out a shallow breath of relief. "My brothers always tell me that my jokes are too dry."

"Well, it *can* get confusing," she said kindly, still studying me. "Trying to figure out when you're actually being a dick and when you're just pretending to be a dick."

"I was pretending."

"Which time?"

"The most recent one."

"Okay, cool. Can we go get food now?"

"Yeah, let's go," I said, grabbing her hand as I headed toward the door.

"You know, I like this hand-holding thing," she said as she followed along behind me. "You're a hand holder, I dig that. I mean it's not good if you actually need two hands to complete an activity, but—"

"You're babbling."

"You freaked me out telling jokes," she shot back. "I feel like I'm in some alternate reality right now."

I didn't even try to stop the chuckle that came out of my mouth.

"I mean, I figured you were too hot to be funny, you know? The whole asshole thing fits better. That made sense. I didn't like it, but it made sense," she continued as we moved down the stairs. "Of course you'd be an asshole. When someone looks like you, they've gotta have a flaw or two, right? But now you're telling jokes, and shit feels upside down."

I paused, making her come to an abrupt stop, and turned to face her. With her on the upper step we were nearly nose to nose.

"I didn't handle it well when we met—"

"Yesterday? So long ago I can barely remember."

"I was dealing with some shit, and you weren't what I was expecting."

"Story of my life," she said. "People always thought they were getting this cute little princess, and boy, were they pissed when they realized they'd been given an angry tomboy with the vocabulary of a trucker."

I wanted to say something flowery. I was supposed to say something flowery. She'd agreed to the mating bond the same day we'd met. She'd jumped in with two feet which was really fucking crazy but also really fucking incredible. Even if she had a hard sarcastic exterior, she still deserved for me to treat her like something special. Everyone wanted that.

But I couldn't think of anything flowery, and the silence was getting awkward, so I just blurted out the only thing I could think of.

"You're growing on me."

Reese's eyes widened before she threw back her head and laughed.

"That didn't come out right," I mumbled.

"I think it came out just right," she countered, looking back at me. "If you would've tried to tell me that you were crazy about me, I would've known you were lying."

"Are you crazy about me?" I asked nonchalantly.

"I tolerate you," she replied, patting my cheek. "But that's good enough for today, right?"

"Works for me."

"Cool. My stomach is eating itself at this point, so if we could get off the stairs?"

"I made lunch," my mom called out, startling Reese.

"Christ on a cracker. I need to remember they hear everything."

"You'll get used to it," my mom answered.

We made our way to the kitchen and stood around the island to eat while my mom asked Reese open-ended questions and laughed at her stories. Mattie Boucher was good at that. She'd never met a person she couldn't talk to. Danny and Zeke were the same way, and I was coming to realize that Reese was, too. I'd never been very good at keeping a conversation going. I was always too focused on what I'd say next to really hear what the other person was saying. I managed to keep myself from looking like an idiot, but no one would ever describe me as a brilliant conversationalist.

I watched as Reese daintily wiped a bit of mayonnaise away from the corner of her mouth in amusement. She had impeccable table manners under the don't-give-a-fuck personality.

"I'm excellent with a rifle," Reese said, nodding her head.

I'd been too busy with my own thoughts and hadn't caught whatever the hell they'd been discussing.

"You're what?" I asked dumbly.

"Your mom—"

"Mattie, please," my mom corrected.

"*Mattie* asked if I had any self-defense training," Reese said slowly, enunciating each word. "And I told her nothing formal, but I throw a pretty strong right hook, and I'm excellent with a rifle."

"I'm not sure where to even start with that," I confessed.

Reese grinned. "Well, I grew up in foster care, and I moved around a lot, so either I taught myself how to scrap, or I got terrorized." She lifted her arms out to her sides. "Lots of new schools, lots of new homes, lots of secondhand clothes. I've never been particularly big, so I had to be fast and know what I was doing."

A flash of rage flowed through me at the thought of my mate having to defend herself, but I shoved it back down. It wasn't as if I could track down every bully she'd dealt with as a child and punish them personally.

"As for the rifle," Reese said easily. "I was fostered with an older couple for a while, and the man liked to hunt. They didn't have any kids, and I was the right age to take out with him. Ed and Cathy. I'm pretty sure she was afraid the old dude would fall and break a hip, so she encouraged me to be one with nature. Turns out, I'm a fantastic shot."

"You're full of surprises," I murmured.

"I've lived a thousand lives," she said cheekily.

"Erik will love that you like to hunt," Mom said. "He doesn't go often anymore, but he'd love the company when he does."

"None of the boys like to go?" Reese asked, taking another bite of her sandwich.

Mom let out a little giggle.

"What?" Reese mumbled around her food, holding her hand in front of her mouth.

"It's just that you call them boys even though the youngest of them could be your great-great-great—"

"Yeah, yeah," Reese said with a wink. "You guys are all ancient."

"They're old," my dad announced, striding in from the garage. "*I'm* ancient."

"How old are you?" Reese asked in fascination.

"Whatever you're imagining," I told her quietly. "Older than that."

"No fucking way."

"Thank you," my dad said as Mom handed him a sandwich. He leaned down and gave her a quick kiss. "This looks great. I'll take care of dinner."

He rounded the island and sat down.

"Reese likes to hunt," my mom said, raising her eyebrows.

"Is that right?"

"I mean, I haven't done it in years, but I think I remember the basics," Reese hedged.

"What do you hunt?" Dad asked as he dug into his sandwich.

"Deer and elk."

"With?"

"A rifle?"

"Amateur."

"Hey," she complained with a laugh. "What do you hunt with?"

"Longbow," he replied. "Knife."

Reese's mouth dropped open. "Bullshit."

I leaned back to enjoy the show.

"All it takes is patience."

"Wait, are Vampires like crazy fast or something? I've seen the movies."

Dad choked a little on his sandwich while Mom laughed.

"Yeah, yeah," Reese grumbled, leaning back against me. "Laugh it up."

"Uh, no," I said, brushing the hair off her neck. "We're not unnaturally fast." I paused for a moment, holding back my laughter. "We don't sleep in coffins or sparkle either."

"You're such an ass," she complained, elbowing me in the gut.

It almost sounded like an endearment.

"We're stronger than humans," my dad explained. "Our hearing is much more sensitive, and so is our eyesight. And as you know, once mated, we're immortal."

"And you don't age past thirty-one."

"Well, actually," my mom said, waving her hand from side to side. "That's an approximation. I stopped noticing changes in Beau around thirty-one years old, but Danny was closer to what?" She glanced at my dad. "Twenty-five?"

"Around then, yes."

"Chance was—" She paused and squinted. "Twenty-nine or thirty."

"Thirty," my dad confirmed.

"Ambrose and Ezekiel were both around twenty-seven."

"Wow. So why are they all different?"

"No one knows," my dad answered. "Just one of those things."

"Maybe it's based upon their mate, right?" Reese said, glancing up at me. "I mean, I'm twenty-seven, so Beau being essentially thirty-one is pretty perfect."

My parents both looked at me and then Reese.

"That could be it," I agreed, running a hand down her back.

"I mean, it would make sense."

"It would."

"You guys should take a poll or something," she mused. "See what the age differences are between mates."

"I'm not sure how many Vampires would be willing to give out that information. We're generally pretty private."

"Well, you should at least say something to your brothers," she said, tipping her head to meet my eyes. "If they know how old they are in relation to their mate, they could narrow down the search a little."

"Yeah, I'll tell them."

"Mattie and I are ten years apart," my dad said gruffly. "I'm not sure how helpful a poll would be in understanding."

"But you two got together in the 1860s, right? So, ten years difference would've been pretty standard back then, more so than now."

"True," my mom said with a small smile.

"I'd bet five years or less," Reese said thoughtfully. "I bet all the Boucher brothers are within five years of their mates' ages."

"Could be."

Reese let out a little uncomfortable laugh and shrugged. "Or I could be absolutely wrong, and there's no correlation at all. Ignore me."

I kissed the top of her head as the conversation turned to other things and a weight settled in my gut.

I understood where she was going with it, and the idea had merit except for one thing. Millie Davies had been twenty-one when we met.

# CHAPTER 9
## REESE

"How did you find yourself working at the bank?" Beau asked as I rolled to face him.

His head rested on the crook of his elbow, the wide expanse of his shoulders bare. I didn't think I'd ever get used to how gorgeous he was.

"Nepotism," I said, pulling the covers up to my chin. God, his bed was comfortable. "I've worked a lot of jobs and got paid okay, but I'd never really found anything I liked. When Noah started Accord, Mr. Miranda asked if I'd like to work there. The rest is history."

"What do you like about it?"

"Beyond being a giant pain in Noah's ass?" I smiled. "I like being able to work independently, just me and my music. Also...I don't know, I like knowing that we're putting out a product that you can't just get anywhere, at least not that kind of quality."

"Accord is well respected," Beau replied. "Expensive, but that's not a problem for most Vampires."

"You get what you pay for," I reminded him. "It's not

like Noah and Mr. Miranda are getting rich or anything. He's still teaching asshole teenagers math."

"You used to be one of those asshole teenagers."

"I was a fucking delight."

"I bet."

"I think he always liked me because I said what was on my mind," I mused. "He's always been kind of quiet. So, what about you? Did you always want to be a commando?"

Beau scoffed, his eyes crinkling at the corners. "It's expected unless a Vampire is a genius or something and can serve some other way until they find their mate. It was part of the alliance that Vampires and humans made. I think it was originally set up to keep humans from looking too close at the Vampires who were mated. I liked it okay. I was good at it."

"What are you going to do now?"

"Live a life of leisure," he teased. "Take up golf."

"I can't see you golfing."

"I'd be excellent at golf."

"Have you ever done it?"

"No."

I snorted.

"I'm not sure what I'll do," he mused. "My parents run a couple of charities, and I could go that route. My brothers still haven't found their mates—maybe something with that."

"Like, research?"

"Yeah." He nodded, his eyes unfocused. "I'm good with computers."

"Just for your brothers?" I asked when his words trailed off. "Or would you help other Vampires search?"

"Just an idea," he said nonchalantly. "I'm not even

sure what kind of parameters we could use to narrow down the searches."

"Noodle on it."

"What?"

"You know, think it over."

"Strange expression."

"You've lived forever, and you've really never heard that expression?" I asked skeptically.

"I've lived a long time," he said wryly. "I haven't lived everywhere."

"I bet you've been a lot more places than me," I replied, tucking my hands under the pillow. "I've never even been out of the state."

"Really?"

"Never had the money," I replied with a shrug. "I mean, I make enough to live well enough, but it's not like I've got the cash to go to London or something."

Beau's shoulders tensed before relaxing again. "Is that where you'd like to go? London?"

"London," I agreed. "There's a castle in Germany I'd like to see. The Colosseum in Rome. There's so much history in Europe, you know? Everything there is old."

"Ah, you like antiques," he said, laughter in his voice.

"I see where you're going with this," I replied, smiling.

"We'll travel," he promised. "Where do you want to go first?"

My mouth opened and closed like a guppy.

"We've already discussed that I can afford it," he reminded me.

"I have to work," I said finally.

Beau looked at me like I'd grown two heads.

"I mean, I'd have to get the time off," I mumbled. "There are only two techs. It's not like I could just take off."

"I wanted to talk to you about that," he replied carefully.

"I already told you I wasn't going to quit my job."

"Yeah, I know."

"Then what is there to talk about?"

"At this point, you're still uncomfortable if we aren't in the same room for more than twenty minutes."

"Yeah, but that'll fade."

"It hasn't yet."

"Well, it has to because I'm going back tomorrow."

"You think that's wise?"

"I think I have a responsibility, and it's shitty for me to leave Noah in the lurch because I can't be away from my boyfriend for more than a few minutes."

"Mate," he corrected.

"Whatever."

"Not whatever."

"I have to go back tomorrow," I repeated, a little flutter of panic rising in my chest.

I'd been taking care of myself my entire life. I'd had a full-time job since I was seventeen years old. The thought of taking days off of work without notice and, more importantly, using the paid days off I'd earmarked for an emergency made me sick to my stomach.

Beau sighed and nodded.

"Did you really just give up?"

"It's your decision," he replied. "You're an adult."

"You're right, I am," I said firmly.

"How do you feel when people say *I told you so*?" he asked curiously.

I glared. "Try it and find out."

"Noted."

"So, how does this immortality thing work?" I asked after a few moments of quiet. "Because your mom doesn't look twenty-two. I mean, she doesn't look almost two hundred years old, but—"

"Parents age as their children do," Beau explained. "So, they started aging when Ambrose was born and stopped when Zeke hit maturity."

I thought about it for a moment. "They don't look fifty and sixty."

"They don't age at the same rate as humans," Beau said with a chuckle. "But they do age."

"Huh." I thought about it for a few minutes. "But what if they had more kids now? Would they keep getting older?"

"Impossible."

"I don't know. Your mom looks pretty capable of having more kids. She seems barely older than us."

"There's a ten-year window after a mating bond is formed when Vampires and their mates can have children. After that, we're no longer fertile."

"Seriously?" I leaned up on my elbow.

"Yes. Biology is a strange thing. I'd imagine it was to keep some kind of balance. If someone lived forever and could potentially just keep having more and more children..."

"You could build your own army," I joked.

"Something like that."

"But what if you're not ready for children?"

"I'm not sure," he replied. "I guess you have ten years to decide, and then you're out of luck."

"That sucks."

"On the other hand, you're immune to all human disease and live forever," he replied dryly. "The trade-off seems fair."

"I guess so. Do you want kids?"

"Yes." The response was immediate.

"How many?"

"However many we get."

I opened my mouth. Closed it again. "That isn't as terrifying of an answer considering there's a time limit," I said finally.

Beau laughed. "Do you want kids?"

"I haven't really thought about it," I confessed. "I mean, there wasn't really any reason to. I've been single most of my adult life, and being a single parent doesn't appeal."

"Understandable."

"But I don't want them *now*," I said quietly. "We just met, and I've already met my quota of impulsive decisions for the rest of my life."

"We'll wait," he replied, reaching out to run his fingertips over my arm. "There's no rush."

"But there sorta is."

"We have ten years. We could wait for a couple and then revisit."

"Okay, yeah." I sighed. "Yeah, that works. I'm on birth control, so—"

"Human birth control doesn't work on mates."

"Fuck."

"I'll take care of it."

"Condoms for the win," I sang glumly.

"I can take a pill," he replied evenly, his lips twitching.

"Men can take birth control pills?"

"*Vampires* have medication that prevents conception, yes."

"Whoa."

"The idea that the female partner should shoulder that responsibility makes little sense if you consider that she'll be responsible for actually growing the child should they choose to have one."

"I agree," I announced loudly.

"That's good since there's currently no birth control option for mates."

"Oh, well." I huffed and laid back down. "What if she doesn't want one and her mate disagrees?"

Beau stared like I was crazy.

"What? It happens."

"Not in our culture, it doesn't."

"That's a pretty broad declaration," I argued. "Do you know every single Vampire on the planet?"

"If a Vampire forced his mate to have his children, he would be ostracized. It's not done."

"I'm sure there's someone—"

"Fine," he said flatly. "There could possibly be a Vampire somewhere at some point that went against his mate's wishes and got her pregnant."

"Both males and females should have the option."

"I think—" He paused.

"What?"

"I think that mates don't have birth control because they're rare. It sometimes takes hundreds of years for a Vampire to find their mate, so once they're found, researchers aren't willing to gamble on trying medication that has the potential to make them sterile. And Vampires sure as hell aren't willing to let their mates be guinea pigs."

"Well, that's annoyingly understandable."

"Don't worry," he said. "I'll take care of it."

"This is weird, right?" I asked, sliding my legs against the cool sheets. "I mean we just met and we're discussing children."

"Mating bonds are for life. Why wouldn't we decide together what that looks like?"

"I just mean, it's really soon to just be putting it all out there."

"Human relationships are bizarre."

"*We're* bizarre?" I widened my eyes at him. "Seriously?"

"The Gods chose you for me and me for you. It's not as if anything either of us do will change that now. We'll figure out the rest as we go."

"As easy as that, huh?"

"I'd imagine being the one to choose a lifelong partner would be stressful. How would you ever know if you'd made the right choice?"

"A lot of people get it wrong," I joked. "That's why there are so many divorces."

"Bizarre," he repeated.

"You're bizarre," I grumbled.

"I saved you from a lot of uncertainty."

I laughed. "Because this whole thing hasn't been a complete mindfuck," I replied sarcastically.

"That's fair."

"I know it is."

"You always have to have the last word, don't you?"

"Yes."

Beau didn't actually roll his eyes, but the expression of exasperation said exactly what he was thinking.

"What was it like growing up back then?" I asked, changing the subject.

"Dirty," he replied with a huff. "Simpler. Scarier, at least as a kid. Back then only the highest levels of government even knew we existed. Humans were more superstitious, so anything remotely strange or different was suspicious."

"The witch trials." I nodded sagely.

"That was before my time," he corrected with a wince.

"Oh, sorry," I teased. "Did I *age* you?"

"You're not as funny as you think you are."

"I'm twice as funny as I think I am."

"It was slower," he said, reaching over to pull me toward him. "We lived in town, so there was always a lot of movement, but at the end of the day, homes were quiet. We'd play, and my mom would make dinner—"

"You didn't have a maid?"

"We were trying to blend in," he said, tightening his arm around me. "And contrary to every show on television, the average household didn't have help."

"Hmm."

"We never went without, but we lived modestly. Our parents chose to raise us that way."

"They clearly changed their minds," I said, gesturing at the room around us.

"My father knows how to invest."

"Obviously."

"I do, too," he said with a grin.

"Good to know."

"We had friends we played with," he said, leaning his head back on the pillow as he tucked me into his side. "Families from church we spent time with."

"Your dad went to church?"

"Trying to fit in, remember? That was what you did back then. It was bad enough that he was covered in tattoos like some kind of pirate. We had to be careful with the face we presented to the world."

"That seems overwhelming."

"They tried to shield it from us."

"Kids see everything."

"Yes, they do. Plus, it was infuriating to an eight-year-old, knowing that we wouldn't actually catch the measles that was making its way through all the children on our street, but had to stay inside like all the other children anyway. We knew that we could never *say* that we were immune, but the urge was there. Thankfully, we had built-in playmates that we didn't have to pretend around."

"Is that why your parents had so many of you?"

"Five isn't that many."

"Five is practically a litter."

"I'm going to tell my mother you said that."

"Please don't."

"I think my parents had five children because as soon as one child was weaned, she got pregnant again until she was no longer able to. Back then, our family was actually considered on the smaller side. Though, I think that the other mothers were jealous of our mom because she didn't lose any of us in infancy."

"She'd lost two before your dad, though, right?"

"It was a long time before she was willing to talk about them," he replied with a sigh. "None of us knew about her previous life until we were older."

"I can't imagine how hard that would be, to have children that no one even knows existed."

"But worse," he said, running his fingers through my hair. "With no proof that they'd ever existed except the family bible."

"She doesn't have—"

Beau shook his head. "She doesn't have anything. They were buried on the farm, and all their things were burned. I'd imagine their markers were made of wood, which would be long gone even if there wasn't a grocery store there now."

"Holy crap," I murmured, sniffling. I blinked away the tears in my eyes. Poor Mattie.

"That won't be our life," he said, sliding down the bed

until we were nose to nose. "Our sons won't get sick. They'll be protected."

"Sons, not daughters, huh?" I joked.

Beau just stared. It was a look that I was beginning to recognize. There was something he was nervous to tell me.

"Vampires are only male, Reese," he said slowly. "I thought—I'm sorry, I thought that was common knowledge."

I let out a snort of embarrassed laughter. "I did know that." I just hadn't considered that it pertained to me, to us. Of course Vampires were only male. Everyone knew that. Mates could be either male or female, but there'd never been a female birth recorded. "Right. Slipped my mind for a minute."

"I'm sorry."

"Why the hell would you be sorry?"

"I know some women would like to have girls—"

"Even if you were human, I wouldn't know what I was getting until the deed was already done," I pointed out. "I could've ended up with all boys anyway."

"That's true."

"And we haven't even decided if that's something we're planning to do," I reminded him.

"Also true."

"Your childhood sounded pretty idyllic," I said, laying my head on his chest. "If we decide to have kids, we should shoot for that."

"Your childhood wasn't?" he asked, running his fingers up and down my back.

"I lived in forty-two foster homes," I replied with a short laugh. "A couple were good. One was great. Most of them sucked. Didn't matter, though. When my time was up, I was shipped off to the next one."

His arm tightened around my back.

"My birth parents were the worst, though," I said, tipping my head up to look at him. "And eventually, I met Rena. So, I guess it worked out in the end."

We spoke long into the night about pretty much everything. I loved Thai food, but Beau's favorite was Italian. He didn't like wearing shoes and warned me that he was pretty much barefoot all summer, just like when he was a kid. I told him about the thrift stores that I liked to go to on the weekends, which stores were overpriced but worth it, and which ones were really cheap but didn't have as much cool stuff. He informed me that his mother liked to go to the fancy estate sales that were invitation only, and he'd tell her I wanted to go with her next time. We discussed Rena and all of the harebrained ideas we'd gone through with over the years.

It felt good to get to know each other, even if it was mostly surface stuff, and I started to wonder if maybe accepting the mating bond hadn't been the stupidest thing I'd ever done.

# CHAPTER 10
## BEAU

I'd spent the first two hours in my car outside of Accord, but for the last twenty-five minutes, I'd been sitting in the lobby, fielding texts from my brothers about Zeke's mate and what they'd found while analyzing the objects they'd brought back from the *Huts of Horror*, as Chance called them. Ambrose was right. Zeke hadn't been the first Vampire tortured in those rooms. They'd been able to identify at least four others so far from the blood samples alone, and they were currently contacting families.

It was impossible to believe that someone was able to capture, much less hold, five different Vampires. The organization must've had unlimited resources or damn good luck. I wasn't sure which of those options was worse, but the more I'd learned, the more anxious I'd been to be closer to Reese while she worked.

Effects from the heat had begun as soon as she'd walked inside the building, and they'd been slowly but steadily increasing as time passed. It was now to the point that my stomach was clenching with nausea. I honestly wasn't sure how she was holding on for so long.

By the time the door to the offices and her workspace swung open, I was pacing the floor while the receptionist tried to pretend she wasn't watching me out of the corner of her eye.

"I'm done for the day," Reese announced, striding out with Noah Miranda-Whittaker following behind her. "Noah wanted to say hi and ask your intentions."

"I never said I was going to ask his intentions," Noah argued. "That's a moot point now."

"Good to see you again," I said, lifting my arm so Reese could scoot in against my side. By the way her body immediately relaxed against me, she'd clearly been wrestling with symptoms too.

"Please," Noah said, gesturing to the open door. "Come back to my office."

We followed him into the back while he ordered the receptionist to hold his calls. As we walked, Reese tucked her hand between the waistband of my jeans and my shirt so she could lay her palm on my bare back. Her body was practically humming with tension.

"I've offered Reese a leave of absence—"

"Which I told him I didn't want."

"I know enough about the Vampire mating bonds—"

I straightened, my body tightening, and his eyes flared for only a moment before continuing.

"I know enough to know that the first few months at least can be painful for mates to be apart."

"And how do you know this?"

"Mr. Boucher, it's a small world. I have clients I consider friends. Reese has been trying her best to hide the fact that she's extremely uncomfortable—"

"I'm fine," Reese countered.

"But I've known her since she was a teenager, and I can see that being separated from you at this point in time is physically painful for her."

"You're such a busybody," Reese griped, glaring at the man.

"She's an integral part of our team here—"

"Oh, brother," she grumbled.

"But I'm not sure how it will be feasible for her to continue working right now while she's, for lack of a better word, sick." The man was stuffy and held himself very carefully, but underneath it all was a very real concern for my mate.

"This is discrimination. I'm going to sue," Reese announced haughtily.

"Reese?" I asked, looking down at her.

Her shoulders slumped. "It sucked," she said quietly. "The entire morning fucking sucked."

Noah smiled sadly at her. "I knew you were lying through your teeth."

"I have bills to pay," she replied tiredly.

"I'll have to hire someone in your absence, but could you make do with half-pay while you're gone?"

"No way," Reese argued. "You're not paying me to stay home. Are you crazy?"

"You're crazy if you think that we'd just leave you high and dry while—"

"That's not necessary," I interrupted. "We can easily afford for Reese to take some time off."

"Not an option," Reese said flatly.

"Excuse us a moment," I muttered to Noah as I tugged her back out the door and a couple of steps down the short hallway.

"You're not going to pay my bills," she snapped as soon as we were alone. "I pay my own way."

"Be reasonable."

"I'm the only reasonable one in this entire fucking building!"

"You can't work while the heat is this bad," I told her gently, wrapping my hands over the sides of her throat. The skin there was so soft, it took a second for me to remember my train of thought. "I can't sit outside all day, every day, waiting for you to be finished. I could barely keep my ass in the car when you walked into the building this morning. So, either you take the time off and half your salary from Accord, like Noah offered, putting him in a tight spot—or you concede with some grace here and let your mate worry about the money."

"Conceding with grace isn't really my MO," she grumbled.

"You and I are connected now," I reminded her, pulling the tie out of her hair so it tumbled down her back. "Consider it a human marriage on steroids. Would you argue with a husband?"

"You know the answer to that."

"I stepped right into that one."

"You really did."

"Let me take care of this, Reese. I know you like your job, but we have the money. Take the leave of absence. Once we're able to spend periods of time apart, you can come right back."

She was quiet for a few moments, her hands stuffed up the front of my shirt so that she could press her palms to the skin on my stomach.

"Things are changing too fast," she whispered with a grimace.

"We'll figure it out. Let's stay at your place tonight."

"Yeah?"

"Sure. I need to fix your door anyway."

Reese nodded and dropped her forehead against my chest with a thud before straightening back up. She pulled her hands out of my shirt and marched back into Noah's office.

"I'll take a leave of absence on two conditions."

"Jesus Christ," Noah muttered as I followed her into the room. "What now?"

"First, I get my job back when all of this mating crap is over with—even if you find someone absolutely brilliant to replace me. You'll fire them anyway."

"Done."

"And second," Reese said, hands on her hips. "You and Mr. Miranda come to dinner at Beau's parents' house later this week to meet them."

I was pretty sure the man wouldn't have been more shocked if she'd punched him.

"His mom really wants to have my family over so everyone can meet each other," she said with a huff. "And I don't have parents, so you're up."

"We'd be honored," he replied, one hand pressed against his chest.

"Oh, don't be a sissy-lala," she said, waving him off. "It's dinner."

"We'll be there."

"Good."

She took a step toward him and then thought better of it and sent a little wave his way before turning back toward me.

"Let's go."

As we headed down the hallway toward the door to the lobby, Reese paused.

"I love you too, you old pain in my ass," she called over her shoulder before reaching for my hand and tugging me along.

Hours later, I found myself lying on her couch while she put dishes away. For some reason, she refused to let me help even though I'd offered multiple times.

"Do you think my landlord will charge me for the new doorframe?" she asked, glancing at me over her shoulder. "Technically, I didn't run it by him first."

I looked at the doorframe in question. The piece we'd replaced looked the same as the old one, only in better shape.

"I doubt he'll even notice."

"You just always see those horror stories of people not getting their deposit back."

"Would it really matter?" I looked around the apartment. Reese kept it clean, but it was impossible to hide how run-down the entire complex was. "How much was your deposit?"

"None of your business."

"It couldn't have been that much," I mused.

"You're a snob," she announced, her face appearing above mine.

"I'm not a snob."

"*It couldn't have been that much,*" she mocked, her face pinched. "Actually, *Beaumont*, it was a month's rent, and even though these apartments were built when disco was big, the neighborhood is expensive."

I couldn't tell if she was actually offended or just fucking with me.

"Come here," I ordered, reaching for her.

"Snob," she grumbled as I tugged her down onto the couch with me.

"How are you feeling?" I asked when she'd gotten comfortable, her body blanketing mine.

"It's bearable," she replied, bracing her elbows by my head so we were nose to nose. "You?"

"Better now."

"You're going to need blood soon," she murmured, brushing my hair off my forehead.

"I'm all right."

"It's already getting a little easier. You haven't needed it since this morning."

"Eventually, it'll only be once a day."

"Really?"

"Your need will supersede mine," I told her quietly. "For now, it's equal, but eventually, it'll be your half of the bond that keeps us from spending any length of time apart."

Reese wrinkled her nose in disbelief.

"Not that I'll ever want to spend time apart," I continued. "I just won't be physically uncomfortable because of it."

"Aw, you won't ever want to spend time apart?" She pinched my cheek.

"You're my mate."

"You don't even like me," she said, rolling her eyes. "It seems like you'd be jumping for joy to get some time apart."

"Rethinking my position on that," I confessed, running my hands down her back.

"I knew it would happen eventually," she replied with mock seriousness. "You just have to give it a minute for my awesomeness to really sink in."

"Oh, is that what it is?"

"Yep."

"I fucked up in the beginning."

"I didn't exactly put my best foot forward." She shrugged. "You probably thought I was a freak for jumping you right after we met. Your mate for eternity, you say? Yes, let's make that commitment even though we know nothing about each other."

"I didn't think that."

"Bullshit."

"I'm serious. Mates are destined. To be completely honest, that was the last thing on my mind."

"What was the first?"

"Damn, she's mouthy."

Reese tipped her head back and laughed. For a moment, I was stunned. It seemed insane to me that I'd ever found her lacking. She was fucking gorgeous when she laughed. She was pretty all the time, but she was a damn showstopper when she laughed.

"Well, that's true," she replied, still grinning. "Maybe the universe thought you needed someone to keep you from being so stuffy."

"I'm not stuffy."

"You're the epitome of stuffy. Poor Beau. Has that stick been up your ass since you were born, or was it a gradual thing?"

The bark of laughter that fell out of my mouth surprised us both.

"You need me to help remove it?" she asked, leaning up until she was straddling my hips. "I mean, I'm not into ass play, but—"

"Mouthy," I shot back, poking her in the sides until she squirmed.

"Stuffy," she gasped as she tried not to laugh, shoving at my hands.

She'd just toppled back toward me, and I'd barely gotten my hands into her hair, remembering how good it had been on that couch the first time when her front door swung open.

"What the fuck?" Reese yelped, jerking back upward.

"You must be the *flu*," her best friend Rena said to me, staring at us from the doorway.

I'd heard people walking up and down the breezeway all day, so I hadn't paid any particular attention when I heard someone outside the apartment. Gripping Reese's hips, I sat up and turned so my feet were on the floor.

"What are you doing here?" Reese asked, scrambling off me. "And how the hell did you get in?"

"I used the emergency key," Rena replied, lifting the key.

"That was for *emergencies*."

"Well, when my best friend, who I talk to *every day*, tells me she's sick and then doesn't answer my calls, I get a little worried."

"I'm clearly fine."

"You're clearly lying your ass off." She looked me over. "Who's that?"

"Beau Boucher," I replied, getting to my feet so I could shake her hand.

"Rena," she greeted suspiciously. "Where the hell did you come from?"

"Knock it off," Reese ground out. "Don't be an ass."

"Oh, I'm the ass?" Rena asked, throwing her hands in the air. "What the hell?"

"It's a long story."

"I've got time."

Reese lifted both hands to her face and pressed her fingers against her forehead.

"What is the big deal?" Rena asked in exasperation. "You couldn't just tell me you were getting banged by Adonis?"

"He's my mate," Reese mumbled, glancing at me.

"Say what, now?" Rena asked, looking back and forth between us.

"We're mates."

"Get the fuck outta here," Rena blustered, her mouth dropping open.

"I know," Reese groaned.

"And you gave me so much shit!" Rena crowed. *"None of that shit is true, Rena. Those magazines are garbage, Rena."*

"They're still garbage."

Rena widened her eyes and pointed at Reese and then at me. "You sneaky bitch. You've just been trying to throw me off the scent. How long has this been going on? Why the hell am I just meeting him?" She looked at me. "I'm Reese's best friend, and I will end you, Vampire or not."

"Noted," I muttered.

"It just happened," Reese said, glaring at her best friend. "I thought I'd give it a few days—"

"A few *days*?" Rena blurted, glancing down at my sock-covered feet. "When the hell did you two meet?"

"Day before yesterday," Reese mumbled quietly.

Rena's back snapped straight.

"I know what you're thinking," Reese said quickly. "It's been a crazy couple of days, and I'll tell you everything. It's just that things have been kind of intense and—"

"Did you already seal it?" Rena asked flatly.

"I don't know what you—" Reese hedged.

"Yes," I replied at the same time.

"Not helping," Reese snapped at me. As if I was the one losing my shit.

"You've known this dude two days, and you've already sealed the bond?"

"What exactly do you think it is?" I asked curiously. She was speaking like she knew all about Vampire mating bonds, but I wasn't sure how that could be possible. There were plenty of news articles floating around, but I'd never seen one that came close to being accurate.

"We need a minute," Rena said, not even bothering to look at me. She shooed Reese toward her bedroom. The door slammed behind them.

As if going into a different room in the tiny apartment gave them some kind of privacy.

"Are you out of your mind?" Rena hissed. "This isn't getting drunk and eloping in Vegas!"

"I know that!"

"You're stuck with that guy. Stuck. There is no escape."

"I'm aware!"

"What could you possibly be thinking? Even if you wanted to leave, you couldn't. They'd never *let* you. Jesus, Reese."

"If you'd give him a chance, he'd grow on you."

"Do you hear yourself? Not, *you'd like him*, but *he'll grow on you*? What's wrong with him?"

"Nothing!"

"It doesn't sound like nothing."

"We had a rocky start."

"Oh, yesterday? Yesterday was rocky but everything is all better now?" Rena asked derisively. "What the fuck?"

"He's—It's—"

"What?" Rena snapped. "You can't even say anything good about him."

"He's really close to his family," Reese snapped.

"Oh, cool. Awesome. That tells me everything I need to know."

"He's protective."

"Try possessive," Rena replied. "They're all fucking possessive. They can't help it."

"We're figuring it out as we go," Reese said firmly.

"You know I love you, and I love that you've always leaped before you looked, but this is bad. This is—I don't even know. Bordering on self-destruction."

Her tone grated along my skin, and I found myself taking a step toward the bedroom. I understood protectiveness toward family, but it was turning from a conversation between the two of them into Rena berating my mate. Fuck that.

"He is the first thing—*the first thing*—that has ever been *all* mine," Reese said, stopping me in my tracks. "Vampires get one mate, and I'm his. He's searched for me his entire life. His mother was so excited to meet me that she made a big dinner with everyone there. His dad called me *daughter*."

"You don't know anything about him."

"I know he's an ass," Reese countered. "He's stuffy, and he's rude."

"You're acting like those are good things."

"He also sat outside the blood bank today for hours so that I could work," Reese said. "He freaked when I cut my arm—"

"How the hell did you do that?"

"And he held me while it was stitched. He kisses the top of my head for no reason. When shit got heavy with his family—nothing to do with us—he leaned into *me* for comfort."

"I see that you're feeling all the things," Rena replied gently. "But you barely know him and you've—you realize this is forever, right? This isn't even *tattoo* forever. This is *death* forever. You will never be able to have a normal life."

"When have I ever tried to be normal?"

"I wish you would've called me," Rena said defeatedly.

"I didn't want to," Reese murmured. "I didn't want you to try and talk me out of it."

"You knew it was a bad idea."

"I knew it was a crazy idea. Not all crazy ideas are bad."

"This one was."

"I don't think so," Reese said stubbornly.

"You have no idea. He's going to completely take over your life."

"He will not."

"How could he not?" Rena hissed. "You're now a Vampire's mate. You're not even considered part of the human race anymore—not legally. You're under Vampire law."

"What?"

"Oh, he didn't tell you that part?"

"How do you know all this?"

"I read," Rena said flatly.

She was lying. Nowhere in any media did it detail our laws. As far as the general public was concerned, we followed and obeyed the same laws they did. If they believed otherwise, it would cause an entire shitstorm.

"I was going to tell you," Reese said after a few moments. "I was just waiting for the right time."

"Right."

"He's actually not that bad," Reese said, and I knew the words were for my benefit. My lips curved. "I mean, he's listened to this entire conversation and hasn't said a word."

"Shit," Rena spat.

The bedroom door swung open again. I was still standing in the middle of the living room when they came back down the hallway.

"You know, you could've stepped outside to give us some privacy," Rena said, glaring.

"Why would I do that?" I asked.

"Be nice," Reese warned as she came toward me, tucking herself under my arm.

"I'm being nice." I looked at Rena. Her entire body was tight, and I couldn't figure out if it was true worry for her best friend or if it was mixed with jealousy. Reese had mentioned more than once how obsessed her friend was. "How do you know so much about Vampires?"

"I read."

"And what else?" I asked, knowing that wasn't the full truth.

"Nothing else."

Reese looked back and forth between us. The silence dragged out as I watched her best friend, waiting for her to tell the truth.

"My grandparents were Vampires," she said finally, her voice so quiet it was almost silent.

"They were what?" Reese yelled.

"Explain," I ordered, tightening my arm around her shoulders.

"My grandmother already had my mom when she met my grandpa," Rena replied, lifting her chin.

"I thought all of your family was dead," Reese said, her voice wavering with hurt.

"They are," Rena replied, meeting her eyes. "My grandparents died in a plane accident when I was two. I never knew my dad, and my mom died when I was ten—which you knew."

"How is that possible?" Reese whispered, looking up at me.

I knew exactly how it was possible. Vampires were *nearly* immortal after they'd mated, and a plane crash could easily cause decapitation. I knew the crash that Rena was referring to. There had been no survivors.

"Your grandparents were Joseph and Irene Rossi," I said.

I remembered them well. Now that I knew there was a connection, I could see Irene in Rena. They had the same dimple in their cheeks and the same eyes.

"Yes," Rena breathed, her eyes wide. "You knew them?"

"Not well," I conceded. "But your grandmother made this pasta dish that she'd always bring to parties, and I swear, I used to eat my weight in it."

"Pasta alla Gricia," Rena said, letting out a little laugh of disbelief. "My mom said it was my grandfather's favorite."

"I didn't know they had a child," I said as Reese stepped away from me to gently urge Rena to the couch.

"She was little when they found each other," Rena said, squeezing Reese's hand. "Grandpa Joe raised her."

I sat down at the other end of the couch, perching on the arm so I didn't seem like I was looming over them.

"That must've been hard for your grandmother," I murmured.

"Knowing that my mother would grow old, and they never would?" Rena asked. "Yeah. My mom said that they were probably relieved that they went first."

"Why didn't your mother reach out afterward? If your family was Vampire—"

"*We* weren't," Rena said flatly. "She didn't know where to look, who to talk to. It's not as if you guys make it easy to find you. She tried searching my grandfather's things, but by the time she was informed that they were gone, someone had already been through the house."

"Shit."

"Basically," Rena said as Reese plopped down on the couch between us, her hand reaching out to rest on my thigh. "Thankfully, my mom was their legal heir, so we got the things that mattered. Then my mom died, and I lost all of it anyway."

"We'll keep looking," Reese murmured. "Every thrift store and pop-up we find, right?"

"Reese has been helping me search for the last ten years," Rena told me with a crooked smile. "There are certain things I remember that I'd like to get back if they're ever for sale."

"I can put some feelers out if you'd like," I offered.

"I doubt your Vampire friends had any interest in some lady's house of inexpensive antiques," Rena joked. "I've got keyword alerts set up on all the resale sites, though."

"We found an old green jar of her grandma's a few years ago," Reese told me with a smile. "We're almost positive it was hers because it had a chip in the bottom exactly the same."

"It was hers," Rena confirmed. "And it was a decanter, not a jar. The lid was gone."

"Whatever."

As they bickered back and forth, I thought about Rena's grandparents. Joseph had been as serious as his mate was bubbly. He'd spend the entire night in one spot, talking to old friends in his deep slow voice, his eyes always following his mate. Meanwhile, Irene would make her way around the room, greeting every single person by name. She'd been cheerful and bright and whip-smart in a way that let you know you'd never get away with anything but that she'd probably forgive whatever you'd done anyway. It made my gut clench to think of her granddaughter never getting to know either of them.

"My father was good friends with your grandfather," I

told Rena, interrupting them. "I bet he'd be glad to talk to you about him."

"That's—" Rena shook her head. "That's so nice. Thank you."

"No problem."

"Okay, he's not all bad," she said to Reese out of the side of her mouth.

"I told you."

"So glad I have your approval," I said dryly.

"And you're right, kind of an ass," Rena continued.

"Remember, he grows on you," Reese said, smiling at me.

Rena stayed for a few more hours, and I got to see a completely different side of Reese as they argued over what to order in for dinner, whether or not Reese should buy a new car, and the fact that Rena needed a maid to bring her coffee in the morning. Rena tugged on Reese's hair and told her she needed a trim. Reese told Rena that her shoes made her look like a dominatrix.

I was superfluous, and I didn't give a single fuck. *This* was the woman I'd hoped for, and ironically, I was pretty sure this was the real Reese. She was still mouthy as fuck, but the hard shell that she usually had around her was completely gone when she was with Rena. It was the softest I'd ever seen her, and after a while, I realized that it was because, in this relationship, Reese was the little sister.

I wasn't sure which of the two was the oldest, and I sure as hell wasn't going to ask, but their dynamic was very easy to see. When Rena was there, Reese let her guard down. She even allowed Rena to boss her. I spent most of the evening saying just enough to be polite and engaging while simultaneously watching them interact.

It was important to Reese for Rena to like me. She

pulled me into conversations that I had no opinion on just to make sure I was included. When I got up to get the dishes and silverware we'd need to eat our takeout, it was impossible to miss the look that the women shot each other. When I walked Rena to her car, Reese watched from the apartment doorway.

"I'm watching you," Rena warned as she opened her car door. "And I'm reserving my opinion for now."

"All right."

She glanced up at Reese and waved before looking back at me.

"I'm serious. Don't hurt her. I'm probably one of the only humans on the planet who knows how to kill a mated Vampire."

She sliced her hand over her throat and climbed into the car, starting the engine as she shut the door.

# CHAPTER II
# REESE

"She's all bark," I said as Beau strode toward me. "And I think she actually liked you."

"Don't care." He pushed me back inside the apartment with his hand on my belly. "She was here for hours."

"She wanted to get to know you," I replied with a laugh, walking backward.

"She barely spoke to me," he countered, slamming and locking the door behind him.

"Well—" I squeaked as he wrapped his arms around my waist and lifted, pressing his lips against my neck with a groan.

"That feels good," I muttered, relaxing against him.

The heat had been a steadily rising hum under my skin, and it was exacerbated by the fact that I'd refused to be all over Beau while Rena was watching every move he made. By the time she left, I'd stripped down to my tank top, and my skin was flushed.

"What are the odds that my best friend's grandparents were Vampire?" I asked as he lifted me off my feet. "That's a strange coincidence, right?"

"It is," he agreed, moving toward the bedroom.

"I wonder why she never said anything." I'd known that her family was dead, but she'd never even mentioned that she'd ever known her grandparents.

"Her mom probably told her to keep it to herself," Beau said, laying me on the bed so he could strip off his shirt.

My mouth watered as I took him in. We hadn't had sex again, just exchanged blood, but I was beginning to forget why I'd drawn that line in the sand. His skin was smooth and taut over defined muscles. Just seeing the v that tapered into the waistband of his jeans made everything inside me clench.

When he reached for the top of my scrub pants, I lifted my hips to help him.

"Fuck," he muttered, running his fingers along the lacy edge of my underwear.

"Workday," I reminded him.

"Not sure if it's hotter when you're wearing these or when you go without," he said, his fingers sliding just barely beneath the lace.

"Let me know when you decide," I joked, stretching.

His eyes met mine as he unbuttoned his jeans, and when I didn't protest, he slid them down his thighs, taking a moment to step out of them and pull off his socks.

"Yeah?" he asked gruffly, crawling onto the bed beside me.

I turned to meet him, and when his skin brushed mine, heat flared, making every place we touched feel like it was thrumming with a current of electricity. I'd never get used to that.

Letting out a sigh, I arched into him as his hand slid down my back and gripped my ass.

"I don't think you fully appreciate the control it's taking not to strip you down," Beau muttered, pressing his open mouth against the notch of my collarbone.

"You're the master of control," I conceded, running my fingers through his hair.

"I know I fucked up," he continued. "But you have to admit that this part is fucking good."

"Very good," I agreed with a shudder.

My nipples were so sensitive that any time he shifted, and my tank top rubbed against them, I felt it in my pussy. I clenched, trying to alleviate the ache, but it only made things worse.

"You took the birth control?" I asked as his mouth traced my collarbone.

He paused for a fraction of a second. "Yes."

Taking a deep breath, I quickly filed through everything that had happened since we met.

"Then why do we still have clothes on?" I whispered in his ear.

Without a word, Beau pushed himself to his knees and pulled my tank top over my head. He tossed it off the bed without bothering to look where it was going, his eyes on mine.

"I'm dying for you," he said seriously, his jaw clenching as he gently ran the tips of his fingers over my breasts, circling them around my nipples.

"You're moving pretty slow for someone who's about to die," I joked, gasping as he pinched.

"Slow?" he murmured, leaning down to pull one of my nipples into his mouth. The hot, wet suction had me arching off the bed. "Or savoring?"

"Savor faster," I ordered, making him chuckle.

He didn't increase his speed, but he did move lower, running his lips over my stomach, his breath hot on my skin. By the time he reached the waistband of my underwear, I was trembling, arousal making my heart race and goose bumps break out over my skin.

I shuddered as he pulled the underwear slowly down my legs and kept them clenched in his fist even as he spread my thighs.

"Gorgeous," he breathed, leaning down to kiss one hipbone and then the other, his nose dragging along the flesh between them.

My hand in his hair clenched as I gripped the sheets with the other.

I'd never experienced anything else like it. We'd had fantastic sex already and exchanging blood was incredibly intimate, but lying there while he traced every valley and groove of me with his eyes was so erotic that I was stunned. No one had ever taken time like he was, as if he was memorizing every centimeter, his hands clenching the insides of my thighs.

When he finally dropped his head, and his tongue flattened on my clit, every muscle in my body stiffened, the pleasure so acute it was nearly painful. The heat roared through me in pulses. As I panted and undulated against his mouth, my fingernails digging into his shoulders, he groaned, the vibration taking me right to the edge.

"Don't stop," I ordered, my voice louder and more desperate than I'd intended when he pulled away.

A second later, his hand was at my lips, two fingers sliding into my mouth, the tang of blood making my eyes roll back in my head. He hadn't nicked his thumb but instead the side of his middle finger, and I shook as he thrust them in and out of my mouth as the fingers of his other hand thrust inside me with the same rhythm.

I couldn't catch my breath. It felt like the room was spinning.

I whimpered as his tongue came out to gently sweep over my clit again and screamed around his fingers as he bit the crease of my thigh, coming so hard that my entire body shook. By the time it was over, he'd flipped me to my belly and pressed my knees wide, sliding inside me easily as I panted.

"You taste incredible," he murmured in my ear, using his finger to paint my bottom lip with my own wetness.

I bit down on his finger and then sucked it into my mouth, making him let out a nearly silent groan.

"Made for me," he whispered, slamming his hips forward.

The next orgasm wasn't as overwhelming, but it was still leagues beyond anything I'd had before Beau. I barely had the energy to roll to my side after he'd pulled out and lay down next to me.

"Come here," he ordered, cuddling me against his chest as he tugged the sheets and comforter over us. "You cold?"

"Surprisingly, a little," I replied groggily. God, he smelled so good. I pressed my nose against his sternum and inhaled deeply. I couldn't imagine ever getting enough of his scent.

His hand fisted in my hair and gently pulled my face away from his chest.

"That tickles," he said, smiling, the corners of his eyes crinkling.

I leaned up but could only reach his chin, so I kissed him there.

"What do you want to do tomorrow?" he asked, smoothing my hair down as I rested my head back on his bicep.

"Stay in bed," I replied, making him chuckle. "I'm not joking. We should never get dressed again."

"That might make dinner awkward," he joked, kissing the top of my head. "But I'm game if you are."

"You're so full of shit."

"You're right. My brothers are never seeing you naked."

"That's what you'd worry about?"

"I'm not worried."

"So, you'd be perfectly comfortable swinging your dick around the kitchen with everyone there?"

"Most of them have already seen me naked," he said with a shrug.

I scoffed as he laughed.

"Sleep," he ordered.

I wanted to argue just to be annoying, but I was too tired. A few minutes later, I passed out.

The next two days passed surprisingly quickly, considering I no longer had a job to go to. If someone had told me on the night we'd met that Beau would be incredible company, I would have laughed in their faces, but it was true. I'd never hung out with someone for so long without getting irritated by something they'd done. Even Rena drove me crazy on occasion, and I loved her.

Love may not have been a prerequisite of a mating bond, but as I sat at a picnic table and watched Beau grab our food and tip the cook in the taco truck, I thought it might be possible for us specifically. I hadn't seen anyone but him since Rena left my apartment. After sleeping in late, we'd driven to the coast to eat at a seafood place Beau loved. Afterward, we'd walked around the town, popping into antique stores and little kitschy shops. On the way home we'd stayed at a hotel that Beau remembered as a poor farm in the early nineteen hundreds. The entire property had been converted into restaurants, a spa, and soaking pool sometime in the 1990s. The history was fascinating, and the fact that Beau remembered it as it had been was a trip.

Today, I was showing Beau around my favorite places. We'd gone to the park I'd loved as a kid, driven by my high school where Mr. Miranda still taught, thrown rocks in the river, and finally stopped for some lunch at the greatest taco truck in the world.

"Careful, it's hot," Beau warned as he set my food down in front of me.

"Thank you."

"The owner knows you," he said with a small smile.

"I come here a lot."

"Clearly."

"He told me that I better treat you right."

"And you still tipped him again?" I asked, picking up my fork.

"That's *why* I tipped him again," he replied easily.

I looked at him in surprise.

"I'm not going to complain that you have people looking out for you," he said, digging into his food. "That's a good thing."

"Your mom wants to have dinner at six, right?" I asked for probably the seventh time.

"Yes," he replied patiently, looking up at me. "Why are you so wound up about it?"

"I want your parents to like us."

"They already like you."

"Well, I want them to like my people."

"They will."

"You don't know that for sure."

"Are they rude?"

"Rena is—sometimes."

"They can handle Rena."

"Mr. Miranda and Noah can get along with anyone," I added. "But I told them to show up at five forty-five because Mr. Miranda isn't the most punctual person on the planet."

"It'll be fine," Beau assured me.

"He's going to be a lot," I muttered. "You should've heard him on the phone."

"We'll handle it."

"He bitched me out for not introducing you to him already," I continued like he hadn't spoken. "It's been, like, five days. You'd think I was twelve."

"He loves you."

"He's a pain in the neck."

"He loves you," Beau repeated.

"Yeah, he does," I murmured.

"You're right," he said, taking a huge bite. "This place is excellent."

"Told you."

"I don't know how I've never been here."

"It's a hidden gem."

"Next time, we'll get it to go," he announced, looking me over. "It's cold out here."

"I'm fine." I was bundled up in a sweater, winter coat, and the hat I'd been searching for the morning we met when I was late for work. Between the clothes and the mating heat, I was practically toasty.

"Your nose is red," he countered.

"We need to head back to the apartment after this anyway," I replied. "I need to get ready for dinner."

"You've got hours."

"Maybe it takes me hours to get ready."

Beau just looked at me.

"You know I'm going to be flat on my back or on my

knees or against the wall the moment I take my clothes off," I reminded him, lowering my voice as I leaned toward him. "I'm just working that into the schedule."

He grinned and butterflies took flight in my belly as he reached out and ran his fingers down my cheek.

"Eat fast," I ordered, making him laugh under his breath.

Less than ten minutes later, I was glaring at him as he pulled into the parking lot of a beauty supply store a few blocks from my house.

"Seriously?" I griped as he parked. "I thought we were hurrying home?"

"You need a hair dryer," he reminded me as he swung out of the car.

I was still sitting there with my mouth hanging open when he opened my door.

"How the hell did you remember that?" I asked as he pulled me out of the car.

"You only told me a few days ago."

"Still," I sputtered. Why in the world was that something he'd remembered? I hadn't brought it up again. Since I wasn't someone who washed their hair every day, it hadn't been that big of an issue. The one time I'd washed it, I'd just let it dry on its own. It was kind of wild that way, but Beau didn't seem to mind it. If anything, he'd seemed kind of obsessed with it.

The memory of him wrapping it around his fist as I kneeled in front of him had my face heating as we walked into the store.

"I'd really like to know what you're thinking about," he said in amusement as we headed for the hair supplies.

"Zip it," I ordered.

He didn't say anything else, but the hand on my back slid upward until it reached my hair, giving a little tug.

"We're in public," I scolded, unable to keep the smile out of my voice.

"Pick a good one," he ordered as I checked prices.

"It's a hair dryer."

"Better to buy one that's going to last and costs a little more."

"You're such an old man," I retorted, squeaking when he pinched my ass.

His hand roamed as I picked out a middle-of-line hair dryer and carried it up to the front of the store. It smoothed over my ass as I walked, slid beneath my jacket as we waited in line, and tangled in my hair again for just a moment as I got to the counter.

I didn't bother trying to argue when he pulled out his wallet. I'd tried that during the first day we were out, and I hadn't won once. Beau was adamant. I wasn't sure if it was because I no longer had a job or if it was just the way he'd been raised, but he hadn't let me pay for a single thing.

"Thank you for my hair dryer," I said as we drove home a couple of minutes later.

"Now you won't be going out with wet hair," he replied.

"I could've bought my own hair dryer, you know," I reminded him, watching him drive. "And my own lunch and the dress I got at the antique store and dinner last night and everything else you wouldn't let me pay for. I'm not destitute."

"I know."

"Okay," I said with a sigh as we parked in front of my apartment. "Glad we cleared that up."

I'd also come to realize that Beau liked opening my car door, so I waited in my seat until he'd rounded the hood. I was a strong independent woman, but I couldn't even convince myself that I didn't appreciate the little acts of service. There was something very endearing about a man who seated you first when you went out to eat, insisted on paying and tipping well, opened every door you encountered, walked on the outside of the sidewalk, and generally acted like a gentleman everywhere except the bedroom.

"We have even less time for activities now," I informed him as I got out of the car, stopping to tip my head back and look at him when he didn't move out of the way.

"You'll need to take a faster shower," he replied. His hand slid over my hip to squeeze my ass hard before stepping out of my way.

If I had any kind of self-control, I would have sauntered up to the apartment and taken my time unlocking the door, but since I was *me* and Beau looked like *that*, I practically jogged up the stairs.

I was naked before I'd made it halfway down the hall, and we barely made it to the bedroom before Beau had me bent over and was powering inside me, his fingers pinching my clit with the same rhythm as his thrusts. I could barely breathe as I reached back for him, my fingers grasping for any skin I could find as I fought to keep my balance. It was mind-blowing. Incredible. I'd thought that the first times we'd had sex were excellent, but it just kept getting better every time. It made no sense. At some point, we had to reach the pinnacle of how we could make each other feel, but I had a weird feeling that we hadn't even scratched the surface yet.

As our bodies tipped forward, Beau's arm came out to break our fall, landing on the mattress in front of my face. His hand flexed against the comforter, and I clenched around him as I stared at the muscles in his forearm. I couldn't look away, whimpering with every thrust that forced me forward and every glide away that I found myself chasing.

I didn't even realize what I was going to do before I did it, biting down so hard on Beau's forearm that the blood in my mouth spilled down my chin.

"Fuck," Beau barked, his hips slamming harder. "That's it, baby. That's it. Take what you need."

My orgasm rushed through me so hard that my knees buckled as Beau bit down on my neck and drank his fill.

It wasn't until afterward that I realized I was crying.

"It's all right," Beau soothed as he closed the bite marks on his arm. "Come on."

I let him carry me into the shower and set me on my feet.

"I bit you," I blurted, staring at the small marks on his arm as he turned on the water.

"Smile at me," he ordered, stepping into the tub with me.

"Why?" I asked, backing into the spray.

"Because you just broke the skin for the first time," he said, smoothing my wet hair away from my face. "Smile at me."

The smile was more like a grimace, but it didn't matter to Beau. His eyes lit up like the Fourth of July as he stared.

"What?"

"Your fangs came in."

"My *what*?"

"Don't panic," he soothed, his hands gliding over me. "Your canines just elongated. They're not noticeable unless you knew what they looked like before."

"I have *fangs*?" I slid my tongue around my mouth, finding the teeth that felt different than before. He was right. They were just slightly longer, but nothing crazy.

"I told you it happened," he soothed.

"You said it usually takes a while."

"Baby, have you noticed anything about us taking a while?"

"Good point," I conceded as he grabbed shampoo and started lathering my hair. Good God, even if we weren't mated, I was pretty sure I'd stay just for the head massage.

"It's a good thing," he said, kissing my nose. "It means you can bite me whenever you need to."

"Will I get anemic if I don't?"

"No, your body doesn't need it the way mine does."

"Oh."

"But you'll still crave it anyway," he said, tipping my head back so he could rinse the shampoo out. "Think of it like sex. People can live without it...but why would they want to?"

"Word," I muttered, leaning into the fingers massaging my scalp.

"Fuck," he said, one of his hands leaving my hair to wrap gently around my throat. "I want you again."

"We don't have time," I argued half-heartedly as he dropped to his knees in the tub.

"Hold on to something so you don't fall," he ordered softly, lifting my leg until one foot was resting on the lip of the tub.

I tore down the little shelf that held my shampoo, and it put us fifteen minutes behind schedule, but the orgasm was absolutely worth it.

An hour after that, I'd finished getting ready, packed an overnight bag with clean clothes, and we were on our way back to Beau's house.

"You keep looking at my hair," I announced, leaning forward to turn the music down. "Does it look bad?"

"Of course not," Beau scoffed, glancing at me. "You know you're beautiful."

"Meh," I honked. "Wrong answer. You just did it again."

"It looks different."

"Yes, because I blow-dried and straightened it."

"I know. I watched you."

"Like a creep."

"Like someone who's seen you naked and would like to see it again."

"No, but really," I said, flipping down the mirror in the sunshade. "Is it sticking up or something?"

"There's nothing wrong with your hair."

"Then why do you keep staring at it?"

"It's smooth," he grumbled, staring out the windshield.

"That's kind of the point."

"My fingers run right through it."

"And?"

"And I like it when they get tangled, all right?" he blustered, glancing at me again.

I bit my lips to keep myself from laughing. He was so out of sorts because he had to explain himself, which made it even cuter that he liked when his fingers got caught up in my rat's nest head of hair. It was the first—and probably the last—time that I'd ever thought of Beau as *cute*. For a moment, I wished I could have known him as a child.

"Don't worry, it'll get all tangled again tonight," I replied, patting his leg consolingly.

"Oh, fuck off," he blurted.

That time I didn't hold back my laughter.

I was still a little giggly when we finally pulled into the garage. Between the last two days that had bordered on blissful, the fact that I'd been able to ruffle Beau's feathers, and knowing that I'd see Mr. Miranda for the first time in weeks, I practically bounced into the house.

Mattie had clearly started cooking earlier in the day because the house smelled wonderful. There was a large pot of something bubbling on the stove, a couple of freshly baked loaves of bread on the counter, and everything was spotless. She'd obviously gone to a lot of trouble trying to get everything just right.

"I'm going to run your bag upstairs," Beau said, kissing my temple. "My parents are in the living room."

"I can do it," I called as he strode off without me. "Or not."

I made my way into the living room and found Erik and Mattie sitting in a couple of armchairs with glasses of wine in hand.

"Well, don't you look beautiful," Mattie called, getting to her feet. "I love your dress."

"Thank you," I replied as Erik came over to help me pull my coat off. "Dinner smells so good."

"It's so cold outside. I thought stew would be nice," she said, smiling as I thanked Erik. "It's not fancy, but I've found that most people like a good stew."

"I'm sure they'll love it," I assured her. "None of them are picky eaters or allergic to anything."

"Did you and Beau have a nice time?" Erik asked as we all sat back down.

"We did! We drove to the coast and ended up staying at a hotel for the night once we got closer to home."

"Isn't it nice to get a night away?" Mattie asked, grinning. "Even if you're close to home, it's like a little treat."

"Exactly," I agreed. "It was fun to step away from real life for a minute."

"I'm glad you two had some time to yourselves," she said sweetly.

"Me and Mattie like to go a bit further afield once or twice a year," Erik added. "Gives us a chance to spend time together without all the responsibilities that come with being home."

"Even when the boys aren't here, there's still a million things to do all the time," she explained.

"I know how that goes. I swear, the first time Beau and I spent any length of time at my house, I felt like I was cleaning the whole time."

"Not the whole time," Beau corrected.

I shot him a glare over my shoulder, and he grinned.

"Rena came for dinner, too, remember?" he asked innocently.

"That's true," I replied, turning back toward his parents. "She pretty much barged in because I hadn't been answering her calls."

"Uh oh," Mattie said with a little laugh.

"It worked out, though."

"She's the one I told you about," Beau said, sitting down beside me with his hand on my knee. "Her grandparents were Joe and Irene Rossi."

"What a small world." Mattie shook her head.

"I remember Irene having a daughter," Erik added. "But I don't think we ever met her, did we, love?"

"No, we didn't." Mattie shook her head. "When Irene and Joe were in that crash, I didn't even think to look her up. We were all just so shocked by the entire thing."

"It doesn't happen often," Erik explained. "Losing mates at the same time."

"Or losing them one at a time, for that matter." Mattie sniffed. "It's not supposed to happen at all."

"What happens if you lose your mate?" I asked curiously, looking over at Beau.

"If the bond hasn't been completed," Erik replied, "The Vampire waits, sometimes for centuries, for another chance."

"Whoa," I breathed.

"If the bond has been completed, then they live without their other half, or choose not to," Mattie murmured, reaching out to grab Erik's hand. "Though it happens so rarely, that it's not something we deal with much. A mated human retains the immortality, of course, but—"

"But living forever alone would be horrendous," I finished for her.

"Yes," she agreed.

"This is probably not the subject we should be discussing right before dinner with your family," Erik said with a good-natured huff.

I leaned into Beau as his parents went off to the kitchen to check on dinner, and we waited for my family to arrive. I couldn't imagine living forever and leaving everyone else behind without the safety net of a partner. I'd already had more than one bad dream about watching Rena get old and gray while I stayed the same age. Thankfully, with everything else going on I hadn't had much time to dwell on it—though I knew those days were coming.

"I'm just so happy," Mattie said, her voice drifting in from the kitchen.

"You've outdone yourself with this one. You should've been a chef," Erik replied. "You could still do that if you wanted."

"I don't want to be a chef," she said playfully.

I smiled, listening to them go back and forth.

"I'm going to have daughters," she continued. "And grandbabies, finally!"

"Don't pressure them, Matt."

"Oh, you know I won't," Mattie replied. "They'll come when they come. I was just so worried after the last time."

"I told you that he'd find her again."

"We didn't even have the chance to meet Millicent," Mattie said as if he hadn't even spoken. "All we got was a black-and-white photo that Beau didn't even realize Zeke had shown us."

"All things happen as they should, love," Erik said gently.

"I never imagined we'd be having *Beau's* mate's family to dinner."

I'd never considered myself slow on the uptake. I could read a room in less than a second and knew whether or not a person was worth talking to in a minute or less. I'd been street smart and book smart, both, growing up. But it took me a moment to notice that Beau had stiffened at my side and another moment after that to understand the context of what Mattie was saying in the kitchen.

The door rang as the floor dropped out from under me.

## CHAPTER 12
# BEAU

She knew.

As we welcomed the Miranda-Whittakers into the house, I watched her out of the corner of my eye. She smiled and hugged the men, maintaining an almost steady stream of teasing as she helped them put their coats on the rack just inside the door, but her eyes were...off. Neither of them seemed to notice that there didn't seem to be anything behind the smile she kept on her face, but I couldn't look away.

"Mr. Miranda, this is Beau," she introduced, gesturing between us.

She didn't even look at me.

"Nice to meet you," the slender man said, shaking my hand as he sized me up. "Call me Pete."

"Likewise," I murmured. I turned to his husband. "Noah, good to see you."

"Hello, Beau," Noah replied, reaching for my hand.

"I'm here," Rena announced breathlessly. "I didn't knock since someone didn't close the door."

"Rena," Pete greeted, reaching out to rub her back as she scooted around him.

"Hey, Mr. Miranda," she said, grinning at him.

She was still smiling as she looked around the group, but the moment her eyes landed on Reese, her expression froze.

"You can put your coat up here," Reese said cheerfully, helping Rena take her coat off.

"Reese?"

My mate just shook her head.

"Come on," she said. "Beau's parents are in the kitchen."

"Just letting you say hello before we add to the mayhem," my mom trilled happily from the kitchen.

I found myself walking with Pete as we headed in that direction. Rena had commandeered Reese, but she wasn't speaking. She must've remembered that anything she said could be heard from across the house.

"Thank you for making this happen," Pete said quietly. "When Noah told me—" He shook his head. "It was a surprise."

"I know the feeling," I replied, staring at the back of Reese's head.

"We know very little about you," Pete murmured. "And I can't pretend to understand all this."

"Pete, you said you wouldn't," Noah said warningly from behind us.

"I'm just glad for the time to get to know you," Pete finished, shooting me a halfhearted smile.

"Welcome," my dad greeted as we entered the kitchen.

As my parents introduced themselves to Rena and said hello to the Miranda-Whittakers, I watched Reese. She grinned and elbowed Pete. He set his hand on her shoulder, saying something that made her wrinkle her nose.

Everyone laughed.

"We were so happy when Beau brought her to meet us," my mom said, her hands clasped in front of her. "They complement each other so well."

"We're working on that stick up his ass," Reese joked out of the side of her mouth.

My dad laughed.

"Can you imagine if you'd found someone like you?" Noah said to Reese teasingly. "I think I would've had to move out of the state."

"You love me," Reese shot back.

"You've grown on me," he conceded. "Like an unsightly mole."

They teased and chatted for a few minutes, but I couldn't make myself join in. My mind was racing. There were too many voices, and I couldn't follow the conversation.

I felt exposed and raw.

Millie was *private*. I didn't talk about her with anyone. Mordecai was the only one who understood what it was like to be cut off from the other half of yourself, and it hadn't been his choice. I'd made that decision and then had to live with it.

"The table is all set," my mom announced. "Shall we eat?"

"It smells so good," Rena said as we made our way to the table.

"It does," Pete agreed.

I dropped into my seat, trying desperately to focus on the people around me. My dad was staring at me from the end of the table, but I could barely look at him. I needed to get Reese alone.

"Thank you so much for hosting us," Pete said from across the table. "You have a beautiful home."

"It's our pleasure," my mom replied, putting a bottle of wine on the table.

I'd just noticed that Reese hadn't taken her seat when she leaned in from behind me to put a basket of bread on the table. Her torso just barely brushed my shoulder as she moved, and she jerked back instantly.

*She'd changed her dress. The light blue fabric brushed against my shoulder as Millie set down a platter of food in the center of the small table. I held back a shudder as she jerked away.*

*A nervous laugh bubbled out of her mouth. "Static," she said, smoothing a hand down her side.*

*"I can't thank you enough for what you did today," Alan said, shaking his head. "I almost killed myself trying to get back across town this morning."*

*"More than happy to help," Zeke replied easily, glancing at me.*

*I nodded in agreement. I was trying so hard to act normal, but I couldn't seem to make my mouth form words. My mate was standing right next to me. I could smell the soap she'd used to clean the grime of the building off her skin.*

*I wanted to ask why he hadn't been home with his wife the night before. Why he'd believed that it was acceptable to leave her alone when the Luftwaffe was terrorizing London. Why he hadn't left her in this small flat that belonged to his parents instead of in the middle of town. I wanted to wrap my hand around his neck until he lost that relieved smile he was wearing.*

*I would've never left her alone. I would've never allowed her to stay in London at all. She'd be safe in some small town in the US if I had anything to say about it, somewhere that had no military targets, where people still left their porch lights on at night and went to sleep without fear.*

*"I knew you'd come, darling," Millie said as she moved*

*around the table to put her hand on his shoulder. "I just had to wait."*

*He lifted her hand and kissed it.*

*It took every ounce of willpower I had not to overturn the table.*

"Reese," my mom called.

I snapped back into the present and turned my head to look at Reese.

"Sorry," she murmured, giving her head a small shake. "Déjà vu."

"Oh, I hate when that happens," my mom replied. "Sit, honey. I think everyone is set."

"This is so nice," Pete said, looking around the table. "I don't remember the last time we had Rena and Reese at the same table."

"That's because no one ever invites me," Rena complained.

"That's not true," Reese argued. "You're just always too busy for us."

"You're always welcome," Noah chided.

"We'll have to make sure Bjorn's brothers are here next time, too," my dad replied.

"Do they live close?" Pete asked as everyone began serving themselves.

"They live here," Reese said, smiling at him.

"Oh, man." Rena grimaced at my mom. "How many sons do you have? That's brave of you."

"Five," Mom replied with a little laugh. "I like having all my chicks in the nest."

I tightened my hand around my fork but didn't correct her. There were four of us now.

At some point I was able to contribute to the conversation, but I didn't remember what was said. Reese's family seemed to have a good time, and the fact that my parents had already met Noah and Pete helped smooth the way. Even Rena kept her suspicion and skepticism at bay for the entirety of dinner, though I felt her gaze on my face more than once.

Reese, on the other hand, was the center of attention. She joked and laughed and teased and generally made sure that there wasn't a silent moment. She described how she and Pete had met when she was a sophomore in his math class when she got detention for talking. Eventually, the two of them had created a somewhat unconventional bond. He and Noah had spent one of their first dates helping her move into her first apartment.

As the night came to an end we said our goodbyes and let Reese walk our guests to the front door alone.

"Look," my father muttered, watching as Reese hugged Pete and Rena and gave Noah a little wave. "Do you see?"

I was still reeling. What was I supposed to see, exactly? I'd watched Reese with them all night. She was pretending, and she was getting away with it. I seemed to be the only one who noticed the tension in her shoulders and the flat look in her eyes.

"*That* man is her father," my dad said, letting go of my arm. "The other, she loves. Clearly. But her father, she can touch."

I nodded. He was right. Reese didn't seem to have any aversion to touching Pete.

"He's worried about her, and you didn't make it any better tonight."

"What do you mean?"

"They were too polite to say anything," my mom scolded. "What's the matter with you? I've never seen you so nervous. You sat there like a darn statue."

"I'm sure it was fine," I replied, still watching Reese.

She stood in the doorway after they'd gone, watching as they drove away.

When she turned around, all pretense was gone.

"Reese?" my mom called out worriedly.

"I'm not your mate," Reese accused, making no move to get closer.

"You are."

"No." She shook her head, wrapping her arms around her waist. "No, we both know that's not true."

"Of course you're his mate," my father said roughly, looking over at my mom for help.

"Thank you for a lovely dinner," Reese said woodenly. "If you'll leave the dishes, I'd be happy to clean them up in the morning."

"Nonsense," my mom replied.

"I'm pretty tired, so I think I'm going to head upstairs."

Without another word Reese turned on her heel and walked away.

"Beau, what's going on?" my mom asked in confusion.

"She *heard* you," I shot back, following Reese. She must've broken into a run once she was out of sight because I didn't catch up with her until I got to our rooms.

A half-empty coffee mug sailed toward me as I stepped inside, flinging cold coffee all over the floor.

"You fucking asshole," she hissed.

"Reese."

"You had another mate?" She looked around the room like she couldn't figure out where she was. "What the fuck, Beau?"

"Drop it," I ordered, slamming the door behind me. I didn't want to talk about Millie with Reese. That part of my life wasn't any of her business. It wasn't anyone's business.

"Fuck you!"

"You're acting crazy."

Reese's eyes widened as she looked around the living room and found a tile coaster on the table and threw it.

"Knock it off!" I ducked as it flew past me.

"You said *I* was your mate. You—you acted like it was fucking fate or something," she yelled, her hands fisted by her sides. "And I *believed* you."

"Because you *are* my mate." I cautiously moved further into the room.

"Who's *Millicent*, Beau?" Reese spat derisively.

I snapped straight. "Stop."

"Yeah, *right*." She laughed. "Who is Millicent? *She's* your mate, right?"

"Let it go, Reese," I warned, trying to keep my temper in check. She was clearly upset, and I didn't want to make it worse, but the way she said Millie's name was like someone poking me repeatedly in the chest.

"I'm not letting *shit* go," Reese retorted. "Who the fuck is Millicent? *Where* is Millicent?"

The most ironic part of it all was that I probably would've eventually told Reese about Millie. Some day when we were settled into our bond and making a life together, I would have explained what had happened to me long before she was even born. But the way she was looking at me like I'd betrayed her when, from the moment we'd met, I'd felt like I was betraying someone else? It made me livid.

"Millie is none of your fucking business," I yelled back.

Reese jerked backward, but her surprise only lasted a moment.

"Oh, *Millie*," she said softly, her tone laced with venom. She laughed humorlessly under her breath.

"She doesn't have anything to do with you," I told her flatly, walking away.

"Bullshit," she argued, following me. "It has everything to do with me."

"It's late," I replied, kicking my shoes off.

I needed to stop engaging. Nothing good would come out of fighting with Reese. It's not as if either of us could leave, not really. Even as she stared at me like she wished I'd fall off a cliff, I knew that the bond's heat was starting to become uncomfortable. She hadn't touched me for the entirety of dinner, and my own body had started to revolt over an hour before.

Reese stood silently and stared as I stripped down to my boxers and went into the bathroom. Maybe a little distance would help. I closed the door between us.

My stomach was in knots. Everything inside me rebelled at the thought of trying to explain to Reese what those years had been like. I didn't even like to think about it, remembering the pain and the disassociation I'd gone through. The shit I'd seen and done.

I was holding on by a thread as I forced myself to lock those memories in the back of my mind where they belonged.

I took my time, but when I went back into the bedroom, Reese hadn't moved.

"We can talk in the morning."

"No," she grit out.

"You're acting like a spoiled brat."

"What is wrong with you?" Reese asked, her voice breaking. "Why won't you just tell me—"

"Because that part of my life doesn't belong to you," I roared, my patience gone. "You get everything else. *Anything* else."

My chest felt like it was going to crack open. Between

the memories that the conversation had brought to the surface and the pain in Reese's eyes, I was fucking drowning.

"I thought we were..." She shook her head, her brow furrowed in confusion. "I thought we were getting closer. I thought—"

"What?" I barked.

"I tied myself to you," she screamed back.

"No one forced you."

Her mouth snapped shut. Then she let out a bark of hysterical laughter, her eyes wild. "You're right. You're absolutely right."

"Can we just go to bed?" I asked calmly, even though my heart was thudding in my chest. I needed her closer. "It's late, and I know that you can't be comfortable."

Reese huffed and shook out her hands at her sides. Her chest was flushed, and her hair was damp at the roots—I could see that the heat was at work—but she didn't bend. Without another word she moved around me, making sure our bodies didn't touch as she went into the bathroom and shut the door behind her.

It was nearly impossible to climb into bed when every instinct pushed me toward her, but I did it. I waited, listening while she ran the tub and climbed in. I lay there, wrestling with memories that I'd thought were long gone, in the silence. Eventually, the tub began to drain. A few minutes later, the sink turned on.

When Reese finally walked quietly out of the bathroom an hour later, neither of us spoke. She was completely silent as she turned off the bedroom light and climbed into bed and she never broke that silence as she scooted across it in the dark and laid down with her back pressed against my side.

She held herself completely stiff as I turned toward

her and wrapped my arm around her waist. The heat under my skin cooled almost immediately, but there was no relief.

Reese didn't relax until hours later when she finally fell into a fitful sleep.

My phone lit up the nightstand, but I didn't move. I didn't care which of my brothers my parents had called. I didn't want to talk to any of them. It wasn't as if a pep talk would fix whatever had just happened with me and Reese.

If I tried to look at the conversation we'd had before bed logically, I knew that I'd handled it badly, but I had no idea how I could've changed it. Reese was confused and angry, but it felt impossible to reassure her. Talking about it, acknowledging that it had ever happened, was torture.

Until that night, I hadn't even spoken Millie's name in seventy years.

I was still awake when the sun rose.

## CHAPTER 13
# REESE

I woke up with a heavy chest and burning eyes. It only took a moment to remember why.

Disbelief and fear held me captive on the bed as I stared at the ceiling of Beau's room.

He'd had another mate.

I didn't know where she was or what had happened, but he hadn't denied it. She existed. I hadn't even known that was possible. *It couldn't be possible.* Everyone knew that Vampires only mated once.

My mind raced as I thought back over every interaction we'd had. Beau had been angry when we met. What had he said? *No. Fuck, no.*

My heart raced.

Beau hadn't been surprised by the heat, but his brothers hadn't known exactly how it worked. Danny had mentioned Beau fucking things up *twice.* The breadcrumbs had been there, but I hadn't even known to look for them.

If I was honest with myself, I hadn't wanted to see them.

Beau had shown me who he was from the beginning, but I'd refused to see it. I'd been so sure that it was fate for us to meet. I'd been so overwhelmed with the idea that, for once, I was being given something special. Every decision I'd made since he showed up at my door had been in line with that belief.

My hands had been slapped so many times when I reached for things that I hadn't even questioned it when I'd been given something without asking for it.

I'd been too grateful for something of my own. Something that was irrevocably *mine*.

The thread connecting me to Beau felt like the curse he'd described as I climbed out of bed and stumbled to the bathroom. My hair was a rat's nest, and the sight of it made my hands shake as I wrestled it into a tight bun at the base of my neck.

I wasn't angry enough to ignore the times that Beau was sweet. It was impossible to forget all the things I liked about him, which made the weight on my chest even heavier. It was impossible to hate the person who'd laughed until he had tears in his eyes when I dropped my ice cream cone on the boardwalk two minutes after he bought it. How was I supposed to forget the way he'd laid in bed beside me, rubbing my back and telling me about the little brother he'd lost?

I couldn't ignore the way he looked at me like I was the center of everything.

My stomach cramped as I braced my hands on the bathroom counter.

Jesus. I'd known him a week. It shouldn't hurt this bad.

"Are you all right?" Beau asked, swinging the bathroom door open slowly.

He was fully dressed, and he looked worse than I felt.

"Are you ready to talk?" I asked, meeting his eyes in the mirror.

"No."

I nodded and looked away. I wasn't even surprised.

"But, I will," he added. "Come out when you're ready."

I took my time getting dressed. Every part of me felt so incredibly exposed already that I needed the armor of clothing.

He must've thought I was such an idiot when I'd so earnestly told Rena that I finally had something that was just mine.

Part of me wondered if I really wanted to know about the woman who'd come before me or if I'd be opening a can of worms that I could never close again, but I also knew that not knowing would eat me alive. I followed him out of the bathroom.

"What would you like to know?" Beau asked as I sat across from him at the small kitchen table. His hands were clasped, and his entire body was stiff.

"Everything," I replied quietly, bracing.

"Her name was Millicent Davies." His voice was flat, almost detached.

"Where is she?"

"Dead."

"When did she die?"

"Twenty-eight years ago," he said roughly.

I frowned as he leaned back in his seat and ran his hand through his hair.

"I thought mates were immortal?"

"Human women are not," he snapped, getting to his feet.

I felt like I was missing something, but I couldn't figure out what it was.

"You're not making sense." I watched as he paced across the room.

"She was married," he said finally, coming to a stop.

"Oh."

"She loved him," he ground out.

"But—" How was that possible? Why was that possible?

A knock on the bedroom door had Beau cursing as he crossed the room.

"What?" he barked, throwing it open.

"Oh, Bjorn," Erik said softly, taking him in. He glanced over at me. "We have company."

"We're in the middle of something," Beau replied. "We'll be down later."

"Mordecai and Helen will wait," Erik said with a nod.

"You called him?"

"I thought it best."

"You overstepped."

Erik nodded again as Beau shut the door in his face.

"Isn't Mordecai your dad's best friend?" I asked, watching him closely as he came back into the kitchen area.

"Is that what you want to talk about?"

"No."

"What else would you like to know?"

"How do you have two mates?" I blurted, my face flaming. I felt like such an idiot. Curling my hands into fists in my lap, I dug my fingernails into my palms.

"I have one mate," Beau corrected. He ran his hands through his hair again.

I'd never seen him so jittery. It was as if he couldn't stand still for even a moment. The heat beneath my skin flared. I ignored it.

"But you said Millicent was your mate."

"Millie," he corrected. "She went by Millie."

It felt as if we were talking in circles and not getting anywhere, but the longer the conversation lasted, the more panicked I got.

"Explain it."

"I have one mate. You."

"Jesus Christ, Beau," I snapped, rising to my feet. "Why the hell is this like pulling teeth?"

"She was happily married, Reese," he barked, throwing his arms out. "We never completed the bond. That's it. That's the entire story."

"No, it isn't," I argued, knowing it instinctively. If it had been that simple, it wouldn't be so hard for him to talk about. "You said that we were made for each other, so why would that be true if you were made for Millie? Why would you have met her after she was married if mates were a part of some grand plan? What you're saying makes no sense."

"He should've died in the war," he shot back angrily, his voice practically vibrating. "All right?"

What war?

"Why didn't he?"

Beau's hands curled into fists at his sides.

"Beau?"

"Because I saved his miserable life," Beau snarled, his face contorting into an expression I'd never seen him make before, even at his angriest. "I followed him, and I kept the motherfucker alive."

"Why would you do that?" I practically yelled in disbelief.

He was changing in front of my eyes. The veneer of detachment that I'd come to expect whenever Beau was pissed had disappeared, and I could suddenly see every emotion he was experiencing.

217

My heart raced as he struggled to control himself.

"Because she loved him," he gritted out, breathing heavily. "Because she was pregnant, and even if he'd died, I couldn't have done that to her."

"Done what?" I asked gently, my heart in my throat as I slowly rounded the table.

"Made her watch while her child grew old and died, and she stayed twenty-one years old," he said so quietly that I barely heard him.

"You walked away," I whispered.

"I barely remember it," he confessed through his teeth. "The pain was—" He shook his head.

"You've probably blocked it out," I murmured, carefully laying my hand on his chest.

Beau was quiet as he wrapped his arms around my back and pulled me closer.

"I don't want to talk about this anymore," he finally murmured tiredly, tipping his head down until our foreheads met. "Can we stop for now?"

The pain in his eyes nearly brought me to my knees.

"Okay." I still had so many questions, but the fact that he'd reached his limit was undeniable. I could've pressed for more, and I was pretty sure he would've given it to me, but I couldn't bring myself to do it.

"I—just say the word," he breathed. "And we can talk about it again."

"Did you sleep last night?" I asked carefully, brushing his messy hair off his forehead.

"No." He swallowed and licked his lips. "You had bad dreams all night."

"I did?" I rarely remembered dreaming at all.

"I didn't want to leave you alone," he confessed almost defensively.

Closing my eyes, I pressed my forehead harder against his.

I'd been so angry that I'd had to force myself to sleep beside him so that the heat wouldn't burn me alive, meanwhile, he'd spent the night guarding me from bad dreams.

"Come on," I ordered, pulling away.

Beau followed me silently into the bedroom and onto the bed. He moved like the weight of the world was on his shoulders, but there was absolutely no hesitation as he wrapped himself around me.

I shuddered as his lips pressed lightly against my throat, and he immediately jerked his head back.

"Go ahead," I murmured, catching the back of his head in my hand. "You haven't had blood since yesterday."

"I'm fine," he murmured, leaning up to meet my eyes.

"Don't make yourself sick," I chided softly, a lump in my throat. "I'm yours, right?"

He bit down so quickly that I let out a breath of surprise before leaning into the sensation. It was different when we weren't aroused, more like a soft warmth cocooning me rather than sparks racing along my skin.

When he was done, he let out a sigh of relief before kissing where my shoulder met my neck in silent thanks. Minutes later, he was fast asleep.

Once I knew that he wouldn't feel the need to follow me, I carefully edged off the bed and left the room. Closing both doors as I went, I wandered into the main house and made my way downstairs, where quiet voices were having a discussion in the living room.

Erik had called his friend, and while Beau had seemed angry about it, I was just curious why he had.

"Reese," Erik greeted gruffly, rising to his feet. He glanced behind me in silent question.

"Beau's sleeping," I answered with a tight smile.

"He looked like he needed it," Erik replied.

Mattie was quietly sitting in a chair with red-rimmed eyes, and she didn't get up as the other two people in the room stood up and turned my way.

"This is Mordecai," Erik introduced, gesturing to a gorgeous black man with long locks and a closely trimmed beard. "And his mate, Helen."

Mordecai was handsome, but his mate was *stunning*.

"It's nice to meet you, Reese," Helen said, her dark eyes kind as she reached out to shake my hand.

Her shoulders were broad and straight, and she stood nearly as tall as her mate, with glossy black hair in a loose braid that hung to her waist.

I gaped.

Mordecai chuckled.

"I'm sorry," I blurted, looking away from Helen, completely mortified.

"No worries," he said with a smile. "She gets that a lot."

"You're the most beautiful woman I've ever seen," I said, looking back at Helen with a grimace of apology.

She smiled. "Thank you."

"Jesus," I muttered, looking back at Erik, who was holding back a laugh. "So, you called in Mordecai. What's the significance of that?"

Erik's expression instantly changed as I moved further into the room and dropped into an empty chair. "I mean, there must be something because Beau was pissed."

"He didn't know you asked me to come?" Mordecai asked Erik chidingly.

"You know Beau," Erik replied cryptically.

"I'm guessing this is because I'm the backup mate, right?" I said, looking around at each of them. "So, let's get to it. How's Mordecai supposed to change the fact that Beau's mate is dead, and he's got a replacement?"

They didn't deserve my anger, but it felt so good to let it out that I didn't even attempt to check it.

I barely noticed Helen's wince.

"Reese, that's not what happened," Mattie said soothingly.

She was trying to be nice. She'd been nice since the moment we met. Logically, I understood that. But her tone made me want to hit something.

"That's exactly what happened," I argued dully. "Let's call a spade a spade. We're all adults here."

Erik and Mordecai shared a look, and I bristled even more, if that was possible.

"You aren't the replacement," Mordecai said, sitting back down, his arm over Helen's thighs as he leaned forward a bit. "You're one and the same."

I just stared at him.

"You're his soul's mate," he said, his words slow.

I couldn't stop the bark of laughter that came out of my mouth. "Right."

"It's where the human phrase *soulmate* originated," he continued calmly. "Life is like a circle. Never-ending."

I huffed out a breath of disbelief even as my heart began to pound at the seriousness of his expression.

"That's some fairytale bullshit," I blustered.

"It's not," Mordecai replied.

"Have you never looked at Beau and thought he was familiar, somehow?" Helen asked softly. "Or felt a sense of...rightness that didn't make any sense?"

I clenched my jaw in response.

"Your soul has searched for his since the beginning,"

Mordecai said gently. "It's what causes the fire in your blood. Once a mate is found, it's nearly impossible to separate from them."

"Beau did," I shot back.

"Not without great cost," Erik said, sitting on the arm of Mattie's chair.

"And what makes you the expert in all this?" I asked Mordecai. "What, you're their leader or something?"

Mordecai scoffed. "Hardly."

"I'd like to see him try and lead me anywhere," Erik grumbled.

"They called us," Helen said, ignoring the men. "Because Mordecai found his mate and lost her long before I existed. It was a very long time before he found me again."

"Are you trying to tell me we're reincarnated until some Vampire finds us?" I asked skeptically. "That's what you're getting at, right?"

"Yes," Mattie said when the others sat silent.

I looked at each of them in turn, wondering how I could politely excuse myself. What they were saying was insane, but they clearly believed it.

"Is it any crazier than believing Vampires exist?" Erik asked quietly as if he was reading my mind.

"I don't know," I shot back. "Vampires have never been something that had to be believed or not. They just *are*."

"So is this."

"So, everyone is just reincarnated over and over again," I said with a laugh.

"We don't know," Mordecai confessed. "This only pertains to mates. We have no idea what happens when humans die."

"Oh, sure," I replied sarcastically. "Because why would you?"

"Reese—" Mattie leaned forward in her seat.

"No. You know, I think I'm going to just let you guys visit. You said your piece, and it's been...interesting. Thanks for that."

I'd just gotten to my feet when Beau strode into the room.

"What the hell is this?" he barked, moving straight to my side.

"Beaumont," Mordecai greeted.

"What do you think you're doing?" Beau asked darkly.

"Just trying to help," Mordecai replied, lifting his hands, palms up. "That's all."

"Does it look like it's helping?" Beau asked snidely, glancing down at me. "Because my mate looks cornered and scared."

I wasn't scared, per se, but I kept my mouth shut.

"I remember the confusion," Helen said. "Knowing I wasn't the first."

"Why the fuck do any of you think this is okay?" Beau asked, his voice rising. "She is my mate. *Mine.* What happens between us doesn't concern any of you."

By the time he finished, he was roaring, his entire body thrumming with anger.

"Beau," I murmured, laying my hand on his back.

"Do not *ever* corner her like this again," he ordered, reaching back to grab my hand.

I let him tow me from the room and straight through the kitchen.

"I don't have any shoes on," I reminded him when we reached the door to the garage.

Without a word, he turned and lifted me, carrying me to the car.

I was expecting to drive back to my apartment or something, but instead Beau pulled the car around the back of the house and into the woods. Gravel crunched under the tires as we wound through the trees.

"Where are we going?" I asked quietly, reaching out to rest my hand on his thigh.

"Just—away from the house," Beau replied, glancing at me.

"What's back here?" It was beautiful. Beyond the narrow road, the forest seemed untouched and wild.

"Nothing really," he said, rolling to a stop. "If we'd taken the right fork instead of the left, we would've ended up at the airstrip, but this way doesn't go anywhere."

"How much property do you guys have?" I asked, turning in my seat to look around. I chose to ignore the airstrip comment. That level of wealth was hard to even contemplate.

"Two hundred acres," Beau replied. "My parents bought it sixty years ago. It's worth a lot now, but it wasn't then."

I nodded like it was the most normal thing in the world to own hundreds of acres of untouched land. Pulling my knees to my chest, I leaned my head against the seat and looked at Beau. He was still stiff with anger, his hands wrapped tightly around the steering wheel.

"I'm sorry they did that," he said eventually. "They meant well."

"Mordecai—" I hesitated. "He said that I'm your reincarnated mate."

"Yes."

"But how is that possible?" I asked slowly. "Do I...Uh, do I look like her, or—"

"No," Beau blurted with a small shake of his head. He still wasn't looking at me.

"Oh."

"She was taller," he said after a moment. "Dark curly hair and it was cut short—to her shoulders. Brown eyes."

"So...when you saw me—"

"I knew you wouldn't look the same," he replied.

"You were disappointed." The realization made me want to curl up in a ball.

"I wasn't." He said it too quickly to be believable.

I turned my head to stare out the windshield. I wasn't even sure what to say. The fact that Beau had a mate before me was enough of a gut punch. To also know that she'd been some dark-haired bombshell that he'd clearly held on a pedestal for God knew how long? It was a lot to process.

"Am I *anything* like her?" I asked softly.

Beau didn't answer.

Suddenly, the car was too small. I couldn't breathe. Throwing open the door I hurled myself out. Mud immediately soaked through my socks as I walked a few steps away.

I was some reincarnated woman that Beau had loved? That wasn't the right word. It was too small for a mating bond. I understood that now that ours had solidified. I was the reincarnation of his *mate*.

My head throbbed.

He was *mine*. That was what I'd signed up for. I'd jumped headlong into an irrevocable mating bond on the certainty that he was mine and would be mine forever. That Vampires were devoted to their mates. I'd forced my way past our rocky beginning on the assumption that it was just one of those things that mates dealt with.

I'd had no idea that I was competing with a ghost.

Of course he didn't even *like* me. He'd been comparing me to a woman he'd cared so much for that he'd kept her human husband safe instead of biding his time so he could be with her himself. That kind of sacrifice was unbelievable.

But he'd happily fucked me within hours of meeting me.

I didn't know that Beau had followed me outside until I felt his hands bracing me as I stumbled to my knees and started to vomit. It just kept coming, like my body was purging me of every terrible realization.

They came too fast to fully process, but I eventually stopped on the glaringly obvious.

He'd touched every centimeter of my body, but he'd never even kissed me.

"Baby, it's too cold out here," Beau said gently.

I felt like a shell as he lifted me and carried me back to the car. The comfort I'd found in touching him, even at my angriest, was missing.

I felt *nothing*.

## CHAPTER 14
# BEAU

"Hey," Chance murmured quietly, swinging open the door. "We just got back."

I nodded, taking another drink of the bourbon that wasn't touching my headache. "Mordecai and Helen still here?"

"Took the guest room," he confirmed. "What the fuck happened?"

"Reese found out about Millie," I replied, glancing at the bedroom door. I'd only left her after she'd fallen asleep. Honestly, she could've been faking it just so I'd go.

She hadn't said a word all day.

"Did Mordecai explain that she's—You know, that they have the same soul?"

I let out a huff of humorless laughter. "Don't think that helped the situation."

Chance scratched the side of his head. "I mean, you never sealed the bond. That must count for something, right?"

"She's—" I didn't even know. She didn't seem angry. She hadn't cried.

I was terrified by the blank expression she'd had since I followed her out of the car.

"It'll work out," Chance reassured me. "It has to, right?"

I nodded to make him feel better, but I had no clue. It was like I'd broken something in Reese, and I had no idea how to fucking fix it.

We'd fought plenty. I'd said terrible things when we'd met, but I'd known that she would hand it right back. Reese was strong and opinionated, and she didn't take anyone's shit—including mine.

The blank stare I'd been faced with this morning made my blood run cold.

"You should go," I told Chance, glancing at the door again. "I don't want to wake her."

"All right," Chance replied slowly. "You'll let me know if you need anything?"

"Sure."

The room was silent again after he left.

The entire time Reese and I had been getting to know each other, I'd known that Millie would come up—eventually. At some point, someone in my family would mention it, and we'd have to have the conversation if we hadn't had it already, but I'd never imagined that it would affect Reese the way it had. Humans had plenty of partners before they settled down. Reese had even brought it up that first night.

I wasn't stupid enough to pretend that Millie was the same as the others. Of course she wasn't, but I hadn't had any idea that it would hurt Reese the way it had. I'd been too afraid to bring it all up again to even worry about Reese's reaction.

Setting the tumbler back on the table, I flexed my fists,

trying to ground myself as I rose to my feet. Walking softly, I moved back into the bedroom.

Reese was still curled up on her side, her eyes closed. She'd been soaked when we got back, but she hadn't made a move to help me as I'd stripped off the soggy clothes. She'd docilely let me tuck her into bed and hadn't moved since.

Grabbing her phone off the top of the dresser, I carried it back out to the living room and searched through the contacts.

I couldn't find Rena, but I found a contact labeled *Favorite Bitch* and gambled that it was the right one.

"Hey, loser," Rena answered on the first ring. "Miss me?"

"Hey, Rena," I croaked, suddenly worried I'd made the wrong move.

"What's wrong?' she asked instantly, all business.

"Reese needs you."

"Where are you?" she asked. "Your house or hers?"

"Mine." My stomach was in knots.

I wanted to be the one who made things right. I wanted to fix it. But I had the distinct impression that my presence was making things worse, not better.

"I'll be there in forty-five minutes," she said quickly.

"Someone will let you in."

She hung up without saying goodbye.

I quietly put Reese's phone back on the dresser and knelt next to the bed. Her breathing was slow and easy, but every muscle was tense as I brushed her hair back from her face. Fuck, how had I ever found her lacking?

We'd known each other for less than a week, and I'd seen at least a thousand different facial expressions. She had eight freckles. Four on one cheek, two on the other, and two on the bridge of her nose. Her skin was the softest thing I'd ever felt.

"Rena's on her way," I said softly, running my finger down her cheek.

The bond felt pulled tight even though she was less than a foot away. My chest ached.

Moving to sit, I kept my arm on the bed, wrapping my hand lightly around her forearm. Until she asked me to leave, I'd stay.

Half an hour later, Rena strode into the bedroom like she owned it.

Her eyebrows pulled together in worry as she moved toward us, going straight to Reese.

"Hey, girl," she said, resting her hand on Reese's hip. "You good?"

Reese's eyes opened slowly, and she tipped her head down just far enough to see Rena.

"I'm going to get this asshole outta here, yeah?" Rena said firmly. "Be right back."

With a stiff jerk of her head, she motioned me out of the bedroom. It rankled, but I got to my feet without argument. She was there for Reese. I'd called her because I'd hoped she'd know what to do. I couldn't complain when she came in and did what I wanted.

"I'll be right outside," I told Reese.

Once we were outside the bedroom Rena closed the door and spun on me.

"What the *fuck* did you do?"

"She's upset—"

"You *think*?"

"She found out that I had a mate before."

"Say what?" Rena snapped in surprise. "That's not possible."

"I didn't complete the bond."

"Why the hell not?"

"Is that relevant?" I asked through my teeth. It was one thing to discuss it with my mate. It was something else entirely to discuss it with her best friend.

"I'd say it's pretty fucking relevant," Rena shot back.

"She knew," I said, shaking my head. "I mean, she knew before she was like that." I pointed to the door. "It wasn't until later that she—" How was I supposed to even describe it? She'd just shut down.

"What else happened?" Rena demanded. "Come on. There must've been something."

"She talked to my parents and their friends," I mumbled, trying to think back. "They wanted to reassure her. They told her about our soul's mate—"

Rena nodded for me to keep going.

"That the soul comes back. I think they thought she'd be reassured that we only have one soul's mate."

Rena stared at me for a long time before her eyes closed.

"You told her that your mate was reincarnated as her," she said, letting out a long breath.

"I didn't tell her shit."

"But that's the basics, right?"

"Yes."

"Right," Rena said, dropping her purse on the chair. "Did you think for a moment that maybe a woman wouldn't want to know that she was her mate's choice because she shared a soul with the woman he'd been with before?"

"I didn't tell her," I repeated. "And that's not how it is."

"I don't give a shit who told her," Rena snapped, glaring. "What the fuck is wrong with you people?"

"They were trying to help."

"Well, maybe they should keep their help to them-fucking-selves. Do any of them even know Reese?" She scoffed. "*You* don't even know Reese. What am I saying?"

"She's my mate," I growled.

"Did Reese tell you anything about her childhood?" she hissed.

"I know that she grew up in foster care," I shot back. Calling Rena had been a mistake.

"Yeah? Did she tell you why she was in foster care?" Rena asked quietly, the venom in her voice burning through me. "Did she mention that the cops found her starving in a run-down motel when she was five years old? She doesn't remember it, but we got her records when we turned eighteen. They think she'd been there for at least a week. There was an empty box of gas station cupcakes that they figured she went through in the first couple of days, because, you know, five-year-olds have no impulse control, and they assume that the food will keep coming. There was tap water in the bathroom, though, so at least she had that going for her."

My throat was so tight it felt like I couldn't drag air into my lungs.

"Yeah," Rena said slowly. "So, I doubt that hearing about how you didn't cement the bond with your mate the first time, and she got reincarnated into a child who was left in a fucking motel room to starve probably didn't give Reese the warm and fuzzies."

I clutched the back of the recliner to stay on my feet as Rena turned away.

"I'll call you if I need you," she spat as she went into the bedroom, closing the door behind her.

My hands shook as I moved toward the door, leaving our rooms. By the time I hit the stairs I was jogging as my heart pounded in my ears.

I wanted to find Mordecai and level him. I wanted to strangle my father for calling him. I wanted to burn the whole world to the ground, starting with Reese's fucking parents. The weight of Rena's words felt too heavy to carry.

Reese found me on the front porch an hour later.

"Rena shouldn't have told you that," she announced, startling me. "That wasn't fair. I don't blame you for that."

"You heard her?" I asked, turning to face her.

"She wasn't being quiet."

"You didn't tell me," I murmured as she sat down in the chair next to me.

She wasn't wearing a coat. It was too cold for her to be outside without a coat.

"You didn't tell me that you'd walked away from your mate and then kept her husband alive so she could grow old with him," Reese countered, looking into the darkness. "Some things take time to share."

"It wasn't that I didn't want you to know," I replied. "I just didn't want to bring it all up again."

Reese nodded. "I can understand that."

"She wasn't like you," I began, making Reese flinch. My gut clenched, but I continued. "She was shy and soft-spoken. She deferred to her husband. She'd say something, and then she'd look at him like she wanted to see how he felt about it."

"Did you know her long?" Reese asked quietly.

"No. Only a few days."

"Is that all?"

"It was horrendous," I confessed. "Being that close to her. The bond just kept pulling tighter and tighter, and I knew she felt it too, but it was different for her."

"How so?"

"I think it was *annoying* to her," I murmured, trying to

remember all the things I'd forced myself to forget. "Like an itch she couldn't scratch. I don't think she even realized that it was me who was causing it. She was so wrapped up in her husband that it wouldn't have even occurred to her."

"It's not annoying," Reese argued. "It's *painful*."

"It wasn't for her. I would've seen it." Once I allowed myself to really think about those days I'd known Millie, so many things stood out. The way she'd kept her distance. The fact that she'd barely spoken when Zeke and I were around. She'd been frustrated that we were taking up time that she could've been spending with her husband before he shipped out. She hadn't felt the pull to me at all. It would've been impossible to hide.

"Why?" Reese asked, turning to look at me. "Why wouldn't she have felt it?"

"I don't think I was supposed to meet her," I said, the realization settling like a rock in my stomach. "She—I don't think it was supposed to happen at all."

"But that's not how it works," Reese said softly, watching me.

"I think I was supposed to meet you."

She scoffed and looked away again as Rena stomped out onto the porch.

"I've given you enough time," she announced, looking at Reese. "You want to come home with me?"

"No," Reese replied, tipping her head back to look at her friend. "But thank you for coming."

"Of course I came," Rena snapped. "Just send an SOS if you need to escape."

"I will."

"Thanks for coming, Rena," I said as she stomped down the porch.

"Eat shit and die, Vampire," Rena called back, flipping me off over her shoulder.

"She'll settle down," Reese said as we watched her best friend climb in her car and peel out as she drove away. "Eventually."

"I wasn't sure what to do," I said, watching the tail-lights disappear. "I thought you might need her."

"I did."

We sat quietly, but it only lasted for a few minutes before I found myself rising to my feet.

"It's too cold out here."

"You're always so worried about the cold," Reese grumbled as she stood up and followed me to the door.

"It's freezing out here."

"You're not even wearing a coat."

"I'm a Vampire."

"Oh, Vampires don't feel the cold?"

"We do," I replied, holding the door for her. "But it doesn't affect us the same."

"I'm immortal, remember?" Reese said as she passed me.

"We don't know if that's true yet."

"How will we know?" she asked, slowly moving toward the stairs.

"You'll stop aging."

Reese looked down at her chest. "Hear that, girls? You're gonna stay nice and perky forever."

I smiled as I followed her up the stairs. She moved like she was eighty years old, and her tone hadn't changed, but the fire was back.

When we got back to our rooms, Reese headed straight to the bedroom. I followed more slowly and found her sitting on the edge of the bed.

"Okay?" I asked carefully.

"I'm not sure where we go from here," she confessed, not looking at me. "I was so—I looked without leaping, you know? I thought things were different."

"What did you think was different?" I asked, rounding the bed as my stomach sank.

"Stupid," Reese muttered. "I thought you'd been waiting for me. I felt—I felt *important*."

"You *are* important."

"No, I'm the one you got stuck with," she said with a shrug, meeting my eyes. "In all of the reincarnations"— she stumbled over the word—"you ended up with the one you didn't even like."

"That's—No, that's not true."

"Let's be real," she said dryly. "We both know I wasn't who you would've chosen."

"You are."

"Stop it."

"You're talking nonsense," I argued. "Of course you're who I would've chosen. You're my *mate*."

"In *this* century."

"Why are you—You're my *mate*," I repeated. Didn't she understand that? What it meant? She was the other half of me.

"You haven't even kissed me," she snapped, shooting to her feet. "So...don't. Just... don't."

I gaped at her.

She hurried to the bathroom, slamming and locking the door behind her.

*I hadn't.*

I hadn't kissed her even once. In the beginning it had felt too intimate. I hadn't wanted to feel the pull to her, and I'd still been fighting it even as we'd completed the bond. But after that?

Staggering over to the bed, I dropped onto it.

Fuck.

I'd still been fighting it. I'd still been holding myself back. Echoes of the past were still fucking me up eighty years later.

Because if Millie had so easily been able to ignore the mating bond, then so could Reese. If I didn't let her get too close, then, when the inevitable happened, maybe I'd still survive it. Maybe.

My self-preservation had made Reese question the bond. It was a self-fulfilling prophecy.

A whimper made my head snap up. I stared at the door. The sound came again.

"Reese," I called, knocking at the door. "Baby, open the door."

The sound came again. Muffled.

"Reese, open the door," I ordered, louder.

Nothing.

Reaching up, I slid my hand above the doorframe until I found the key.

When I opened the door, Reese was sitting on the floor, her back against the wall with her knees pulled up to her chest. Her head rested on her arms, and she didn't look up as I crouched in front of her.

"Hey," I called softly. "Look at me."

Her hair was even more tangled than usual, and I swallowed hard when it curled around my fingers as I brushed it off her shoulder.

"I don't want to feel like this," she rasped, tipping her head back to meet my eyes.

"I'm sorry," I ground out, the sight of her red-rimmed eyes like a punch to the chest. Her face was wet with tears.

"I don't want to feel like this," she repeated angrily.

"I'm sorry," I whispered, cupping her face in my hands. Gods, she was *made for me*. What the hell had I done?

When I leaned forward and pressed my lips to hers, I was sure she was going to hit me. Her entire body stiffened with anger.

"I'm sorry," I said again. Kissed her again. Her mouth softened.

How had I deprived myself for so long? Her lips were plush and soft. I wanted to drown in her. Gods.

"I'm sorry." Kneeling, I pulled her toward me and kissed her again.

"I'm a fucking idiot," I murmured against her mouth. "I'm so sorry."

"You don't have to do this," she said, her body shuddering. "Just—" She shoved at me half-heartedly. "You don't have to."

"I fucked up," I breathed, holding her steady. "I keep fucking up."

"Then stop," she whimpered, sniffling.

"I promise," I choked out.

She was everything I'd ever needed, and I hadn't seen it. I'd been too stubborn to even acknowledge it. Reese called me out constantly, and she forgave me just as often. She never let me get too far into my head because she couldn't stand for it to be quiet. When I leaned into the bond, which I'd only allowed myself when I was inside her, it was as if everything about her was familiar. I *knew* her. The details were irrelevant. We were matched pieces in a set.

"You don't have to do this," she repeated. "I'm already here. I'm not going anywhere."

"Do what?" I asked, cupping her face in my hands.

Gods. In less than a week, she had me wrapped around her finger. There wasn't anything I wouldn't do for her.

The realization settled inside me like it had always been there.

# CHAPTER 15
# REESE

"Y ou don't have to pretend," I ground out, forcing myself to maintain eye contact. "I signed up for this, remember? So, we'll figure it out. You don't have to pretend."

"I'm not pretending anything," he replied quietly, his thumbs wiping at my cheeks. "Gods, Reese. Haven't you noticed? I can't get enough of you."

I didn't cry. I grit my teeth, and I dug my fingernails into my palms if necessary, and I moved the fuck on. I'd been doing it since I realized that tears served no purpose. They changed nothing and usually just made me feel worse.

But I couldn't fight the stinging in my eyes. It was as if I'd been turned inside out, and I couldn't figure out how to fucking fix it.

"It's the heat," I reminded him with a shudder. "It's not real."

"It's the realest thing I've ever had," he countered. "The physical ache, yeah. That's the heat. Breaking down your door because you weren't answering it—even though I've known how to pick a goddamned lock for the last hundred years? That's not the heat. Wanting to murder my parents for cornering you and putting this shit in your head? That's not the heat. Calling your friend who hates me because I didn't know how the fuck to help you? Not the heat. The mating bond physically pulls us together. It doesn't make me care that you're upset."

"Vampire instincts—"

"Would force me to keep you from harm, yes. They don't care what kind of food you like or make me follow you into antique stores all day."

"You could've had someone else. If we hadn't met at the bank—"

"Then I would've seen you walking down the street, and I would've pulled the fuck over. I would've run into you at a restaurant or a grocery store or somewhere else, and we would've ended up exactly where we are now," Beau argued. He winced and shook his head. "And maybe I would've figured shit out earlier and realized what I had the moment I met you, and you wouldn't be on our bathroom floor arguing with every single thing I say because you don't trust me."

Someone knocked on the outside door, and Beau's head shot up angrily.

"Go *the fuck* away," he yelled.

"It might be important."

"Not as important as this," he assured me, leaning forward to brush his lips over mine.

God, he was trying. He was trying so hard. I could see the sincerity in his eyes. He meant everything he said—but I couldn't get past it.

I'd *never* been anyone's first choice. No one had ever looked at me and thought, that's her. I have to have her. She's mine.

I grew on people. That was my superpower. I wore them down until they thought I was funny and cool and worth knowing. I'd done it with Rena when we were kids, I'd done it with Mr. Miranda in high school, and now I'd done it with Beau. Even with the mating bond pulling us irrevocably together, it had taken him *days* to actually want to be around me.

Why couldn't I have that one person who thought I was incredible the moment they met me? Why couldn't my mate be that person? I'd learned early that life never gave you what you wanted and rarely gave you what you needed, but why couldn't I have that one thing?

I stared at Beau.

Maybe I didn't get *that*, but I did have him. He was there in front of me—all of him. Every barrier between us was gone. I could *feel* it.

That should be enough. I'd make it enough.

Gripping his shirt, I pulled myself toward him and pressed my mouth to his. It would be enough.

So what if I wasn't his first choice? He was choosing me now.

"Baby," he murmured, pulling me into his lap as he tumbled to his ass. "Fuck. *More*."

His tongue slid into my mouth, and my skin tingled from my scalp to my toes.

I needed more of him. Grappling for the hem of his shirt, our lips parted briefly as I pulled it over his head.

"Are you sure?" he asked, pulling me closer. "You're upset."

Instead of answering him, I pulled off my own t-shirt.

"Hold that thought," he rasped, gently untangling our limbs.

He helped me to my feet and moved carefully around

242

me, disappearing into the shower. A moment later, the sound of running water filled the room.

"What are you doing?" I asked, looking into the massive shower.

Beau was standing next to the tub, his jeans unbuttoned and hanging precariously on his hips.

"Taking you to heaven," he said, his lips quirking up on one side.

He remembered what I'd said about the tub.

*He remembered everything.*

We spent an hour in the water. Kissing slowed us down. It added another layer to what had already been incredible sex. Exploring each other in soft touches and gentle movements, our skin slick from the bath oils he'd added, Beau dismantled me in a way I wasn't sure I could come back from.

By the time we got out, my fingers were wrinkled, and the rest of my body was pliant. I wasn't sure if I'd ever been more relaxed, and I stood with my hands in Beau's hair as he carefully dried me off. The strands were spiky and wet, clinging to my skin.

"Get in bed, baby," he ordered, kissing my sternum softly. "I'll be right in."

My hair was huge, and goose bumps covered my skin as I left the bathroom. Beau had never turned on the light in the bedroom, and everything was in shadow as I slid between the sheets, shivering. It was the first time I'd been actually *cold* since we'd met, and the implications weren't lost on me.

I couldn't feel the heat.

Trying not to let myself worry, my mind still raced as Beau finished up in the bathroom. Why couldn't I feel it anymore? The heat had become so normal that I hadn't even really noticed it except when it was amplified. Now that I couldn't feel it all, the lack was making my chest tighten with panic.

"I'm going to light the fire," Beau said as he crossed the room, naked. "If we leave the door open, it'll keep things warmer in here."

I barely noticed the flex of his bare ass.

He didn't feel the heat anymore, either.

What did it mean? Had we somehow broken it? Was that even possible?

"I'm wrecked," Beau said as he climbed into bed, immediately pulling me into his arms. "Fuck, you're like an ice cube."

"It's cold in here," I replied, pushing in closer.

"It'll warm up quick," he assured me, his hand briskly rubbing up and down my back as he wrapped his legs around mine. "Kiss me."

"In what universe would I take orders from you?" I replied, hiding my fear with a joke as I tipped my head back to look at him.

"This one, apparently," he said smugly, leaning in. The kiss was deep and wet. My toes curled, and my arm around his back tightened, my nails digging into his skin as his hand gripped my ass.

I wanted him closer. Dread made my heart pound as I pressed myself against every inch of flesh I could reach.

"Warmer now?" he asked, lifting his head a little as his body relaxed into the bed.

"A little," I agreed. I wasn't freezing anymore, but I still couldn't feel the comforting presence of the heat.

"Sleep, baby," he murmured, tucking my head beneath his chin. "It's late."

"I wonder who came to the door," I mused, closing my eyes.

"They'll still be here in the morning," he replied easily. "If it was an emergency, they'd have used the intercom."

I thought about how the intercom system worked until I fell asleep, refusing to let myself spiral.

That night I woke up too many times to count, my pulse racing. I couldn't remember the nightmares that had held me captive, but every time I escaped them, Beau was there. He held me through the night, never once loosening his grip.

When morning finally dawned, I opened my eyes to bright light coming through the curtains. Beau rolled to his back with a groan as I climbed out of the bed and walked over to the window. Outside was a blanket of white. Snow covered every surface, making the entire property look like some kind of wonderland.

"Too bright," Beau grumbled as he walked up behind me, kissing my bare shoulder. "Ah, snow. No wonder it was so cold in here last night."

"It's gorgeous," I murmured, leaning back against him.

"You're gorgeous."

Rolling my eyes, I stepped away.

"I'm sure I'm a regular beauty queen this morning," I said dryly, pushing my hair away from my face.

"I like it," Beau said easily, moving to his dresser. "You look thoroughly fucked."

I let out a surprise bark of laughter. "I'd say that's accurate."

Something had changed between us, but we were still careful of each other as we got dressed and ready for the day. Beau let me brush my teeth alone. I didn't stay to watch as he put his clothes on. By the time we were ready to join the rest of his family in the main part of the house, a strange tension had built. It wasn't uncomfortable, really.

As we made our way downstairs, I realized what it was. After the day before, when we'd shown each other all the little broken pieces that we normally hid, neither of us knew how to behave. It would've been funny if I'd known how to handle it.

"Sounds like everyone's here," Beau murmured.

I paused. I wasn't ready to face them yet.

"I'm going to go check out the snow," I said, trying to smile. "You go ahead."

Beau searched my face. "Okay. Wear a coat."

"Yes, sir," I replied, giving a halfhearted and very dorky salute.

He watched as I grabbed my coat out of the closet by the front door, but by the time I had it zipped, he'd disappeared into the kitchen.

It was cold as hell outside, but I welcomed the chilly breeze on my face as I sat on the porch swing. Beau hadn't mentioned the lack of mating heat, and I wondered if he was as worried as I was. Nothing in our relationship had been normal, that had become startlingly clear, but the fact that I didn't feel the physical urge to be in his presence already? It scared me. If the heat was gone, then what the hell would hold us together?

"Do you mind if I join you?" Helen asked kindly as she stepped out of the house. "I love the snow."

"It's pretty," I agreed as she sat down in a chair a few feet away.

"I wanted to apologize for yesterday," she said immediately. "Sometimes, when my mate gets something in his head, it's hard to dissuade him."

"Sounds like a man," I granted.

"And Vampires are worse," she joked. "Especially the old ones."

"What's considered *old* in Vampire time?" I asked curiously.

"I'm sure it's different for everyone," she mused. "But I think it's safe to say anyone born before the Europeans reached this continent."

My laugh came out wrong, and I ended up choking, coughing for a moment before I got it under control.

"When we tried to explain yesterday," she said softly. "About our souls reincarnating, I hadn't considered the fact that your experiences would shape your feelings about that differently than we'd intended. I was raised to believe that reincarnation was just another part of life, and so..."

She shrugged.

"Knowing that Mordecai had known the life before mine, however briefly, was a comfort to me. A sign that I was on the right path."

"You didn't feel like second choice?" I asked, the words tripping off my tongue before I could stop them.

"No," she replied in surprise, frowning. "It is the same choice."

"But the woman he met before you was different," I argued. "She didn't look like you or act like you or—"

"Why should that matter?" Helen asked curiously.

"It's *not* the same choice."

"Our souls are matched, Reese," she said gently. "There is no better match for me than Mordecai, no better match for him than me."

"Or the woman he met before you," I retorted impatiently. "Maybe she would be a better match."

"You're speaking of Beau. Why would you think such a thing?" Helen asked, aghast.

"Because he loved her so much he couldn't even talk about her." I shot to my feet, the swing jerking behind me. "I'm supposed to compete with that? I don't even *want* to compete with that."

The woman beside me made a noise of dismissal in the back of her throat.

"Sit," she ordered.

I dropped back down.

"I still believe you're viewing this in the wrong way," she said shortly. "Your soul is a match for his. Two pieces of a puzzle that fit together flawlessly. Nothing else is of any concern."

She lifted her hand to stop me when I opened my mouth to argue.

"But I will tell you this." She looked me in the eye. "She was no match for him. I'm sure that is why the bond wasn't completed. I met her."

"You did?"

"Mordecai was concerned for Beaumont," she said with a sigh. "We traveled to London so my mate could check on him. I suppose I was curious. Millicent was beautiful, yes. Sweet. Very kind to her neighbors. Devoted to her spouse."

I swallowed hard.

"Beaumont would've walked all over her," Helen said flatly. "His personality is too strong for a weak mate. She also showed no signs of the mating heat. Beau was overcome but she was only concerned with the departure of her human husband. I don't believe the Boucher brothers crossed her mind once out of sight."

"How is that possible?" I asked in confusion. The heat had been unbearable before we'd completed the bond. Even directly afterward, I'd felt like I was coming out of my skin.

"Erik mentioned that your experience has been more acute than he'd encountered before," Helen said, lacing her fingers in her lap. "I have a theory on that."

I nodded when she paused.

"Because Beau walked away by his own choice," she said slowly. "I believe your bond started out stronger than others so he wouldn't be capable of it again."

"So, he *should've* bonded her," I said, pointing at her.

She side-eyed me. "Perhaps you should be thankful that your mate recognized, however unconsciously, that it wouldn't be a successful mating bond in the ways that matter."

"Is that even possible?"

Helen let out a small laugh. "Oh, yes. I've met many mates who were bonded in all ways and chose to never move beyond that. Building a life and family with someone creates a sense of intimacy, of course, but without love, what is the point?"

"Beau doesn't love me."

"Do you love him?"

"No."

Helen scoffed. "If you did not care you, would not be concerned with the mate he never bonded."

"I don't like being second choice," I shot back.

"You really believe that is the reason for your heartache," she said in sympathetic surprise. "Child, you would not be jealous if you did not care for Beaumont. The opposite of love is apathy, an emotion that I'm not sure you're capable of when it comes to my godson."

"He's your godson?"

"He is. He and Daniel, both. As my sons are the godsons of Erik and Matilda. It's a custom my mate insisted on."

"You didn't agree with it?" I asked curiously.

"In my experience, a person's loved ones take care of children if the parents are lost. There is no need for specific plans."

For a moment, as her eyes grew unfocused, I wondered what her story was. She was obviously Native American. Her beautiful bone structure and sleek black hair were evidence of that. How long had she and Mordecai been together? Where was she from? When? What had she seen in her long life?

"What are the two of you doing out here?" Beau asked, sticking his head out the front door.

"Visiting," Helen replied, looking at him over her shoulder.

"Are you warm enough?" he asked, his eyes rising to meet mine.

"I'm fine."

"We'll be in soon," Helen said, shooing him back into the house. She turned to me. "He worries I will say something that upsets you."

"He doesn't like it when I get cold," I countered.

"The heat should take care of that for the time being," she joked.

I jerked in surprise. I wasn't cold. The heat that had become a part of me was back, and it throbbed gently when Beau was close.

I let out a shuddery breath of relief.

"You and Beau are an excellent match," Helen said, smiling gently at me. "Your soul has found his again in *this* life, when the time was right. Your experiences had shaped you into true equals, and perhaps most importantly, when the two of you needed each other most. It was the same for Mordecai and me. He appeared precisely when he was supposed to. Something to consider."

She rose gracefully to her feet and went back into the

house while I turned her words over in my head. Was that the secret? Had we met again in this life because that's when we needed each other?

I thought about it as I headed back inside.

I hadn't been in any particular need when Beau and I met. I loved my job and liked my apartment. I had friends and a social life. It wasn't anything special, but I hadn't been unhappy. I hadn't been particularly happy, either, but I figured that was pretty normal. Happiness happened for me in moments. It had never been a sense of being.

*Beau*, though.

I carefully hung my coat in the closet, remembering the stiff way he'd stood at the receptionist's desk the first time I saw him. The flash of anger and fear in his eyes when the heat had pulsed between us. The way he'd asked to hold me, like the words were torn from him. The stillness of his body later, when Ambrose had begun detailing the place where their brother had been tortured.

He'd been so angry, and I didn't think it stemmed from finding me. I thought that maybe he'd been angry for a very long time, and losing Zeke had been a trigger that made everything worse. By the time he found me, he'd shielded himself so well that it was a miracle I'd ever broken through.

Without the intensity of the bond, Beau may have never shown up at my apartment that first day.

"I was just coming to get you," Beau said, breaking me out of my thoughts as he strode toward me. "Breakfast is ready. My mother made a feast since we're all here."

"Great," I said distractedly, still grappling with everything Helen had said and what it meant.

"You okay?" he asked, cupping my face in a motion that was becoming familiar. "I didn't realize Helen had gone outside."

"I'm fine," I assured him. "It was a nice visit."

"Did she tell you about all the trouble I used to get into with her boys?" he asked with a small smile. "When we moved west, we lived near them for a time. We were technically adults, but you'd never convince our parents of that."

"No," I said, curling my hands around his wrists. "She told me about Millie."

"Shit."

"No, it was okay," I assured him quickly. "She was mostly apologizing for freaking me out yesterday."

"Maybe we should go somewhere," he said, leaning down to brush his lips over mine.

I didn't think the sensation would ever get old.

"Just me and you," he continued. "And a private beach."

"Sand," I replied, wrinkling my nose.

His lips tipped up as he kissed me again. "Fine, somewhere else. You pick."

"I liked that hotel we stayed at," I mused, leaning in. If I was honest, I didn't really care where we were. I had a lot to consider about how our lives would unfold going forward, but as long as Beau was beside me, I could do that anywhere.

"England?" he asked, pulling back a little. "You said you wanted to go to London."

"Not London," I blurted. I guess it did matter where we were. I did *not* want to return with him to the place where he'd found Millicent Davies.

Beau winced. "Right. Italy, then. The Colosseum."

"We don't need to go anywhere," I argued.

"Our mother's making us wait on you," Chance called loudly. "Move your asses."

I hadn't even realized that Beau's brothers were home.

I wondered if that meant they had news about Zeke's mate.

"There are too many people here," Beau breathed, kissing me once more before pulling away. He took me by the hand and tugged me toward the kitchen.

Another leaf had been added to the table, and Beau's entire family sat around it with Mordecai and Helen, waiting on us.

"You could've eaten," Beau chided, pulling out my chair. "I told you we'd be back in a minute."

"That's rude," Mattie argued primly.

"Nice to see you again, Reese," Danny said cheerfully. He smiled at me, but it didn't reach his eyes. In fact, all of Beau's brothers looked absolutely exhausted.

"You, too," I replied, smiling at him and then at Chance.

"I hope my brother isn't being an idiot anymore," Ambrose said from across the table.

"Ulf," Erik said in warning.

"It's touch and go," I replied easily.

Beau pinched me under the table.

"Actually, it was your father being an idiot yesterday," Erik said, setting his glass down as his eyes met mine. "Was it not?"

"It's fine." I waved him off.

"No, it wasn't," Beau countered stiffly.

"We apologize, Beau," Mordecai said quietly.

"It's not me you should apologize to," Beau shot back.

"Beau, stop," I whispered, putting my hand on his thigh. The muscle under my hand was rigid. I tightened my fingers as if I could hold him in place.

"We overstepped," Erik said with a sigh.

"What the hell happened?" Danny asked, glancing around the table.

"Reese heard Mom and Dad talking about Millie," Beau said flatly, making his brothers straighten in their seats. "And instead of realizing that they'd done *enough*, they invited Mordecai and Helen over to...what?" He stared at his father. "Do damage control? Which backfired after they cornered her while I was sleeping."

Ambrose cursed under his breath. The tension at the table was palpable. My face burned.

Mattie spoke quietly. "We thought they could help you both understand—"

The look Beau shot his mom was so full of rage that my breath caught.

Erik's fist slammed onto the table, the sound as loud as a gunshot. Dishes rattled.

Everyone braced as Beau looked to Erik. Ambrose placed his hands on top of the table like he was going to vault out of his seat. Daniel carefully put down his water glass. Chance pushed his chair back from the table. Mordecai's gaze sharpened.

"Beau," I murmured, my heart pounding. "Hey." Reaching up, I cupped his cheek the way he always did to mine. "Beau."

I held back a flinch as his gaze met mine.

"It's okay. We're okay. Leave it."

"They made you—" His teeth snapped together, his cheek flexing under my hand. "You were hurt."

"We've already gone over this," I whispered, running my thumb over his jaw.

I was acutely aware of the table full of people watching us, but I was terrified that the moment Beau looked away from me, he'd do something stupid, like lunge across the table at his father.

"I'm okay," I reminded him. "It's over."

"They *hurt* you," he ground out.

The bottom of my stomach dropped out at the vibration in his words. I'd known that Beau was upset when I'd gone into my own head the day before—it had been impossible to miss—but I hadn't understood the depth of it.

I'd scared him.

"You disappeared," he said, the sound so soft that I barely heard him. "I couldn't reach you."

I hadn't realized how much it bothered him that Rena had been the one to snap me out of it. She'd gone through it with me before and had the tools to reach me. She'd known to throw the blankets back and pull me to my feet. She'd known to force me to meet her eyes and bully me to respond to her. She'd known that I needed to let it all out, however it came, before I could move forward. Someday, I'd explain it all—but not with an audience. It was something Beau deserved to know, for both our sakes. It didn't belong to the others.

"It was good that they came," I assured him as he leaned closer. "Helen explained some things this morning that—"

I barely held him in place as his head jerked in her direction.

The table was achingly silent.

"We're moving past it," I reminded him, leaning up to brush my lips over his. "Remember? Let it go."

Beau let out a long breath, and I watched as the worst of the tension drained out of him.

Finally, he nodded.

As I let go of his face and turned toward the others, Beau's hand drifted up to wrap securely around the back of my neck like he was grounding himself.

"Shit," Chance said, sliding his chair back in with a screech. "Thank Gods Reese is the Bjorn whisperer. I thought things were going to get rowdy there for a minute."

"Do you ever shut up?" Ambrose asked with a glare.

"Nope," Chance and Danny replied at the same time.

Chance flipped Danny off, and his mother reached over, backhanding his chest in rebuke.

Helen met my eyes across the table, lifting one of her brows.

"What are you guys doing here?" Beau asked as the flow of breakfast began again, and everyone started serving themselves.

"We have news," Danny said, glancing at Ambrose.

"Which we would've told you last night if you would've answered your door," Chance complained, his mouth full.

"We were busy," Beau said flatly.

"We have to head out after breakfast," Ambrose said, setting his fork down. "We think we might have a lead on Zeke's mate."

"You're kidding," Beau said, stiffening.

"His name is Charles Franklin," Ambrose replied with a nod. "Facial recognition pinged him pretty quickly. Finding an address has proved a bit more difficult."

"His last known address was in Baltimore a year ago," Danny added. "Chance and I went out there and spoke to the neighbors. No one knew him." He rolled his eyes. "But one lady—you know the type—had quite a bit to say. Charlie and his sister were supposedly going to Europe. She was really put out that they'd saved up so they could take the year off and travel. Like it had anything to do with her bitchy ass."

"They're traveling?"

"That's what she said," Danny replied with a shrug.

"So, who the fuck knows where they are now. Ambrose has been searching for where they've crossed borders—"

"Nothing since Zeke was captured," Ambrose cut in. "Dead end."

"But we know he's in Europe," Beau said, as his hand wrapped around mine. I didn't even think he realized what he was doing as he laced our fingers together.

"His passport hasn't left Belgium," Ambrose confirmed.

"Unless he's traveling under the radar," Chance said with a little whoosh of his hand. "If he knows Zeke is gone, he might've decided it was best to lay low."

"There's no way he hasn't realized his mate is gone," I blurted, even though I knew I had no role in the conversation. My stomach clenched. I wasn't sure how Zeke and his mate had separated in the first place, but I knew down to my bones that if it was Beau, I'd know the moment he was gone.

Just the thought of it made the fire under my skin flare.

"It's time to start searching," Danny said, glancing at us. "And we could use some more eyes out there."

"You're due for a trip anyway, right?" Ambrose asked as he dug back into his food. "You were just talking about it."

Right. Because they always heard everything Beau and I discussed unless we were in his rooms.

"You want me to go?" I asked in surprise. I'd never even been out of the country. I wasn't sure what kind of help they expected me to give.

"It's not like dumbass could go without you," Chance said with a shrug. "We're just looking for Zeke's mate so we can introduce ourselves and let him know that he's got family. We're not doing any cool shit."

"It'll be safe," Ambrose told me with a sigh. "But we can cover more ground if Beau's with us."

"Okay."

"We'll discuss it," Beau said at the same time.

"What's there to discuss?" I asked, lowering my voice as Mordecai and Ambrose started talking.

Beau glanced around the table and then stood, snatching a few muffins as he pulled me out of my seat. I hurried to catch up to him as he marched toward the stairs.

"Your mom made breakfast for everyone," I reminded him, glancing over my shoulder.

"I got muffins," he replied, tugging me toward his rooms.

As soon as he stepped inside, he closed the door behind us, locking it for good measure.

"What's your damage?" I asked in exasperation.

"What?"

"*Heathers*?"

"I don't know what the fuck you're talking about."

"Nothing." I waved him off. "What's wrong? Why are we up here?"

"Because I'm sick of having every conversation with an audience," he replied with a scowl.

"You don't want to go to Europe?" I asked, trying to figure out what his issue was.

"Of course I do." He tossed me a muffin and set the others on the table. "But we don't know how long this could take."

"Okay."

"It could be months, Reese," he said, watching my face. "You have a life here. What about your job?"

"Will I be able to go back to my job in the next couple of months?"

"I don't know," he confessed, running his hand through his hair. "The heat calmed down last night but—"

"You noticed?"

"Hard to ignore," he said with a grimace.

"Is that normal?"

"Sure," he replied easily. "For short periods of time. Why do you think I started a fire last night?"

"Oh." So, we hadn't broken anything.

"I'm guessing it was a reprieve after the bathtub," he said, his lips twitching. "Our bodies needed time to recover."

"Speak for yourself," I blustered. "I could've gone all night."

"I'll hold you to that."

"Promises, promises," I sang.

Beau's expression fell. "We don't know what we're dealing with yet," he warned. "This Charles guy might not want anything to do with us."

"But you have to try, right?" I asked gently. "You want to go?"

"Yes." He sighed.

"Then we'll go."

I didn't have a sibling, but if I knew that Rena's mate was somewhere in the world, devastated and possibly scared? I'd be on the first flight out.

"I'll run down and tell them," Beau said, scrubbing his hands over his face. "I—this is bad timing."

"We've got plenty of time," I reminded him. "Go tell them, and I'll call Rena and Mr. Miranda to let them know we're headed out of town."

He nodded and moved, stopping in front of me. "Thanks, love," he whispered, leaning in to give me a soft kiss. "I'll make it up to you."

He was gone a moment later, and I stood dumbly in the middle of the room, the muffin crushed in my palm.

Our relationship had shifted. It was no longer Beau and Reese, pushing and pulling to see where the limits of our bond were. Suddenly, we were a single unit who decided together whether or not to do something.

There had been no pressure from Beau. He hadn't tried to persuade me. He'd been fully willing to stay behind, *again*, if I'd wanted to.

Ignoring the lump in my throat, I walked to the bedroom to get my phone.

## CHAPTER 16
## BEAU

"Where are we starting?" I asked Ambrose, standing in the doorway to his rooms.

"You guys can drop me and Chance in Belgium," he replied, tossing a Dopp kit into the open suitcase on his kitchen table. "See if we can catch any threads there. You and Danny go to Germany and meet up with Matthias."

"Matthias is in Germany?" Mordecai and Helen's oldest had found his mate the year before, and the last I'd heard, they'd settled down in Montana on the family property.

"He and his mate saw Zeke while he was there," Ambrose replied, pausing to look at me. "It seemed like he didn't really want to discuss it over the phone."

"You think he knows something?"

"Possibly. You know how paranoid he is."

"Fair enough."

"I'm guessing Reese needs to pack?"

"Yeah. We'll have to run to her apartment."

"She should just move in here."

"Why don't you tell her that," I joked. "Make sure it sounds like an order. She loves that shit."

"I don't want to hear about your sex life."

"Fuck off," I shot back, grabbing a shoe he'd left by the door to toss at him.

"Go get packed," he ordered. "We want to head out as soon as possible."

"On it," I mumbled, turning away.

"Hey, Bjorn," Ambrose called before I could get very far. "Congratulations."

I grinned.

"Things are good now?"

"Getting there," I replied with a nod.

"Good. She's the other half of you, brother. Protect that."

"I know."

When I got back to my room Reese was already off the phone and was waiting impatiently.

"All set?" I asked as I pulled my suitcase out of the coat closet.

"Rena is jealous as hell, and Mr. Miranda said to make sure my passport is still valid."

"Is it?"

"I don't have one," she muttered, her cheeks pink. "I'm sorry. I've never needed one. This screws up our plans, right?"

She shifted nervously, waiting for...What? Did she think I'd be angry? Fuck, we still had so much to learn about each other.

"You'd need a new one anyway," I said, dropping the suitcase so I could reach for her. "You're considered part of the Vampire Federation now, remember? Your passport should reflect that."

"But this time we could've just used my old one if I had one," she said, wincing. "I know we're in a hurry."

"I should've thought of it before," I assured her, brushing her hair back from her face. "Ambrose is across the hall. Go let him know that we need to stop in Vermont on the way to get your papers."

"Vermont?"

"Headquarters," I murmured, leaning down to kiss her. Now that I knew what I'd been missing, it was hard to be so close without the contact.

"I didn't know your headquarters were in Vermont," she said, pulling away. "Are you sure he's not going to be pissed?"

"That's by design, and no, Ambrose won't be pissed. He'll be annoyed that he didn't think of it first. I'm going to get my shit packed, and we'll leave for your place in fifteen."

"If your brother gives me shit, I might sling it back," she warned, stepping away.

"Make it sting," I replied, tapping her on the ass as I headed toward my bedroom.

I felt lighter than I had in longer than I could remember. We were getting close to finding the last piece of Zeke. My brothers and I would find Charles Franklin and his sister. Command was searching for the people who'd gone after my baby brother, and I knew they wouldn't stop until they got answers.

Reese and I were falling into the bond that I'd imagined when I was a kid and my parents promised me that she was out there somewhere—a mate that was made just for me. She didn't trust me yet, and she had every reason not to, but I'd prove myself. I had no doubt that we'd get to that place eventually. I just had to be patient.

I thought about Zeke's other half as I threw clothes

into my suitcase and grabbed my Dopp kit. It was wild to think about my baby brother's other half. All of us probably felt that way. Knowing that your sibling had a match out in the world somewhere had always been something that the five of us wondered about. Would Ambrose's mate be as serious as he was? Would Chance's be sarcastic and borderline rude? Would Danny's be as easygoing? Would Zeke's mate be like Reese, full of piss and vinegar, or would he be quiet and gentle?

The protectiveness I felt when I thought about Charles Franklin was almost as strong as when I thought of my brothers. He was one of us even if he didn't realize it yet.

"Danny wants to come with us," Reese announced, storming into the room. She looked at the zipped suitcase. "You're already done?"

"I've been a soldier since before your great-grandfather was born," I reminded her, lifting it. "I know what I need to pack."

"I hope you're not expecting the same when we get to the apartment," she said, hurrying over to her bag. She haphazardly stuffed back in the clothes that were spilling out. "Because I have no clue what to bring."

"Anything you forget we can just buy when we get there," I told her, setting my hand on her lower back as we left the room.

"Yeah, okay, moneybags," she replied dryly.

"Danny's coming with us?" I asked, bringing the conversation back around.

"I think he wants to scope out where I live," she joked, glancing over her shoulder at me as we left our rooms. "I told him it's nothing special."

"He probably wants to make sure we don't take too long."

"I'll take as long as I take," she replied formally. She hurried down the stairs, belying the words.

I was glad that no one was around as we headed out to the garage. After the scene at the table, I wasn't in a hurry to deal with any of the older generation. I'd dropped it, and Reese was right, we'd worked shit out, but I wouldn't forget what they'd done any time soon. They hadn't always been so intrusive, but after I'd walked away from Millie, they'd worried.

"You didn't have to sit in the back," Reese told Danny as she climbed in the car. "Aren't you squished back there?"

"I'm fine," he replied, sitting in the center with his arms spread out across the backs of the seats.

"He knows I would've made him move," I informed her as I backed out. "You're not sitting in the back seat."

"I'd fit fine back there," Reese argued.

"You sit next to me."

"Oh, good grief."

I listened as Reese and Danny chatted about her apartment and Europe and a hundred other things as we drove to her apartment. The conversation never lagged, and I relaxed into the seat. They got along well. Actually, Reese got along well with my entire family. At some point when I wasn't looking, she'd settled into our unit like she'd always been there.

The apartment complex was quiet when we got there. Most of the people living in Reese's building worked during the day, and we didn't see anyone as she led us up to her door. She and Danny were bickering good-naturedly, and I was enjoying the fact that they were in such good moods.

I think that's why I didn't realize that things were too quiet.

The sound of Reese's scream was something I'd remember until they burned me.

Vampire instincts were nothing if not efficient, and before she ran out of breath, I'd shoved her between Danny and me, taking in the scene in an instant.

Reese's long-haired neighbor was on the couch, and he was absolutely mutilated. There was blood everywhere. The floor, the table, the lampshade, the wall. The couch was saturated.

"Behind," Danny said sharply.

Reaching back for Reese, I yanked her inside the apartment with me and listened as Danny slammed the door closed behind us. He was already on the phone, calling in help.

Reese made little mewling noises, but I couldn't focus on her yet. I was still taking in the apartment.

All of her books had been pulled from the shelves. Every cupboard in the kitchen was open. The pillows on her couch had been sliced open. It was chaos.

Then I saw the boot prints.

Bloody and headed toward the back of the apartment.

"Danny," I said quietly, shoving Reese toward him.

I strode quietly toward the hallway, but my silence made absolutely no matter because before I'd even reached it, a man came out of Reese's bedroom, and he didn't hesitate.

Smart man, but he should've brought a knife.

I rushed him as he fired, the bullets hitting me center mass. He'd been trained well, but he'd never had a chance.

Making sure that I kept my body between him and my mate, I met his eyes as I reached out and slammed his arm into the wall so he'd drop the pistol. It took seconds.

His head was in my hands in the next moment, and I'd

never been more satisfied by a sound as when I snapped his neck.

Before his body had even hit the floor, I rushed into Reese's room. Trashed but empty.

Bathroom—the same.

"Beau?" Danny called.

"Clear," I called back, bracing my hand against the wall as I blinked. Shit.

Giving my head a shake, I strode back out to the front of the apartment. Danny had tipped one of Reese's bookcases in front of the door.

"How many?" I asked, slowing.

"Not sure," Danny replied, peeking out the curtains. "Two that I can see."

I nodded and found Reese. Danny had tucked her in the little corner where the two couches met. She was unhurt and shaking so hard that I could see it from across the room.

"Pull back the bookcase," I ordered, looking back at my brother.

"Ambrose is ten out," he argued. "Fifteen tops."

"Move it," I ordered again.

His eyes lingered on my chest, but I refused to look down. If I saw how many times I'd been hit, I'd feel it.

I needed just a few more minutes.

"I'll go," Danny said, pulling his Beretta out of the shoulder holster he never went without.

"No, you fucking won't," I ground out. "Stay with her until I give the all-clear."

"We can wait them out," he argued, even as he tried to hand me the pistol.

"Not taking that chance." I shook my head. "Keep it."

"Bjorn."

"Move the bookcase, Arne," I said, reaching out to

squeeze his shoulder. If he kept me inside much longer, we were fucked.

As he slid the bookcase back, I met Reese's terrified eyes.

"I'll be right back, baby," I promised.

"Don't," she rasped.

"Right back," I repeated.

The next thirty seconds passed by in a blur, muscle memory carrying me through as I took down the man outside the door. Another bullet hit my thigh as I jumped over the railing and landed on the top of a piece of shit sedan, but I kept moving. Stopping wasn't an option.

The last one ran. He wasn't fast enough.

Scanning the parking lot, I let myself pause, waiting for anything to stand out. There was nothing.

Straightening my shoulders, I ignored the black spots that danced in my vision as I forced myself back up the stairs. I'd barely made it to the breezeway when the sound of chopper blades sounded from somewhere behind the building. Ambrose.

Danny stood in the doorway when I reached it.

"All clear," I mumbled, stumbling against the doorframe.

"Got you," he said, helping me slide to the floor.

"Beau," Reese screamed as I closed my eyes. "Oh, god."

Fuck, it hurt.

"Hey, asshole," she said frantically, her hands cupping my face and brushing the hair back from my forehead. "Look at me."

"Did you just call me an asshole?" I grumbled, dropping my head back against the wall as I opened my eyes.

"I'm going to kill you," she stuttered, her face covered in snot and tears. "What did you do? Oh, god. What were you thinking?"

"Stings a bit," I grunted as someone pressed against my gut.

People were moving around us, but all I could see was her. Gods, she was beautiful.

Beautiful and safe and whole.

"Danny," I called, not looking away from her. Damn, I wished that my arms didn't feel like they had weights holding them down. I wanted to touch her.

"Right next to you, Bjorn," Danny said calmly.

"Stay with Reese."

"He's helping *you* right now," Reese said gently, hiccupping. "I'm okay."

"I'll stay with her," Danny promised.

Someone helped me lay flat, and I grit my teeth to keep myself from yelling as pressure against my chest felt like it was going to crack my ribs. People were talking, and there was movement around the room, but the entire time, Reese's face stayed close to mine.

"You're okay," she whispered as I arched, trying to get away from whoever was tearing my leg off. "It's okay, Beau. Let them help you."

"Reese," I groaned.

"I'm okay," she replied, brushing her lips over mine. "I'm right here."

"Stay with Danny," I muttered, repeating myself twice because my tongue didn't seem to be working correctly.

"I'll stay with Danny," she agreed.

I let my heavy eyes fall closed.

## CHAPTER 17
# REESE

"Stop it," I ordered, jerking my arm away. Fire raced under my skin as I pushed closer to Beau. "Why isn't he waking up? He was just talking."

A hand touched my waist, and I jerked to the side, leaning further over Beau.

"Wake up," I whispered. "Wake up."

"We have to go," Danny ordered.

The hand on my shoulder burned.

"Stop touching her," Erik snapped at his son.

Danny's hand disappeared.

"Reese," Erik boomed, jerking my attention away from his son. "We have to get him out of here. Stand up so we can lift him."

"I'm not leaving him," I argued, my hand tightening on Beau's shoulder. They'd have to tear me away, and by the way Erik was staring at me, I didn't think he'd do it.

"Of course you're not," he said gently. "We're all going."

"Okay," I mumbled, getting to my feet unsteadily as

Mordecai grabbed one end of the red plastic stretcher and Erik grabbed the other.

I kept my hand on Beau's shoulder near his neck as we made our way out of the apartment. Vaguely, I noticed that there was a helicopter in the center of the parking lot with men I assumed were Vampires standing at regular intervals around it.

"I'm in the back with Reese," Danny yelled as we got closer, jogging next to us.

"I'll co-pilot," Mordecai replied with a nod.

Beau's head rolled to the side, and I caught it gently with my hand.

God, he looked so bad. There was blood everywhere. His skin was nearly blue he was so pale.

The males around me gestured for me to climb into the helicopter first, Beau's stretcher sliding in beside me.

"How is he?" Ambrose asked from the pilot's seat.

"Not great," Danny spat, kneeling down beside me.

I wasn't sure how long we were in the helicopter. Time seemed to have warped the moment I saw Kenny's body on my couch, alternately speeding up and slowing down with no warning.

Beau's breathing was labored. There was blood in his mouth.

Erik and Danny moved carefully around me as they worked on Beau.

I kept my mouth shut, frozen. If I opened it, I was afraid I'd start screaming, and I wouldn't stop. What the hell had just happened? We were supposed to be on our way to Europe.

"Landing in five," Erik yelled, meeting my eyes. "Then we're on the move."

I nodded, looking out the window for the first time since we'd climbed in. Trees surrounded us as we flew

271

forward and eventually lowered, gently landing on a wide slab.

"Everything's prepped," Chance hollered as he threw open the door. His eyes landed on Beau and widened. "Fuck!"

"Moving now," Erik told me.

I followed closely as we climbed out of the helicopter. Chance and Danny grabbed each end of Beau's stretcher, and I lost my grip on him as they jogged toward a path in the trees. My heart in my throat and fire burning in my veins, I ran behind them. Somehow, they managed to move swiftly, barely jostling Beau as they went.

My heart stopped when the familiar gables of the house came into view.

"He needs a hospital," I argued, glaring at Erik, who kept pace beside me. "What the hell are you doing?"

"No human doctor would know what to do with Beau," Mordecai replied from my other side. "It's good we're here."

"Someone should—"

My words cut off as Mattie raced onto the porch, Helen and a woman I didn't recognize following her out. The new woman was covered from head to toe with scrub gear, similar to what I wore at work.

"How the hell did Aunt Alice get here so fast?" Danny called over his shoulder as we got closer to the house.

"They were in town already," Erik replied.

"Uncle Sven's here, too?"

"Well, he wouldn't let me have all this fun myself," the woman in the scrubs called out, striding down the steps.

Helen wrapped her arms around Mattie, holding her in place.

Danny and Chance slowed as Alice met them in the

gravel, but we all kept moving around the side of the house as she looked Beau over.

"Aw, Bjorn," she murmured. "What have you gotten yourself into?"

A door on the back of the house was open, and they disappeared inside. The few seconds before I crossed the threshold was agony, and I grit my teeth as I raced after them.

"You must be Beau's mate," Alice greeted as Chance and Danny lifted Beau onto a narrow bed in the center of the room.

My mouth dropped open as I reached Beau's side. It looked like a hospital room. There was a bright light shining down on my mate, illuminating his blood-soaked clothes and slack face. Cabinets lined every wall, some of them open with medical supplies stacked neatly inside. A stainless-steel sink stood in the corner.

"Reese, right?" Alice said brusquely, snagging my attention again. "I'm Alice. I want you up here at the head of the table, all right?"

She waved me toward a stool near Beau's head.

"Are you squeamish?"

I shook my head and then nodded as the room moved quickly around me. Erik scrubbed his arms at the sink. Ambrose stood impatiently behind him, waiting his turn.

Danny stood the stretcher on end against the wall.

Chance was doing something by the door I couldn't see.

Mordecai had disappeared.

"I need you there," Alice reminded me, pointing at the stool. "If you're squeamish, keep your eyes closed."

Slowly, I moved around the table to the stool and carefully sat down. My hands shook as I brushed Beau's hair back from his face. He was so still. He'd thrashed a little in the helicopter, but since we'd landed, he hadn't moved at all.

"Erik?" Alice asked, her gloved hands in loosely held fists by her chest. "You're up."

Freshly gowned and gloved, Erik stepped in next to the table and quickly started cutting Beau's clothes off with a pair of scissors.

My stomach twisted, and I slammed my eyes shut as pale bloody skin came into view.

"One, two, three, four," Alice said, her voice almost monotone.

"And one in the thigh," Erik added.

My head grew light, and I swayed in place, refusing to open my eyes.

"Head down," Danny ordered somewhere near my shoulder.

Bracing my hands on the end of the bed, I leaned forward.

"That's right," he said gently. "Put your head right next to Beau's."

I shuddered as the smell of my mate's skin permeated the nightmare. Turning my head, I pressed my lips to the spot above his ear.

"That's good," Alice said. "Talk to him, Reese."

They spoke in quiet voices as I sat there, hunched over Beau with my lips pressed against his face. Tuning them out the best I could, I listened to his breathing. It was steady. In and out. In and out.

"I'm going to kill you," I whispered. "You fucking idiot."

The sheet beneath us grew wet, but I didn't open my eyes even once as the tears slid down my face. I couldn't see his wounds. I was too afraid to look.

"He's doing well, Reese," Danny said at some point.

Time had no meaning. We could've been there for hours or minutes. I had no idea. My only focus was Beau's little puffs of breath.

In and out. I synced my breaths with his.

"They've exchanged blood?" Alice asked someone.

"The bond's complete."

"Reese," she called. "We're all finished, sweetheart."

I was afraid to raise my head. I was monitoring his breathing, and I couldn't do that if I moved away. If someone wasn't making sure he was breathing, then all of this was for nothing. Someone had to make sure he was still breathing.

"Reese," Danny said. Air moved by me like he'd started to put his hand on my shoulder but stopped himself. "Reese, they're done."

"I need you to lean up for me," Alice ordered, not unkindly.

"What's wrong with her?" Chance asked.

"Shock," Erik replied quietly.

"Beau needs blood, Reese," Alice continued. "I need you to lean up for me."

When I lifted my head, Beau was bare from the waist up, a sheet covering the rest of him. Large bandages peppered his chest. One near his heart. Another on his sternum. On the opposite side over his ribs. To the left of his belly button.

Gripping the sheet in my fists, I pushed myself straight.

"If you put your arm near his mouth," Alice said with a nod. "He'll drink. Instincts are a beautiful thing."

Sliding to my feet, I leaned over Beau and pushed my coat and sweater up my arm, pressing the bare skin against his mouth. Nothing happened for a minute.

It felt like everyone held their breath. No one moved.

When his mouth opened and immediately clamped down on my wrist, I let out a sob of relief, my legs going out from under me.

"Got you," Alice said, her strong arms wrapping tightly around my waist. "He'll only take as much as he needs. Don't worry."

I almost pushed her away. Don't worry? I wasn't worried Beau would take too much. He could have anything he needed. I'd never been *less* afraid for myself. There wasn't any room for self-preservation, not then.

"Good," I whispered to Beau, pressing my lips against anything I could reach. His forehead. Cheek. Nose. "You're okay. You're okay."

Beau's eyes opened slowly and met mine, panicked as he let go of my arm and swiped the tiny beads of blood with his tongue.

"You're okay," I repeated. "I'm okay. We're at the house."

Cupping his cheek in my hand, I watched as his eyes scanned the room, taking in the family that surrounded him. He let out a small, relieved puff of air and looked back at me.

"Kiss me," he ordered, his voice broken and rough.

Alice laughed quietly as she let go of my waist and stepped away.

"I don't take orders from you," I argued with a small sob, leaning down to press my lips to his.

Before I'd even lifted my head, he'd lost consciousness again.

"No," I yelped, jerking back to look at him. "No, wake up."

"It's okay," Erik said, tearing his gown off as he moved toward us. "He needs the rest."

"He woke up," I argued, shaking my head as I stared at Beau. "No, he was just awake."

"This is just sleep," Alice said, carefully laying her hand on my shoulder. "Sleep will help him heal. This isn't a bad thing, I promise you. He's just sleeping, Reese."

My heart felt like it was going to beat out of my chest as I traced the contours of his face with my fingertips.

They spoke quietly behind me. I wished they'd all go away. I just wanted to be with Beau.

"Reese, we're going to take him into a bedroom, all right?" Ambrose said, stopping on the opposite side of the table. "Somewhere more comfortable." He paused. "For both of you, okay?"

Why was he still bothering me? Couldn't they see that I wanted them to leave us alone?

Raising my head, I looked at Beau's older brother. He looked almost as devastated as I felt.

"Just into a bedroom," he repeated. "We've got a spare downstairs that's all ready."

I forced myself to nod. It was too bright in there anyway. There was no way that Beau could get any rest with a light shining in his face.

I shuffled out of the way as Beau's brothers rolled the table toward the door by the sink.

"Come on," Danny said softly, walking beside me as we followed them into the downstairs of the massive house. The door opened up to a place under the stairs near the kitchen—one I wouldn't have thought was anything more than a closet if I'd seen it from the other side.

"Erik," Mattie called, hurrying toward us.

"It went well," Erik replied tiredly as Mattie reached Beau's side. She murmured words I couldn't hear.

There was a dull roar in my ears.

The room they took us to had a wide window with the curtains pulled back. There were no dressers or anything on the walls, but two plush chairs sat on either side of the bed. I hovered as Ambrose and Chase transferred Beau carefully onto the crisp white sheets of the bed, pulling them up to his waist before taking the operating sheet away.

I dropped numbly onto one of the chairs as the room began to clear.

Chance and Ambrose strode away, asking Alice about something I couldn't hear. Erik stood on the opposite side of the bed while Mattie leaned over it, fussing with Beau's bedding.

Looking down at my hands, I shuddered.

I was covered in blood. It was caked around the cuticles and beneath my fingernails. There were smears of it disappearing into my sleeves. Dropping my chin, I looked down at my coat. The originally purple fabric was nearly black.

Erik practically carried Mattie out of the room as she began to cry.

Leaning over, I set my hand on Beau's bare arm, resting my cheek on the bed between us.

Sometime later Helen strode quietly into the room, carrying a bowl and a stack of something I couldn't get a clear look at.

"Up, child," she said gently as she closed the door behind her.

I didn't have the energy to fight her, so I rose to my feet.

"You're a mess," she continued, shaking her head as she sat her things at the foot of the bed. "You don't look much better than poor Beaumont."

Standing like a doll, I let her unzip my jacket and pull

it off. My guts twisted at the realization that blood had seeped through near the neckline and gotten all over the sweater I wore beneath it. Lifting my arms, I let Helen pull that off too. Then my shoes and jeans. She dropped every-thing into a pile on the floor.

Next, she dipped a rag into the bowl at the end of the bed and reached carefully for my face.

Closing my eyes, I let her gently wipe away the blood. It was down my neck. In my ears and hair. Covering the bottom half of my arms and hands. She kneeled in front of me and wiped down the fronts of my legs where it had soaked through my jeans.

I didn't even know that people had that much blood in their bodies. How in the world had Beau lost so much?

"I grabbed some clothes out of Beau's dresser," Helen said as she rose to her feet again. Reaching behind her, she handed me a soft gray t-shirt. It smelled like Beau.

I pulled it over my head.

"The boy doesn't have sweatpants," she informed me, handing me...leggings? "But I found a pair of thermals."

I pulled the soft base layer leggings up my legs, folding and rolling the waistband to keep them from falling off.

"That's better," she said with a small smile. She lifted the bowl of water off the bed, and bile filled my mouth at the sight of the dark liquid inside. "You climb in with Beau. I'll tell them all you're sleeping."

"Thank you," I croaked.

"Anytime," she replied, pausing by the door. "I've patched Mordecai up a time or two."

"Was he ever this bad?" I asked in a whisper, looking down at Beau.

Helen was quiet for a moment before she spoke. "A couple who looks like us were targets for all kinds of fools," she said finally. "But they always got what they deserved in the end. Rest, child. I'll come back and get those dirty clothes in a few minutes."

As soon as she was gone, I crawled onto the bed and curled up next to Beau on his least injured side. The heat was a steady thrum under my skin, so I didn't bother getting under the blanket. He was so still, his arms down at his sides and his head tilted just slightly toward me.

"As soon as you wake up, I'm going to rip you a new one," I whispered on a shuddery exhale.

Lacing my fingers through his, I closed my eyes and pressed my lips to his bicep.

I must've fallen asleep because when I woke up the sky was darker through the window, and my clothes had disappeared from the floor. The door was open, and Ambrose's head was barely visible as he peeked inside.

Movement next to me had me lifting my head just in time to see Beau gesturing for Ambrose to leave.

"I'm awake," I announced groggily, pushing myself up so I could see Beau's face.

He looked terrible. There were dark circles around his eyes, and his expression was strained—but his eyes were clear.

"I'm going to kill you," I growled, getting to my knees as Beau let out a painful sounding huff of laughter.

"I second that," Ambrose agreed, striding into the room.

"I'm fine, baby," Beau said with a wince, his hand clasping my thigh.

"You...you..." I stuttered, staring at him in disbelief.

"What the hell were you thinking?" Ambrose barked, dropping into the chair next to the bed as people started filing in.

Ambrose must've been what broke the dam because I

was pretty sure everyone on the property had crammed themselves into that little room.

"We were less than ten minutes out," Erik chided.

"You were shot five times, Bjorn," Alice said, censure dripping from her words.

Beau's jaw firmed as I scooted in closer, moving to sit at his shoulder.

"You didn't even have a weapon," Chance drawled. "What kind of suicidal shit was that?"

Beau's arm moved out slowly, crossing over my thighs. His thumb rubbed along my kneecap.

"Well," Erik said when my mate refused to respond.

"Is this some kind of intervention?" Beau asked curiously. I wondered if anyone else heard the thread of venom in his voice.

"I've already lost three children," Mattie said softly.

Beau jerked almost imperceptibly.

I didn't think that this conversation was going to go the way everyone had planned. "I think this is too much—"

"I'm a mated male," Beau snapped. "None of them had a knife large enough to *remove my head.*"

"You didn't know that," Ambrose argued.

"Yes, I did."

"And what if you'd fallen?" Mordecai asked sternly. "Then it would no longer matter whether or not they carried a blade. They could've taken you anywhere."

"Bjorn, we don't even know if your immortality has been cemented yet," Alice scolded gently.

My heart pounded as I turned to look at Beau.

"My mate was in that apartment," he said emotionlessly, his gaze scanning over the people in the room. "There was no other option."

"You could've let Daniel—"

"Danny hasn't mated," Beau cut Mordecai off. "He was safest inside protecting Reese."

"All you had to do was wait," Erik thundered.

"Until what?" Beau replied angrily, shoving himself up in bed.

I scrambled to brace him, but he didn't seem to need the help.

"Until a stray bullet hit her? Danny could take two, maybe three? Reese could *not*."

I gently laid my hand on Beau's back. His entire body was trembling.

"You could've died," Ambrose said angrily. "You could've been taken."

"And it *still* would've been worth it," Beau yelled, the tendons in his neck bulging.

"Hey," I whispered, smoothing my hand over the clammy muscles of his back as my eyes began to sting. "Hey, calm down."

"Get the fuck out," Beau ordered, his hand tightening on my leg. "All of you."

"Beaumont," Erik scolded.

"I swear to the Gods," Beau snapped, reaching for the sheet like he was going to throw it off and climb out of bed.

"Out," Helen ordered, speaking for the first time as she gazed up at her husband and then back at us. "They need some time."

Mordecai nodded and led her out of the room. The rest of them trickled out slower than they'd entered, but, eventually, Beau and I were the only ones left in the room.

He was sweating as he lay back down, his chest heaving.

"Do you feel like a big strong Vampire now?" I admonished, glaring at him.

"I don't need shit from you, too," he replied, closing his eyes as he let out a long slow breath.

"What were you thinking?" I asked, wishing I could smack him. "They were ten minutes out? Beau."

"One minute was too fucking long." His eyes snapped open to glare at me. "Thirty seconds was too fucking long."

"It wasn't."

"Those men were in *your* apartment."

"I know that."

"They ruined your stuff," he continued. "They killed your friend."

Oh god. I hadn't even thought of Kenny since Beau was hurt.

"I thought you were going to die," I grit out angrily.

"I told you about the mating bond—"

"Well, excuse-the-fuck-out-of-me for forgetting that little tidbit when you were bleeding everywhere!"

"I don't know why you're angry," he growled. "It's my job to keep you safe."

"I thought you were going to die," I repeated, my voice going all high and screechy. "Do you know what that felt like?"

"I wasn't going to die."

"Oh, really? Because your brothers and your dad looked like they were going to shit their pants, too." I pointed at the door. "It wasn't just me that thought it."

"I won't apologize for keeping you safe."

"Fuck you," I hissed, jerking away from him. "You would've left me all alone!"

"What are you talking about?" he asked, reaching for me as I scrambled off the bed.

"You would've just—" I struggled to speak around the lump in my throat. "You would've just left me forever.

And I just would've...would've...been stuck here without you."

Beau's expression changed instantly.

"Come here, love," he murmured gently.

"I don't want to," I shot back, still angry. "You could've waited for help."

"No, I couldn't have," he said, throwing the blankets back.

"Stop it," I ordered as he slowly and carefully got to his feet. "Get back in bed."

"Let me hold you," he said breathlessly, shuffling toward me. "Come here."

I was still angry, but I met him halfway. I told myself it was because he was hurt, and he was going to end up ripping open his stitches, but the truth was that I *needed* his arms around me.

"I'm sorry you were scared," he murmured against my hair.

"You should've stayed with me," I mumbled.

"I would make the same decision a thousand times more," he argued, his voice soft. "There will never be a time when I hide while you're in danger."

"You were so pale," I whispered, tipping my head back to meet his eyes. "You were bleeding everywhere."

"I'm right here," he whispered back. "I'm fine. I took a calculated risk."

I opened my mouth to argue but snapped it shut again when he gave my hair a slight tug.

"It is a risk I will *always* take, no matter the odds."

"That's stupid," I grumbled.

Beau's lips tipped up at the edges, his eyes crinkling at the corners as he reached up to run a finger down my cheek. "You are the beginning and the end of me, Reese Matthews."

"Shit," I breathed, staring into his eyes.

The moment he started laughing...I knew I loved him.

## CHAPTER 18
# BEAU

Everything hurt, and I wanted more than anything to fall asleep with Reese, but the moment Chance poked his head around the door, I waved him inside.

"You look like shit," he said, sitting on the bed near my feet.

Danny came in next with Ambrose on his heels.

"I feel like shit," I replied, running my hand down Reese's back as she stirred in her sleep. "What do you know?"

"Other than the fact that you eliminated anyone we could've interrogated?" Ambrose asked sarcastically. "Not much. All three were former human military. Their truck was found around the block, filled with food wrappers—"

"And piss bottles," Chance added. "Fucking animals."

"It looked like they'd been surveilling Reese's apartment for at least a day. Maybe two."

"Why?"

Danny looked at Ambrose. Chance looked at Danny.

"We don't know," Ambrose replied. "But we know

now that Zeke was taken just after he'd found his mate. Now, Reese."

"Fuck," I spat.

It couldn't be a coincidence that two members of our family had been targeted.

"It's not like she could go back to her place, anyway," Danny said quietly. "But we need to move Reese into the house. She shouldn't go back there."

I sighed. "She's got a job and a life—"

"She'll be up your ass for the next year at least," Chance said, waving me off. "Hopefully, by then, we'll have taken care of whatever shit this is."

"Did you call command?"

"Arthur is headed out here in the morning," Ambrose confirmed. "We need to know everything they've found in the last few days."

The four of us grew quiet as we thought about what we already knew. It wasn't much. Someone was targeting Vampires and if our suspicions were correct, they were looking for newly mated ones. In order to stop whatever was happening, we needed to find the head of the snake.

"Who did you call in today?" I asked curiously.

"Who says I called anyone in?" Ambrose asked innocently.

"Because the three of you wouldn't be inside this room if you didn't have someone out keeping an eye on the property."

Danny laughed quietly.

"Just some mated locals," Ambrose replied, his lips twitching. "Makes it easy to round them up when they all have prior training."

"Paying them well?"

Danny scoffed. "Like any of them would expect

payment after they saw those humans you left in the parking lot."

"To be fair, one of them was at the top of the stairs," Chance corrected.

"Vampires get itchy when humans decide to play games," Ambrose said, stretching his arms above his head. "A problem for one of us is a problem for all of us."

"When are you guys heading out?" I asked tiredly, letting my head drop to the pillow.

"Once you're back on your feet," Danny replied.

I shook my head. "Don't wait."

"We're not leaving you here," Chance argued.

"This one's going to take weeks, Happ," I reminded him with a grimace. "You guys need to get over there now and find him."

"Another couple of weeks won't matter," Danny said stubbornly.

Looking down to the end of the bed, I met Ambrose's eyes. If these humans were searching for Zeke's mate, too, he may not have *days* to wait. He nodded.

"We'll leave in the morning," he conceded.

"We'll catch up as soon as we can," I promised. "Once I'm healed and Reese has settled."

"She did well today," Danny said, glancing at my mate. "Kept it together."

I barely remembered anything once I'd made it back to the apartment. The only vivid memory was Reese's face. "Yeah?"

"I mean, she's kind of a princess when it comes to blood," Chance said, pulling out a pocketknife so he could fiddle with it. "But she didn't pass out."

"She sat with you during surgery," Ambrose explained. "But she kept her head down."

"Probably best," I mumbled. "How'd it go?"

"Alice got all of them out," Ambrose replied soberly. "One was tucked in right next to your heart."

I nodded, realizing how close I'd come. I could've survived a shot to the heart, but I wouldn't have been able to keep my feet. If the human had been slightly less terrified of me and his shots cleaner, I might've woken up in a hut somewhere. Reese and Danny, too.

It didn't matter. I still would've made the same choices.

My eyes grew heavy.

"We're losing him," Chance joked, straightening from where he'd been leaning against the wall. "Better let him get his beauty rest."

"Let me know before you leave," I ordered as Ambrose stood.

"Of course," he said, smacking my foot.

Once they were gone, I looked down at Reese.

Her face was still swollen from crying, and every few minutes she twitched in her sleep like she was dreaming. Carefully rolling toward her, I grimaced as my chest and thigh pulled tight and sharp. The shot in my gut felt like it was already healing, but the others still hurt like hell.

I should've known that Reese would hold up well under pressure. My mate came out swinging when she was scared. She'd been doing it since we met.

"Why are you awake?" she rasped, her eyes half open. "You want me to turn the light off?"

"No, leave it on." I wanted to be able to see her.

Nothing had prepared me for the fear that filled me when she'd screamed. Nothing had prepared me for the moment that I'd realized we'd closed ourselves into her apartment with one of the humans who'd come for her. It was terror on a level that I couldn't have anticipated.

It was nothing like the moment when I'd realized my

mate was under the rubble in a bombed London street. Up until that morning, I'd thought that was the most terrifying experience I'd ever have. It didn't even come close to when I'd realized that Reese was in danger.

"You're looking better already," she murmured, smiling softly.

"I told you we heal fast."

"I didn't think you meant within hours."

"I'm going to feel like shit for a couple of weeks."

"That's what you get for scaring the hell out of me," she said smugly, her worried eyes looking me over.

"I was talking to my brothers—"

"I heard you," she said, laying her head on her arm. "You want me to move in here."

"Thoughts?"

Her skin was so soft. Tucking my hand under her shirt, I curved it around the dip in her waist.

"I don't want to go back there," she said instantly. "Actually, I'd prefer if we just burned the entire building to the ground, but, you know, other people live there, too."

"I'll relocate them," I joked.

"Nah, let them stay." She shot me a small smile before dropping her eyes. "Why do you think they killed Kenny?"

"No idea," I murmured. "My best guess is that he saw them going into your apartment and hassled them about it."

The man was tortured, probably for information on Reese, but I wasn't going to mention that if she didn't ask. Her friend had died horribly in her apartment. That was enough to deal with.

"He was nice," she whispered. "Really flaky, but nice. I wonder if his parents know yet."

"Someone will have let them know."

Reese nodded.

We slept fitfully that night. Reese was incredibly careful not to jostle me, keeping her hands to herself, but I was still in quite a bit of pain. Any time I shifted my position, I woke up with a start, and it took a long time to fall back asleep. By the time the sun began to rise, I was wide awake again, watching her sleep.

She'd cleaned up at some point, but there was still blood in her hair. It wasn't a lot, but as I ran my fingers through it, I could feel the little dried bits catching on my fingers. If I was a better male, I'd feel guilty that she'd been targeted for being my mate, but I just couldn't regret the fact that she was mine. Finally, after waiting for so long, the other half of my soul slept beside me. I'd do anything to protect that. Protect her.

Swallowing hard, I looked away from her neck.

My stomach clenched angrily, and I took a deep breath, trying to ignore it.

"Come here," she murmured, sleepily, lifting her hand to my face. "You need blood."

"Go back to sleep," I ordered softly, kissing her palm. "I can wait."

"Why?" Her thumb brushed over my bottom lip. "Take what you need."

"Reese," I groaned.

"You feel it?" she whispered, her drowsy eyes meeting mine. "Heat's building again."

"Yes." I'd felt it for the last two hours.

Leaning forward, I brushed my lips over hers. Her hand slid tentatively around the back of my neck.

I moved slowly, ignoring as my body protested.

She smelled so good. She felt so fucking good. The fact that I could've lost this—that *we* could've lost it—was inconceivable. There was no longer a place in this world for me if she wasn't in it. I belonged by her side.

"You're hurt," she protested weakly as I slid my hand down the front of her leggings. She was soft and wet, and I wanted to *live* just like this. If we never moved from that bed again, it would be too soon.

"My hands are fine," I argued, running my lips over her jaw as I slid my middle finger inside her slowly.

My heart pounded as she arched off the bed, a small mewl falling from her mouth.

When my mouth reached her neck, she tipped her head back in offering. Relief and arousal rolled over me as I bit down, every muscle in my body clenching, mixing pain and pleasure until I wasn't sure which was which.

Her cunt pulsed as I added another finger, her orgasm soaking my hand.

It was over too soon.

"Sweet relief," she joked, her breath catching as I gently pulled my hand away and brushed over her swollen clit. Cupping my face in both hands, she searched my face. "Better?"

I nodded. "The heat?"

"Calm again," she assured me with a smile. "You should try and sleep a little longer."

"I feel like I've been sleeping for a week," I argued.

"It hasn't even been twenty-four hours, and you need the rest."

"I'll stay in bed," I conceded, relaxing into the mattress again. "But I'd enjoy it a lot more if you took off my clothes."

Reese scoffed and leaned up on her elbow. "You're already naked."

I flicked at the t-shirt hanging off her small frame. "You're not."

"I'm not getting undressed when people are coming in here whenever they want."

"I'll lock the door."

"Not happening," she said dryly, perching her head on her hand. "You look so much better today."

"I'm betting anything would be better than how I looked yesterday."

Reese's eyes grew unfocused for a few moments. When she looked at me again, they were dark. "I was so scared," she said quietly. "I've never been so scared."

"I'd never let anything happen to you," I promised, curving my hand around the side of her neck where her pulse beat furiously.

"I know that," she replied. "I wasn't scared for *me*."

"I had to make sure that none of them could get to you."

"There was so much blood, Beau." She winced. "First Kenny and then you...you were bleeding *everywhere*. When you came out of the hallway, it didn't seem that bad. With your coat on, I couldn't really see any of it. But when you came back from outside..." She paused. "I couldn't understand how you were still standing."

"Moving around outside probably got things moving," I explained. "I had to chase one of them."

"God, Beau." She grimaced.

"It's over, love," I reminded her.

"I still see it when I close my eyes. It's like it plays on a loop. Over and over, I see you stumbling back through the doorway. I thought you were dying. *I thought I was watching you die.*"

"I'm right here." Pulling her closer, I let my eyes drift closed as her face tucked into my neck. "Bite, baby."

"No," she replied quickly, jerking her face back. "No, you need every drop of blood you have left."

"It won't hurt me," I countered, catching the back of her head in my hand. Pressing her forward, I tilted my head away. "You need it."

"I don't. It's a want, remember? It's not a need. I won't get sick without it."

Tipping my head back down, I met her gaze. Her pupils were still shot.

"It is a need," I told her gently. "You thought I was going to die. I'm your *mate*. You need that connection as much as I do. Bite."

She didn't fight me as I pressed her face back to my neck, but she didn't bite, either. She sniffled, her body shuddering as her tongue laved my neck. I couldn't understand why she was fighting it so hard. We both knew that the blood exchanged was minimal. She needed the taste of me on her tongue, and I should've realized it earlier. That was on me.

"Bite, my love," I whispered soothingly, smoothing my hand down the back of her head. "Do it now."

I nearly groaned when I finally felt her pierce my neck, but I was afraid that if I made any noise at all, she'd stop.

Her body relaxed against mine as she licked the small punctures just seconds later, the same way I did to hers when I was finished. I didn't need her to close the wounds, my body did that itself, but the small aftercare made my chest ache. She was taking care of me the same way I took care of her.

Reese's face was wet as she lifted her head.

"Better?" I asked softly.

"I love you," she replied with a sob. The words were almost defiant.

"That pisses you off?" I teased, wiping at her tears.

"You're an asshole," she cried.

I couldn't stop the bark of laughter that made pain radiate through my torso.

"Stop laughing!"

"I hate to break it to you," I said, kissing her. "But so are you."

"I am not."

"You are, but I love you anyway."

"This is not how it's supposed to go," she complained, wiping angrily at her face. "You're supposed to say it first, and you're supposed to say a bunch of other sweet shit, too."

"Sorry," I replied dryly. "First timer here."

Reese glared. I smiled.

"Your soul matches mine, Reese Matthews," I whispered against her lips. "I was made to love you."

Reese was quiet for a moment, her tongue coming out to slide along my bottom lip.

"That'll do," she grumbled, her eyes twinkling.

"As soon as I can move without these stitches ripping, I'm going to fuck you for hours."

"Ooh, that's even better," she joked.

We were still smiling at each other when a knock at the door interrupted us.

"Come in," I called, untangling from Reese so I could sit up.

"Such an idiot," Reese mumbled under her breath as she stacked pillows behind me.

"Hey, we're heading out soon," Ambrose announced, leaving the door open as he strode into the room. "We got a hit on the sister's passport. She left Belgium for France yesterday."

"But not Charles?" Why would they have separated?

"He could be using a different passport, thinking no

one would be looking for the sister," Ambrose said with a shrug. "I have a feeling if we find her, we'll find him."

"Is Danny still going to meet up with Matthias?"

"Yeah, he'll drop us at Albert-Picardie first."

"Keep me updated," I ordered, frustrated that they had to go without us.

"Of course," Ambrose said with a nod. "We've got a rotation going outside. Four on at all times, so stay put for a while until you're healed, would you?"

"Security," Reese mused. "I feel like a celebrity or something."

Ambrose scoffed, but his lips twitched. "Keep this fool out of trouble."

"I'll do my best," she said dryly.

"We're all set," Chance called out as he appeared in the doorway. "Love you guys. See you in a couple of weeks."

"Love you, too," I replied as he disappeared again.

"Take care of yourself," Ambrose said, reaching out to grip my shoulder. "We'll see you soon."

"Soon," I agreed.

"Reese," he said with a nod.

"Happy hunting," she replied with a smile.

"Love you." Why the hell was I so torn up that they were leaving without us? We'd gone our own way for most of our lives. It was rare for all of us to be in the same place at the same time for more than a couple of days a year.

"Love you, too, Bjorn," Ambrose said seriously. "Don't rush the healing. We'll see you when we see you."

Once he was gone, Reese tucked herself into my side, her head on my shoulder.

"It'll be kind of weird having them gone," she said as we watched the open door.

"We're not here much," I replied, kissing her forehead. "They're still part of command. They've been given time to search for Zeke's mate because it aligns with the objectives of command, but once that's done, they'll be separated again."

"Unless they find their mates," Reese replied, looking up at me. "Right?"

"Right."

I wasn't sure how to explain to someone who was only twenty-seven years old that it could be another century before my brothers found their mates. She had no concept of that kind of time.

"Have to make this fast," Danny said as he strode into the room. "Or Chance is going to have a fucking conniption."

"He can't leave without you," I pointed out. Danny was the only one of us with a pilot's license. "Take a seat."

My little brother laughed. "I'd still have to spend the day flying with him," he pointed out. "It would catch up to me eventually."

"You're all set to see Matthias?" I asked as he stopped near the foot of the bed. "You know he won't say shit unless you ask the right questions."

"I know him as well as you do," Danny responded dryly. "I've got it handled."

"And you packed extra socks, right?" Reese teased. "You never know when you'll need a spare."

Danny grinned at my mate. "Take care of him."

"I will."

"Let me know when you get to Germany," I ordered.

"I'll send you a telegram," he joked. "We've got plenty of security, but keep your eyes open, yeah? Love you."

"Don't worry about shit here," I replied. "Love you, too."

"Bye, Reese," Danny said with a small wave as he backed out of the door.

She waved back.

Dropping my head back against the headboard, I stared at the ceiling. Letting my brothers go to Europe without me felt wrong. Danny would be alone after he'd left Chance and Ambrose in France. I'd feel a lot better after he'd met up with Matthias. The Vampire might be a suspicious pain in the ass, but he'd protect any one of us like his own brothers.

"I'm sorry we have to stay behind," Reese said, kissing my shoulder. "We'll catch up as soon as you're able."

"Two weeks," I replied firmly.

"As soon as you're healed," she countered as her stomach gurgled.

"Come on," I ordered, pushing the sheet off my lap. "You need food."

"What the hell are you doing?" she griped as I turned to set my feet on the floor.

"What does it look like I'm doing?"

"Getting out of bed," she hissed, scrambling around me to reach the floor before I did. "Should you be up?"

"I'm a Vampire, Reese," I reminded her.

"You were shot five times," she muttered distractedly as I rose. "You should not look like *that*."

I let out a huff of laughter even as my cock seemed to notice where her attention was focused.

"You need to put some pants on," she ordered. "And a robe. And a parka."

"All my clothes are upstairs."

"I'll run up and get them," she said, finally looking away when I was completely hard. "Helen said you don't have any sweatpants. What should I get?"

"I have a pair in my suitcase." Which reminded me. "Do you know if anyone brought my car back?"

Reese looked at me like I was nuts. "Sorry, I was a little preoccupied."

I grinned as she stomped out of the room, waiting until she was gone to sit back down on the mattress. Damn, I was weak. I'd had injuries before—I'd been shot more times than I could remember—but I'd never had so many wounds at the same time.

Is that how they managed to capture Zeke? We no longer had his body to check, but command must know. He wouldn't have had time to fully heal before he'd died. There should've been some evidence.

A few minutes later, Reese came back with my clothes and watched as I insisted on dressing myself. When we got to the kitchen, my mother, Helen, and Alice were sitting around the table with cups of coffee.

"On your feet already?" Alice commented with a raised eyebrow.

"We're hungry, and my nurses disappeared," I joked as I shuffled across the room.

"He insisted he could walk around." Reese glared at me. "I could've made something myself."

"There are cinnamon rolls in the oven," my mom said, looking me over. "I just left them in there to keep them warm."

"Thanks, Mom."

I stopped and sat on a stool as Reese went to get us breakfast.

"Beau," Helen called. "Do you believe they're targeting newly bonded mates?"

I glanced at Reese. We hadn't had that discussion yet.

"That's what it looks like," I confirmed. "But we don't know enough to be sure."

"Matthias," Helen said worriedly. "He and Misha have only been mated for less than a year."

"Danny's on his way there now," I reassured her as Reese set a cinnamon roll near my elbow. "But you know Matthias. He's being careful."

"Why in the world would they target new mates specifically?" my mom asked. "What's the point?"

"Someone wants to know the secret to immortality," Alice replied flatly, watching as she twisted her coffee cup in a slow circle. "I'd bet you every penny I have that our secret is no longer a secret."

Helen's face paled, and my mom jerked in her seat like she'd been slapped.

The pieces started to fall into place as I turned to look at Reese.

"First, we'll find Charles," she said softly, brushing the hair back from my forehead. "Then we'll deal with whatever this is. One thing at a time."

# CHAPTER 19
## REESE

"Where the hell is my hairdryer?" I called, riffling through one of the boxes that covered the living room. "It's not in the bathroom box."

"How would I know?" Beau called back. "I didn't touch it."

"Well, maybe if you'd let me pack my shit instead of hiring a moving company," I grouched. "I'd be able to find things when I need them!"

"I wasn't in any shape to pack your apartment, and neither were you," Beau pointed out as he wandered into the room.

It had been nearly two weeks since Beau had been shot, and as he passed by in nothing but a loose pair of jeans, I marveled at the smooth, healed skin. He didn't even have a scar to remember what we'd gone through that day.

Part of me thought that it was strange, but I was mostly just glad that the visual reminders were gone. I still saw his body sliding to the floor whenever I closed my eyes. I didn't need to think of it every time I saw his bare chest.

"I can't find it anywhere." I sat back on my heels, looking around at the half-empty boxes. A lot of things in my apartment had been ruined, but I still had too much stuff to fit in our suite of rooms.

"Have you checked the bathroom?" Beau asked dryly, pulling a yogurt out of the fridge. "That's where normal people keep it."

"I already looked in there," I shot back, heading for the bathroom anyway, just to be sure. "It was at the apartment. I didn't bring it here."

"I think you're wrong," he called.

"Shit," I muttered, finding it under the sink.

"I knew it was in there," he said smugly, raising his voice so I could hear him.

"Fuck off," I said quietly.

"You're welcome," he replied, still in the kitchen area.

I couldn't help but laugh as I pulled the hair dryer out and plugged it in. He was such a pain in the ass.

The last two weeks had been hard. Not only had Beau been a terrible patient, pushing himself every day even though it freaked me out, but I'd had nightmares every night that left me exhausted all day long. It was probably a good thing that I'd given up my job because there was no way I would've been able to work.

Learning to live together with the added benefit of trauma and serious medical issues wasn't for the faint of heart, but we'd managed it. Beau irritated the hell out of me, and I drove him crazy half the time, but we'd started to lean into it. It was us. He was still the first face I wanted to see when I woke up and the last I wanted to see before we slept, so I figured we'd be okay.

Mordecai and Helen had left once they knew that

Beau was on the mend, planning to meet up with their sons to warn them about the theory that new mates were being targeted. Matthias and his mate had already met up with Danny and planned to meet them back home in Montana.

Matthias didn't know where Charles was, but he *had* met him. He said it was the happiest he'd ever seen Zeke. He also said that Charles's sister was protective, and there was no way that they would've split up.

The Boucher brothers were still trying to track her passport. Charles's passport hadn't turned up.

"We're just going to dinner," Beau said, leaning against the doorway as I blow-dried my hair. "You don't need to do that."

"It won't dry by the time we leave," I explained patiently, meeting his eyes in the mirror.

"We have a couple of hours. Think of all the other things we could be using that time for," he said, moving into the room.

"Origami?" I asked innocently, turning off the hair dryer so I didn't accidentally blast him in the face with it. "Checkers?"

"We're leaving that thing here when we go," he replied, ignoring my joke as he wrapped my damp hair around his fist.

"That would be inconvenient," I blustered as I blindly set the hair dryer on the counter. "But you did say we could buy anything we forgot at home."

"I like it like this," he murmured, giving my hair a soft jerk.

"It's wild," I countered, arching into him. I'd never get sick of the way his body surrounded me, one hand on my belly, his feet bracketing my own.

"It's you," he argued. "Fucking chaos."

"I seem to remember you not liking chaos," I reminded him with a moan as his hand slid up my torso.

"I'm embracing the chaos." His hand slid from my breast and trailed down the skin of my stomach before sliding under the hip of my panties. "Why the hell are you wearing these?"

"Because you like them," I replied, shimmying my hips to help him pull them down.

"Bullshit," he countered.

"Because we're going to dinner with your family," I conceded. "And I'm wearing a dress."

"So?"

"So, I'm not going commando around your parents."

"Pity," he muttered as he dropped to his knees behind me. "I like it when you're bare."

The first swipe of his tongue had me rising onto my toes, my hands sliding along the top of the counter until they smacked into the wall. I groaned in disappointment when his mouth lifted away, but I should've known he wouldn't leave me. Wrapping his hand around the back of my thigh, he shoved it upward until my knee was braced on the countertop.

"Stay right there," he ordered.

"I don't take orders from you," I gasped, my back arching painfully as he dove back in.

The feel of his lips and teeth and tongue brought me close to the edge so quickly that my head spun. I was right there—so close—when he pulled away again.

Seconds later, he was on his feet behind me, thrusting inside so forcefully that my arms strained as I held myself in place.

"Made for me," he whispered into my ear, his lips trailing down to my neck as he lifted my torso. "All mine."

"Maybe you were made for me," I moaned, grinding

my hips against his. He felt so much deeper after I'd straightened. "My soul was probably here longer than yours."

Beau smiled against my neck as our eyes met in the mirror. "I like that explanation better."

"God, you feel good," I whispered, dropping my head back against his shoulder as he glided in and out of me.

His teeth pierced my skin, and I came, the waves of pleasure throbbing with my heartbeat as his hand covered my mouth. Biting down, I let his blood trickle into my mouth, and my orgasm intensified. By the time his orgasm ended and his hips stilled, I was a quivering mess.

"Your hair's dried," he informed me as he gently pulled out.

"I look insane," I stated, staring at my messy hair in the mirror. It was huge.

"You're gorgeous, Reese Matthews," Beau argued, kissing my shoulder blade as he pulled up his jeans.

"You know," I said nonchalantly, throwing the hair dryer back beneath the sink. "I'm not committed to that name."

Beau paused behind me. "What do you mean?"

"You know, Matthews. It's not like I have any emotional attachment to it."

"That's good to know," he said slowly.

"So, I could change it."

I knew the instant he realized what I was saying.

"Are you asking me to marry you?" he teased, raising his eyebrows.

"I'm saying I would be open to it," I corrected, turning to face him. "You know, if at some point—"

"How about tomorrow?" he asked seriously. "We'll do it before we get your passport. Danny will be here to pick us up."

"Not tomorrow," I blustered, rolling my eyes. "If we get married, I want a dress and all that."

"You do?"

"Is that so surprising?" I griped, my cheeks heating.

"A little," he replied, catching me as I tried to escape. "You can have your dress, baby. You can have whatever you want."

"Forget it," I grumbled.

"Fuck that." He immediately dropped to his knees.

"What are you doing?"

"I was going to propose like a human," he replied, leaning forward a little, his hands on my hips. "But when I got down here, you smell so good." My entire body broke out in goose bumps as his hot breath drifted over my sensitive skin. "And I don't know what to say."

"Yes, I'll marry you," I answered anyway, holding back a grin.

"You want my last name?" he asked, resting his chin on my belly.

"It's better than Matthews." I shrugged. "Reese Boucher sounds pretty good. It's French, right?"

Beau laughed.

"What? Wait, your dad's not French."

"No, he's not."

"Then why does he have a French last name?"

"He thought it sounded best," Beau said with a shrug as he led me out of the bathroom. The amusement in his voice made me even more curious.

"Explain," I demanded, stopping by the bed so I could pull my dress on.

"He didn't have a last name," Beau replied, grabbing his shirt.

"Oh." I paused to watch him dress.

Beau's eyes met mine. "But for a time, he was known as Erik the Butcher."

It took a moment for his words to sink in.

"Erik Boucher," he continued with a flourish.

"Holy shit."

Beau nodded.

"Your dad is *really* fucking old."

He grinned.

"How is this my life?" I breathed, walking back into the bathroom to grab my underwear.

"Leave them off," Beau ordered.

I ignored him and pulled them up my legs. "Our kids are going to ace their history tests," I informed him as I walked back into the bedroom. "You know that, right?"

"We're having kids?"

"At some point," I replied distractedly. If Erik was old enough to have no surname how old was Mordecai? Or Sven?

"You knew he was old," Beau said consolingly, laughter still lacing his words.

"Yeah, yeah."

I searched the dresser for a pair of socks and went searching for some boots to wear in my plethora of boxes. The entire process was a nightmare. We couldn't live out of boxes but there was nowhere to store any of my stuff.

"This isn't going to work," I announced, pulling the top half of my body out of a box that I'd only found one boot in. "We need to build some shelves or a closet or something. I'm going to lose it."

"What are you missing?" Beau asked, walking out of the bedroom fully dressed. "I'll help you look."

"My boot."

"Which box did you find it in? The other one is probably in the same—" His words trailed to a stop as I glared.

"It's not just the boot. I can't find anything in this mess, and I don't have anywhere to put anything." Frustration made my eyes sting as I stood up and looked around the room. "This isn't working."

"Do you want to move?" he asked quietly.

"I know this is a thing," I replied, waving my arms at the room. "Vampire families live together, and I get that. I understand it. It's *nice*. But we don't fit here. What if we have kids? Where are we going to put them? *I don't even have anywhere to put my shoes.*"

"Hey," he soothed, stepping over boxes to reach me. "I hear you."

"I can't find anything," I huffed, relaxing against him. "This sucks."

"Why don't we build our own house?" he asked after a moment. "Would that be better?"

"Are you serious?" I asked dubiously, jerking my head back to look at him.

"We've got plenty of land," he replied. "My parents have always said that if we wanted to build once we had mates that—"

"Yes," I answered.

"It'll take a while," he warned. "We won't be able to get started until we're back from Europe."

"Yes," I repeated. If we built on the Boucher family land, we'd still be close, and I wouldn't feel like I was tearing Beau away from his family—but we'd have space and privacy. I would've thought of it myself, except I'd never been in the position to just nonchalantly decide to build a freaking house.

"It doesn't help the situation now," he said, looking around at the boxes.

"Shelves," I said, giving him a squeeze. "That will

work for now. Plus, once we leave, I won't have to look at it anymore."

"True," he said, reaching into a random box. When he pulled back, he was holding my other boot.

"How the hell did you just do that?" Dropping onto the couch, I pulled them on.

"I saw it when you were looking in that box earlier."

"Figures."

"Hey, did you ever talk to Rena again?" he asked as he grabbed his phone off the table.

"About the baby thing?"

"Yeah."

"She's determined," I said with a shrug as I pushed myself to my feet. "She said she's tired of waiting for a relationship. She'd rather pick some sperm from a catalog."

"Just like that?"

"I think she's been considering it for a while," I replied.

Rena had just mentioned it to me the week before, but I knew she'd been preparing for much longer than that. I wasn't even surprised by the decision. She'd always wanted to be a mother.

"Brave of her," he said, walking over to pick up my coat from where I'd flung it over the back of the couch. "You ready?"

"We still have time." I glanced at the clock.

"My mom mentioned doing drinks beforehand since Sven and Alice are leaving tomorrow."

"Oh, sure. Give me a minute."

It took longer than a minute, but Beau waited patiently as I found a sweater and slapped on a little makeup. The minute I tried to tame my hair, though, he walked straight into the bathroom and towed me back out.

"I have to pull it back or something," I complained as he pulled me straight through the suite and out the door.

"I love it like this," he countered, pausing to kiss me. "Leave it."

"You're awfully bossy about my grooming habits when you wouldn't even let your beard grow in," I chided as we went downstairs.

"It itches when it's growing in."

"Poor baby."

"You want me to grow a beard?" he asked seriously.

"I mean, I wouldn't mind feeling it between my thighs," I mused.

Beau's eyes widened in glee, and I nearly tripped over my own feet.

Goddammit.

"Hello, Erik," I said quietly, just to test the waters.

"Hey, Reese," he called back. "We're in the living room."

"Fuck," I muttered.

"They can still hear you," Beau said unhelpfully.

Lifting my chin, I swanned forward like they hadn't just heard me talking about Beau's potential beard between my thighs. The older couples were seated around the room, and all of them greeted us as we walked in. It was fine—everything was fine—until Alice inconspicuously toasted me with her glass and tilted her head toward Sven. He had a full beard.

I felt my face go up in flames.

"Reese and I are going to build a house," Beau announced as he pulled me toward a chair across from his parents, tugging me onto his lap once he'd sat down. "Is that still on the table?"

"Of course, Bjorn," Erik replied. "We'd love that."

"I was thinking at the end of the lane," Beau said, glancing at me. "What do you think?"

"Where we drove—"

Beau nodded.

"It's pretty out there."

"Plus, you'll already have a driveway," Erik pointed out.

"What kind of house would you like?" Mattie asked quietly as the men discussed the steps they'd need to take to get the property ready. "Two story? Ranch?"

"I have no idea," I confessed, feeling a little strange. Did she care that we were moving out? "We just don't have enough room right now."

Mattie winced, and I felt like an ass. "When we built the house, we didn't plan very well. We knew the boys would need their own space, but we didn't anticipate their mates and the things they'd bring with them."

"I don't have much left," I replied. "But it's enough to make walking around the living room pretty impossible."

"I can imagine," she said kindly. "Well, start thinking about the kind of house you'd like to build. Once the two of you are home from Europe, you can start planning."

The conversation went on, with Mattie and Alice giving tips about what I didn't want to forget when picking out the details of our new place. Apparently, a laundry sink should be nonnegotiable, and we needed to make sure that we had enough electrical outlets in the kitchen. My mind spun as they went on and on about shit I would've never even considered or cared about. I was just about to cry mercy when Beau's head snapped up.

"Danny," Erik said, rising to his feet.

"I thought he was getting in tomorrow," Sven said. "Did he tell you he'd be here early?"

"No," Erik replied, striding toward the door.

As Beau lifted me off his lap, I looked at each of them. Something was wrong.

"You're sure it's Danny?" Mattie asked worriedly as she followed Erik to the front door.

"Yes, I'm sure," Erik replied, striding out onto the porch.

I was glad for the coat Beau had carried downstairs as I pulled it on, following him outside. He took the porch steps in one leap.

"Beau?" I called.

Without answering or pausing, he held out his hand. The moment I gripped it, he tugged me along faster.

"Why does it matter if Danny's here earlier?" I asked in confusion as I practically jogged to keep up with him. "We knew he was coming."

"He was supposed to stop in Montana for the night," Beau replied as lights shone through the trees. "If he came straight here, something is wrong."

"What could be wrong?" I persisted. "Why wouldn't he have just called?"

Beau didn't have time to answer before Chance and Danny came striding quickly through the trees.

"Get back to the house," Chance ordered, quickening his pace as he came toward us. "Back inside."

"What the fuck?" Beau barked.

"Get her back inside," Danny ordered, jogging toward us.

Beau's arm wrapped around me, and he nearly lifted me off my feet as he hurried us back to the house.

"What's going on?" I asked, scanning the darkness around us. I hadn't been worried when we'd walked into the dense trees because Beau was with me, but now that we were trying to escape them, my heart was racing.

"It's fine," Danny assured me, swinging his head from side to side. "We just need to get back inside."

"Inside," Chance called to his parents as we reached the driveway.

Our feet hit the porch just as Erik stepped back inside the house, and I was jostled between the brothers as they ushered me in behind him.

My throat felt thick with fear as I got a good look at Danny and Chance. They looked like they hadn't slept in days. Chance's long hair was pulled back in a messy French braid down the center of his scalp, and he had dark circles around his eyes. Danny hadn't shaved in at least a week, and his red beard was scruffy. They looked like shit.

"What's going on?" Erik asked, wrapping his arm around Mattie.

"We found them," Danny said baldly. "We tracked the sister back to fucking Baltimore."

"They went back?" Beau asked doubtfully.

"She did," Chance replied. "By the time we caught up with her, they'd separated."

"Where is *Charles*?" Mattie asked.

"She wouldn't say," Danny replied, scratching at his beard angrily. "But she had quite a lot to say about everything else."

"They're far more organized than we thought," Chance said, falling back against the wall. "She knew so much shit. Zeke told them all the things he'd figured out before he went back to his unit. They were supposed to hide until he could get back, but then he never came."

"Why would he leave his mate?" Sven asked in bewilderment.

"Because he was convinced that someone in command was telling tales. There was no other way that humans would even know that a Vampire had found his mate unless they were getting official records."

"I didn't report it," Beau said in confusion, pulling me tighter against him. "That can't be how they're finding out because I didn't report Reese."

"I did," Mattie said softly.

Beau let out a huff of air like he'd been socked in the gut.

"He wasn't sure if it was someone in the United States command or in Europe command, but since they were working together in South America, he thought he could poke around a little," Danny said, shaking his head.

"Someone is leaking classified information to the humans," Erik said slowly, like he was letting it sink in.

"That's not even the most interesting part," Chance said bitingly, tearing the rubber band out of his hair. "The head of all this, they're pretty sure that it's that billionaire with the tech company that's cozying up with the president."

"Unlimited resources," Beau said, pinching the bridge of his nose.

"What's the one thing money can't buy?" Alice asked rhetorically. "A long life."

Fear covered me like a suffocating blanket. Money like that made people invincible. The Bouchers were wealthy, but the man they were speaking about had more money than he could spend in a hundred lifetimes. He could just keep sending people. No matter how many times Beau stopped them, they'd just keep coming.

"Where is Ambrose?" Beau demanded.

"She'd only agree to take one of us to get Charles, and she refused to fly," Danny said angrily. "She's more paranoid than Matthias, I swear to the gods."

"And she agreed to take *Ambrose*?" I asked in disbelief.

Out of the three brothers she could've chosen, he was the least personable. It wasn't that he was rude. He just wasn't as outgoing as the other two.

"Well, yeah," Chance drawled. "Since she's his fucking *mate*."

"Oh," Mattie said, her eyes widening.

"We might not want to report this one," Danny said tiredly.

Erik snapped something at Danny, but I wasn't paying attention. My thoughts had looped back to the realization that one of the most powerful men in the world was kidnapping Vampires and their mates. Did Charles and his sister have proof? What exactly had Beau's baby brother found before he was killed?

I didn't realize that I was breathing heavily until Beau's hand wrapped around the lower half of my jaw and tipped my face toward his.

"What?"

"They're never going to stop, are they?" I asked, fear tightening like a band around my chest. "What are we going to do? How can we live our lives if they're just out there waiting for us—"

"No one is going to touch you," Beau promised, backing me into the corner by the door. "Do you understand? No one."

"They'll just keep coming. There will always be someone willing to take that job."

"We just have to cut off the head of the snake, my love," he murmured, leaning down until our noses were almost touching. "And if Zeke's information is right, we know who that is."

"What do we do now?" I whispered, wrapping my hands around his forearms.

"Nothing," he whispered back. "You're safe inside this

house. So, I'm going to order dinner in, and then I'm going to fuck you—"

I slammed my hand over his mouth as I glanced over his shoulder at the people crowded in the foyer. "Shh."

He kissed my palm and pulled his head away.

"And we're going to wait for Ambrose to bring his mate and Zeke's mate home."

If someone had told me a month before that I would be standing in the foyer of a mansion, staring into the beautiful brown eyes of my mate, surrounded by family, and feeling safer than I'd ever been in my life despite all that had happened to us? I would've laughed in their faces.

Family was a joke. Mates were something from tabloids and fairy tales. Safety was an illusion.

And then suddenly, because a surly Vampire decided that he wanted to see a blood bank for himself, my entire world had shifted.

He'd changed my life.

"I could go for some Thai food," I said, sinking against his chest.

"She comes out swinging," he murmured against my lips.

"Love you."

"You're the beginning and the end, Reese," he whispered back.

# A LOOK AT BOOK TWO

**A bond neither asked for. A war they never saw coming.**

Ambrose Boucher isn't looking for love—he's looking for blood. After the brutal murder of his younger brother, vengeance is all that fuels him. Step one: track down the mysterious mate his brother died protecting. Step two: burn the shadowy organization behind it all to the ground. But fate has other plans. Instead of Zeke's mate, Ambrose finds his own—and she's the last person ready to believe in destiny.

Lucille Franklin knows exactly what being a vampire's mate means. She watched her brother fall headfirst into a bond that was beautiful... until it turned tragic. With vampires being hunted and their mates targeted, Lucy swore she'd never let herself get pulled into that world. But Ambrose is impossible to ignore—relentless, dangerous, and already tangled in the grief that nearly broke her once before.

As the Bouchers dig deeper into a deadly conspiracy, Lucy and Ambrose are forced to rely on a bond she never wanted and a connection he can't control. But when enemies close in and secrets unravel, trusting each other might be the only way to survive.

Can a love forged in loss be strong enough to rewrite fate—or will history repeat itself in blood?

***AVAILABLE AUGUST 2025***

# ACKNOWLEDGMENTS

To my fella, my kids, my parents and parents-in-law: thanks for pitching in to help me finish this novel without completely losing it. Love you!

To my betas: thanks for assuring me Vein & Vow didn't suck before I sent it to the editor.

To Donna: thanks for blogging about my first book. I wouldn't be here without you.

To the readers who've come with me this far: thank you for your support and love these past 12 years. I couldn't do what I do if you weren't doing what you do.

And to Ellie, who read the premise of the Bouchers series and said, *I want it*. Thank you a thousand times. Love you, dude.

Nicole Jacquelyn started writing before she started elementary school, however she didn't start publishing her stories until her senior year in college. Today, she's the author of the bestselling Aces series, the Fostering Love series, the Kellys series, and The Bouchers series. She loves to read, drinks too much coffee, and lives in Oregon with the coolest children in the entire world.